Books may well be the only true magic.
—Alice Hoffman

Bait and Witch

Angela M. Sanders

KENSINGTON
PUBLISHING CORP.

www.kensingtonbooks.com

KENSINGTON BOOKS are published by

Kensington Publishing Corp.
119 West 40th Street
New York, NY 10018

All Kensington titles, imprints, and distributed lines are available at special quantity discounts for bulk purchases for sales promotion, premiums, fund-raising, educational, or institutional use.

Special book excerpts or customized printings can also be created to fit specific needs. For details, write or phone the office of the Kensington Sales Manager: Attn.: Sales Department. Kensington Publishing Corp., 119 West 40th Street, New York, NY 10018. Phone: 1-800-221-2647.

First Printing: January 2021
ISBN-13: 978-1-4967-2874-6
ISBN-10: 1-4967-2874-2

ISBN-13: 978-1-4967-2875-3 (ebook)
ISBN-10: 1-4967-2875-0 (ebook)

10 9 8 7 6 5 4 3 2 1

Printed in the United States of America

CHAPTER ONE

I scanned the passing countryside in vain for signs of life. Fir trees pressed in over the pitted asphalt. After a few miles, the forest opened to a valley sparsely dotted with farmhouses, only one lit in the night. I prayed I hadn't made a fatal mistake.

The driver hadn't said more than a few words the whole hour-long drive from the airport.

"This job looks fascinating," I said, hoping to spark conversation. "Why did the last librarian leave?"

The driver was a tall gent with a cowboy hat and an inscrutable expression. Every time the pickup hit a bump, his hat dented against the roof. "Didn't work out," he said.

I waited for more, but nothing came. I lightened my tone and tried a different approach. "When will we be in Wilfred?"

"Ain't no Wilfred."

My heart lodged in my throat. "What do you mean?"

Had they tracked me down already? The driver didn't look like a for-hire killer, but I was no expert. My hand crept to the door handle. I was ready to jump, no matter how fast the truck was going, when he finally responded.

"Ain't no Wilfred since the mill closed."

"I was hired as the Wilfred librarian."

"Sure. Folks still call it Wilfred, that's all."

Calm down, I told myself. I was still shaky. When the plane had passed somewhere over the Midwest, I'd felt a visceral snap and jerked so violently that the woman in the next seat had fanned me with her magazine and asked if she should call the flight attendant. I'd gulped from my water bottle and forced myself to breathe. After a moment, the internal earthquake had mellowed to tremors. I hadn't felt the same since.

The truck slowed. There was nothing around us but a copse of trees intersected by a dirt lane.

"What are you doing?" I asked.

"Slowing for the speed trap," the driver—Lyndon Forster, he'd told me—said. He shifted up. "Never mind. We're clear. We're just about to the library."

A minute later we passed a few storefronts and a tavern with a nearly empty parking lot. I knew Wilfred was a small town, but I'd expected at least a stop sign. Rural Oregon couldn't be more different than the crowded sidewalks and high-rises I was used to back home in D.C.

We crossed a narrow river, then hooked an immediate right to climb a gravel lane. Lyndon parked in a circular driveway and cut the lights. In front of us loomed a three-story Victorian mansion replete with gingerbread trim and a central tower. We might have driven into a Victoria Holt gothic novel.

"We're here," he said.

"You've got to be kidding."

The woman who'd hired me had said I'd be living above the library, and I'd envisioned a modern apartment atop a generic municipal building, not much different from my one-bedroom apartment back home. I hadn't had time to ask a lot of questions.

Too late now. I stepped out of the truck. Crisp autumn air filled my lungs. It had to be near midnight, and a chiffon veil of moonlight filtered through the oak trees ringing the mansion.

"Just point me toward the door, and I'll take my bag and leave you to the rest of your night. I hope you don't have a long drive." In fact, I hoped he had a very long drive to somewhere far, far away. The man gave me the creeps.

"Nope," he said. "I'm the caretaker here. Got a little place out back." He grabbed my suitcase and ambled up the steps but bypassed the double doors in front. He stopped before rounding the corner. "This way. We use the service entrance."

I took a deep breath and followed. Maybe it was for the best. They'd never find me here, that was for sure.

We climbed a narrow staircase, Lyndon hefting my suitcase over his shoulder like a sacrificial goat. The hall was cold and smelled of beeswax. Two flights up, he extracted a ring of keys from his Levi's and unlocked the door. He set down the suitcase.

We stood in a hall that looked over the old house's

central atrium, open all the way to the third-floor ceiling. A stained-glass window set in the roof glowed dull red and blue with moonlight. Below us, two floors of shadowed rooms that must have once been the house's bedrooms and parlors held bookshelves.

"Here we have the living room," he said.

I stuck my head into a dark room with mullioned windows and the dim shapes of a sofa and chairs.

"Next is the bedroom." He waved his hand toward the next door, closed, but made no move toward invading those quarters.

"Here's the kitchen. Not too large, but plenty big for you, I reckon." The bloated form of a midcentury stove was all I could make out in the dark. Lyndon turned to examine me as if for the first time and drew his bushy eyebrows together. "You feeling okay? You seem kind of jumpy."

"I'm fine," I lied. We moved on.

"The bathroom." The mint-green bathtub and sink clearly hadn't been updated since the Eisenhower administration. "Here are the keys. I'll show you more once you get settled in." He touched the brim of his hat and disappeared down the hall. After a moment, I heard the door shut and the solid *thunk* of a bolt thrown in place.

Well.

The apartment was quiet but for the faraway sound of crickets. I rolled my suitcase to the bedroom and clicked on the lamp on the dresser. Pale light showed an armchair and a bed with an elaborately carved headboard that stretched nearly to the ceiling. Someone had left a jug of wildflowers on the dresser, a reassuring note.

A pink envelope next to it was labeled "Josephine

Way." I opened it to find a handwritten note from Darla Starling, the woman who had hired me by phone.

"Dear Josie," it read in a girlish hand, each letter painstakingly formed. "Welcome to Wilfred. I hope you find your rooms comfortable—we changed the sheets, and there are fresh towels in the bathroom. We'll see you downstairs at nine tomorrow morning. I look forward to meeting you in person. Sincerely, Darla." A banner reading SWEET GEORGIA PEACHES ran across the stationery's edge.

I crossed the room to the window to draw the curtains and stopped short. Amber eyes stared back. It was a black cat, perched on the roof outside my window. I wasn't being watched, I reminded myself. No one knew I was here. They couldn't. It was just a cat.

Just as I was about to jerk the chintz drapes closed, the cat sat on his haunches and paddled his front paws comically on the windowpane before falling on his back in a move Buster Keaton would have envied. The cat opened one eye to make sure I was watching. I couldn't help but laugh.

Feeling calmer, I turned to the task I'd been dreading. I'd seen a rotary phone on the kitchen wall. It had been years since I'd used one, but there was no question of using my cell phone. I'd left it at home so I couldn't be traced. First I dialed 1-1-6-9 to block my number, then my sister Toni's number, even though it was three in the morning back home. I let it ring twice and hung up. Our signal. Then I called again, again blocking my number.

Toni—Marie Antoinette was her full name; our historian father had named each of the three of us after French queens—answered with a hesitant "Yes?"

"It's me, Josie."

"What time is it? Is everything all right?" In those few words, her voice went from drowsy to alert. "How's New York?"

"About that." I screwed my eyes closed and opened them. Out with it. "I'm not in New York."

She groaned. "Oh, Josie, you haven't—"

"I won't tell you where I am. But I wanted you to know I'm okay, just in case you called the hotel and found out I hadn't checked in."

"So. You ran."

"I'll come home after the trial. It'll only be a few months. I already gave my deposition. They don't need me now."

"I knew this would happen. Couldn't the feds hide you somewhere? What about the witness protection program? I don't feel good about this."

"After what happened to Anton, I didn't want to take the chance." The week before, my coworker and fellow whistleblower Anton had vanished, leaving a wife and toddler daughter with no idea whether he was dead or alive.

"Are you okay?"

"Yes—that is, I'm not sure. I had this weird episode on the plane, like my innards were exploding. Is that what a panic attack feels like?" Toni was a physician. She'd know.

"Not usually. Stress does weird things, though."

I'd had plenty of stress. I pulled aside my collar and pressed a finger on the star-shaped birthmark on my shoulder. Ever since I was a girl, I'd touched it for comfort. Tonight, it almost burned.

"I'm sure I'll be better in the morning."

"You really won't tell me where you are?"

"No. You know I can't. But you should see it here. It's crazy, like I stepped into *Cold Comfort Farm*. The guy who drove me from the airport could have been nicknamed Lurch. I'm waiting for a raven to appear on a tree branch outside."

"Just give me your town's name. What if something happens to you?"

"No. I can't. It's better this way." I toyed with the phone's coiled cord. "I'll call Mom tomorrow," I said, replying to Toni's unspoken question. All our lives, my sisters and I had shared a tacit communication. We could work elbow-to-elbow in Mom's kitchen and never get in each others' way. We'd pass a half cup of milk or plug in the mixer or set the oven's timer for another sister without saying a word. "It's late. I need to get to bed. I just wanted you to know I'm all right."

After hanging up, I laid my nightgown on the foot of the bed. On impulse, I heaved up the bedroom window. Oak trees vanished into the night. Beyond the trees was a cabin that couldn't have been more than a few rooms. The caretaker's, I guessed. Beyond that, maybe fifty yards away, was a house as large as the library, but squat and wide. I made out the glow of a light in an upstairs window. As I watched, a window shade pulled shut and blocked it out.

A breeze whooshed through the dry leaves, carrying a few to rattle against the roof. "Good night, wind," I said, almost hearing my grandmother whisper the words in my ear. Funny, I hadn't greeted the wind since I was a girl.

The black cat returned, too, padding up the shingles below my window.

"Who are you, little guy?"

He took two steps forward, mouthed a silent "meow," and leapt away into the darkness.

CHAPTER TWO

That night I dreamt for the first time in decades—vivid images of my grandmother's garden with lavender-scented laundry on the line and bundles of herbs drying on a sunny windowsill. One dream in particular stayed with me. I was a little girl, outside in my nightgown. Stars spangled the night. My mother was encouraging me to drink something from a crystal tumbler, but I didn't want to. In another, darker vision, a woman in a black jacket circled the house, trying doors and windows.

But that was last night. This morning, sun seeped through the cracks in the curtains. I swung my feet to the braided rag rug and pushed the drapes open to blue skies. It was the first day of my new life.

I'd never managed a library before. Sure, in library school I'd supervised a few interns and staffed the infor-mation desk, but at the Library of Congress I'd specialized in cataloguing the folklife collection. It had been just me, a computer, and stacks of old documents.

To tell the truth, I was surprised the Wilfred library had hired me, given my lack of experience. I felt a twinge of guilt that I wouldn't be staying long. Still, while I was here I'd be the best librarian I knew how to be. All I had to do was act normal—unremarkable, even. Do my job and draw no attention to myself.

When I'd interviewed, I'd glossed over my work at the Library of Congress and focused on the job I'd held before at the University of Maryland. My former boss had been happy to give me a recommendation and play down my dates of employment. Darla hadn't seemed to mind my relative lack of experience. If I hadn't known better, I'd have thought she'd planned to hire me no matter where I'd come from.

For my first day of work, I chose a professional cotton skirt, cardigan, and the librarian's regulation clogs, perfect for hours on my feet. My hair, a long nest of red curls threaded with frizz, would spoil the efficient look I wanted to project. With the help of the dresser mirror, its face spotted black here and there, I managed to wrangle it into a low bun studded with bobby pins.

As I popped in the last bobby pin, I noticed a book on the nightstand. Funny, I could have sworn it hadn't been there last night. *Folk Witch*, it was called. I bit off a laugh. Must have been left by the last librarian, probably some hippie girl who made love potions and did astrological charts. I tossed the book on the bed with the intention of reshelving it later.

As I made my way down the staircase, voices drifted up. And, thank goodness, the aroma of coffee.

The staircase led into a bright, blue-and-white-tiled kitchen with a long wooden table in the center. Around the table, three heads turned toward me. All at once, I felt apprehensive. Had I made a huge mistake?

"Hello, everyone." I took a deep breath. "I'm Josephine Way, the new librarian. You can call me Josie."

"Ma'am." Lyndon Forster, the caretaker and last night's chauffeur, nodded. I knew better than to expect a long-winded greeting. He looked less ominous in the morning light, just craggy and sun-darkened. "Sleep well?"

"Yes, thank you."

"Not that it will matter much longer," a graying brunette said from across the table. She must have been in her early fifties, and she seemed to be made entirely of curves. Jeans and a blue plaid shirt barely held in a plush body, and the theme continued in cheeks rounded like apricots, blue eyes, and even a ball at the tip of her nose.

"What do you mean?" I asked. They couldn't have found out about me already, could they?

"Hush, Roz," said the third person, a comfortably built woman with pink frosted lipstick, big hair, and a leopard blazer over a T-shirt and jeans. "Don't you listen to her. She's never been a glass-half-full gal. I'm Darla, the trustee in charge of the hiring committee. You interviewed with me." Darla rose and stuck out her hand. "It's a pleasure to meet you at last. Bet you'd like a cup of coffee about now. You had a late night."

"Roslyn Grover," the brunette said, offering a hand. "Everyone calls me Roz. I'm assistant librarian."

Darla poured a mug of coffee with the flourish of a longtime waitress and pushed a jug of cream across the table. "The library will be closed today while you settle in. Before we get down to your responsibilities, I wanted to meet with you first thing. We have something"—she stole a glance at Roz—"sensitive to talk about."

Lyndon sucked the rest of his coffee from his mug. "Got to rake the side yard. Best be moving on."

"Sure. What is it?" I asked hesitantly as the kitchen door shut behind him. I had to wonder if I'd be bundled into his truck in a few hours and sent back to the airport.

"Now, I don't want you to get alarmed."

"Okay," I said, my apprehension deepening.

"It has to do with the Wilfred mansion. And the library." Darla took her seat again at the table.

"It's getting ugly," Roz said. "The whole town's divided." Her skin reddened, and she flipped open the fan on the table beside her. "Hot flash. Caffeine brings them on." The fan moved double-time. "That, and stress."

"Roz, you stay out of it."

Wide-eyed, I looked from one woman to the other. It didn't sound like the issue had to do with me, but I wasn't ready to breathe a sigh of relief just yet. On the other hand, whatever the situation was, as long as it didn't involve hit men, I'd deal with it.

Darla set down her mug. "I'm sorry to spring it on you like this, but you see—" "Georgia on My Mind" erupted from her purse. "Excuse me." She pulled out her phone, then wrinkled her nose and dropped her phone back into her bag. "We have a situation, and I've got to run." She turned to Roz. "Why don't you bring Josie to the diner? I'll explain it all then."

A moment later, the door shut, and only Roz and I were left in the kitchen.

Worry—a feeling I'd been all too familiar with

lately—sparked in my chest. "What's happening with the library?"

"Come on," Roz said. "I'll tell you about it on the way to breakfast."

"Darla never hinted at any kind of trouble in the job interview," I told Roz as we left through the kitchen door. I noticed a cat door and was about to ask about the black cat I'd seen last night, when Roz spoke.

"I told her she shouldn't hire you on false pretenses. But does she ever listen to me? Does anyone?"

"What false pretenses? What should she have told me?"

"Darla's a library trustee."

I nodded. "Got that."

"She also owns Darla's Tavern and Diner and the Magnolia Rolling Estates trailer park. Basically, she's Wilfred's de facto mayor."

"I didn't know you had magnolias in the Pacific Northwest." A sudden memory came to me of fat, creamy petals falling in my grandmother's garden.

"We don't. Not native ones, anyway, but Darla loves the South. Always has grits on her menu. The library subscribes to *Southern Dame* because of her." Roz stopped just on the other side of the library and turned toward the river below. "Isn't that a view? I never get over it."

The sky was bluer than I'd ever known a sky to be. Every throatful of air was fresher than spring water after a run. My senses were working on all pistons. I felt like life had exploded into Technicolor, as if I'd boarded my flight as one person and left as another.

Down the bluff, beyond the river, the tiny town we'd driven through last night hugged the road. Imagine a cross, with the road as the north-south axis and the river running east-west. The library, including its grounds, the caretaker's cottage, and the other large house, filled the southwest quadrant. Wilfred proper straddled the road on the northern squares of the cross.

"That must be Darla's restaurant." I pointed to the low-slung tavern I'd seen last night. This morning, dirty pickup trucks and SUVs filled the front lot.

"Yep, that's it. Closer, here by the Kirby—that's the river's name—is the trailer park where I live."

"What's that building, the one with the bay windows?"

"The old commercial block. Built in the twenties. Next door is the post office. It's a grocery store now. Across the highway"—she pointed to the woods on our side of the river—"is the old mill site. The mill is long gone, but the mill pond is still there."

We stood a moment, each thinking our own thoughts, mine having to do with the "crisis" I'd heard about. Birds cooed. The proud old library sat up like a spinster aunt at church, tidy and straight.

"It's crazy that the house's best view is over the river toward town, but the front—the big driveway and porch—faces the other direction," Roz said.

"Hmm. Maybe they liked seeing the woods."

"More likely they didn't like seeing everyone else. That would be just like the Wilfreds."

Town history was interesting, but my immediate future grabbed me more. Time to get to the point. "So, Darla owns land in town. What does that have to do with the library?"

Roz led me to a wooded trail along the bluff. "We'll take this to the bridge. It's shorter than going by the driveway and road. See that house?" She seemed almost deliberate in her attempt to keep me from asking questions.

"Yes." It was the house I'd glimpsed last night through the trees.

"We call it Big House. Even though, technically, the library is bigger."

"Who lives there?"

"Right now? No one. It used to belong to the Wilfreds. Marilyn Wilfred—old man Thurston Wilfred's daughter—stayed in the original Wilfred mansion and turned the bottom two floors into a library. The next generation had to build a place next door."

We were past Big House now. "I saw a light there last night."

"Couldn't have," Roz said decisively.

"Okay." No use arguing. "Let's get back to Darla. What does owning a tavern and trailer park have to do with the library and this 'sensitive situation'?" I asked, feigning patience.

Roz didn't respond.

She started across the bridge, but I stayed put. "You have to tell me what's going on here. I haven't even been on the job an hour and I've been warned about something dire that has to do with the library. Plus, this place seems to be a revolving door for librarians. What's the story?"

Roz looked at the river, then at the tavern just down the road. Finally, she met my gaze. "Okay. Darla said to wait, but I guess . . . Sit down." She pointed to the bridge's wide railing.

The cement was cold under my skirt. "I'm listening."

"Tourism has been picking up lately. Campers, bicyclists, people touring wine country."

"That's good, right? More tourism, more business."

Roz stood. "It's shaking things up, that's all. Let's go have breakfast. You've got to try the shrimp grits."

That was it? That was the "sensitive" issue? "You're not telling me everything. Be straight with me. What does tourism have to do with the library?" Roz marched straight ahead. I suppressed the urge to yank her back by the waistband of her jeans. "Stop it! You're avoiding my question. Please, Roz. Answer me."

She felt around in her pocket, probably for her fan. Yes, there it was. Despite the fall breeze, she flipped it open.

"I'm waiting."

"They want the library." The words came out in a rush.

"What?"

"Some people want to buy the Wilfred mansion and bulldoze it and put up a retreat center."

"When?" The word came out as pure breath.

Pricks of moisture gathered on her forehead. "If the sale goes through, it could be as early as next month."

"Oh no. No wonder—"

"Don't panic. We're doing everything we can to make sure it doesn't happen. Even if the Wilfred mansion goes away, the county says they'll build a new library."

Which I knew would take years, if it was built at all. "I can't believe it. You guys flew me all the way across the country for this?"

"We don't know for sure what will happen, and in the meantime we really need a librarian."

"How can you need a librarian when you might not even have a library?"

Roz pursed her lips. "Nope. I told you all I'm going to for now."

* * *

Darla took one look and pushed us into a booth. "She told you, didn't she?"

"She wouldn't wait," Roz said. "I tried."

I was still shocked—and angry, even though I hadn't been planning to stay, anyway. How dare they hire me to run a library slated for the chopping block?

Darla pressed menus into our hands. "Knowing Roz, you didn't hear the whole story. Before you do anything rash, hear me out. I need to wait on a table first. I had the day off, but people heard you were in town, and, well—"

The tavern was split into two. On the left was the tavern proper. Roz and I were seated in the building's right half, a comfortable diner with gingham curtains, linoleum-topped tables, and country-western music on the radio. A counter ran along the back of the diner, with the kitchen behind it and a cash register at one end. Above the cash register big letters read SAVE THE LI-BRARY. The room was packed. Diners had put down their forks, and besides Dolly Parton's imploring of Jolene to leave her man alone, the room was silent.

"People, mind your own business," Darla shouted from the counter.

She was used to being obeyed, and it showed. Slowly, forks clinked on plates and conversation picked up.

A moment later, glasses of water appeared on our table, leaving rings of condensation on their paper coasters. I turned over my coffee cup, and Darla filled it.

Roz didn't even look at her menu. "Shrimp and grits."

That sounded good to me. I pushed the menu with its SAVE THE LIBRARY sticker to the side.

Darla slid into the bench next to Roz. "What did Roz tell you?"

I was preparing to respond when a pimply boy in a Portland Blazers T-shirt delivered two bowls of shrimp and grits. He stared at me, and I smoothed my hair. Sometimes a curl decided to make off on its own, but I didn't feel any wayward corkscrews. He'd just wanted to check out the new person in town.

"We haven't even ordered yet," I said.

"I took the liberty of ordering for you. On the house," Darla said. "Okay, so what do you know?"

Roz swallowed a generous mouthful of grits. "I told her a couple wants to knock down the library and put up a retreat center; library might be demolished next month; folks are split." She dug her spoon into her bowl again.

Darla looked at me for confirmation. Roz's summary really drove it home.

"That's about it," I said, still shocked.

"Those are the facts," Darla said. "Some of them. The sale isn't a done deal."

"You mean the buyers might not want the library?"

"Oh, they want it alright," Roz said. Her bowl's contents were diminishing rapidly.

"Then what?" I tentatively poked at my breakfast and raised a forkful to my mouth. Savory with thyme, the scent of the ocean, lots of good butter. Even food tasted better here. "Then why did you hire me, knowing the library might not be around?"

"We don't know it for sure, plus the trustees put aside a month's salary as severance," Roz said.

"Let me back up a bit," Darla said. "Marilyn Wilfred founded the library."

"Old man Thurston's daughter," Roz added.

It seemed I was doomed to a history lesson whenever someone spoke of the library. "I've heard about him."

"All the firstborn Wilfred men are named Thurston, so we use 'old man' for the town's founder," Darla said. "Anyway, when Marilyn died, she left the library and a trust to Wilfred with certain conditions."

"Sounds normal," I said. The pimply boy stopped by to refill my coffee.

"One condition was that nothing in the library change, unless it was for the 'betterment of Wilfredians.'" Darla had clearly quoted the last part.

"Surely, demolishing the library can't be the best for the town?"

"Remember how I told you about the mill shutting down?" Roz said. She'd pushed her empty bowl out of the way and leaned back into the booth with her coffee. "People here are struggling."

"When did it close?"

"Almost twenty-five years ago, it—"

"Twenty-five years," I said. "People haven't moved on?"

"Families have been here for generations," Roz said. "And have worked in the mill since it opened over a hundred years ago. They planned their futures based on the mill. Then, when it closed so suddenly—"

"Middle of the night. The mill caught fire and burned to the ground. When the firemen came around, the Wilfreds were gone. Big House was empty. Nearly a hundred jobs lost. A hundred families without support," Darla said.

"Nothing. No final paycheck, no explanation," Roz added.

"Still," I said. "Twenty-five years."

An older woman with a sun-roughened face illuminated by bright pink lipstick approached the table and stuck out a hand. "You must be the new librarian. Helen Garlington."

I stood to shake her hand, and she gave me a complete head-to-toe assessment.

"Bookish but approachable. Marilyn would have approved," she said.

"I'm glad I pass muster," I said, with a glance at Roz, who propped her chin in a palm and watched with a barely noticeable smile.

"The library has meant so much to all of us." Helen Garlington's voice rose a wavery notch, as if she were lecturing a crowd. "It has been a place of gathering, respite, and strength, the ship that carries us as the world buffets around us, tossing waves of pain and confusion."

"Mrs. Garlington's a poet," Roz said.

"I hope the library will continue to be important to Wilfred," I said.

"When the mill closed," Darla continued as the older woman found a booth, "Marilyn—Marilyn Wilfred—welcomed everyone to the library."

"I thought you said the mill owner's family had left town."

I shrugged off my jacket and noticed something in a pocket. The copy of *Folk Witch*. But I'd left it back at the library. I set it on the table and stared at the cover's landscape of heather and moonlight.

"Reading about witches?" Roz asked.

"No. I'm more of a vintage mystery fan."

Roz picked up the book and examined the back cover. "Looks like nonfiction. A history of witchcraft in Scotland, in fact. I didn't even know we had it in the collection." She set the book on the table. "I'll reshelve it for you."

"Please. I'm not sure how it ended up in my coat." Where the heck had the book come from? It almost seemed to sigh as Roz slipped it into her tote.

Diners through the room watched us, lifting heads every once in a while to check me out and monitor Darla's reactions. Their chatter blended with the clinks of plates and the ring of the cash register. The crowd wasn't overly prosperous. No surgeon-inflated lips or Dior handbags or key fobs for German luxury cars.

"As I told you, when Marilyn Wilfred died, she left the library to the town with the stipulation that nothing change unless it was for the betterment of Wilfred as a whole," Darla said.

"So, you're making the case that the library means more to Wilfred than the retreat center would," I said.

"Exactly. We're suing the library's trustees for voting to sell the library."

"But you're a trustee."

Darla nodded. "It's awkward."

Roz snorted.

"The other trustees have filed a motion asking the judge the drop the suit. They have some complicated study showing the long-term economic benefits of the retreat center. Plus, they say the library grounds are a nuisance and attract troublemakers after hours."

"All backed by Ilona." Roz gave both of us a knowing glance.

"Ilona?" I said.

"Ilona Buckwalter, the real estate agent handling the sale. It means big money to her. Plus, she's a trustee."

"How did she do that? Seems like a conflict of interest for her to benefit financially and have a vote in taking down the library," I said.

"So we've told the judge," Darla said.

In coming to Wilfred, I'd thought I was landing somewhere I'd be safe for a while. What a mistake. I didn't have the money to stay on the run indefinitely, and I had no backup plan. It had all happened too quickly.

"When will you know whether your suit is thrown out or not?" I asked.

"Anytime now," Darla said. She leaned forward, her reading glasses dangling from a beaded cord around her neck. "Will you stay? At least until then? Please. Just give it some thought. Just for a few days. The judge might side with us."

"You didn't tell me any of this when I applied for the job."

The ad, the phone interview, the charming photos of the Oregon countryside—everything had looked so simple and honest. If only I'd known. But I couldn't return home. Not yet.

"I'll think it over."

CHAPTER THREE

We were back at the library's kitchen, and Roz, supposedly my assistant, was laying down the law.

"I only work mornings, Tuesday through Saturday. Afternoons, you're on your own. Dylan comes in twice a week. He's our intern from the high school. Once a year the knitting club helps with a top-to-bottom cleaning, but otherwise you're responsible for tidying up. I don't vacuum or do windows. Lyndon takes care of maintenance."

If I'd known I was staying, I'd have made some motion toward taking charge, but it wasn't worth the fight. Not now.

"Why didn't you apply for the head librarian job?" I asked when she paused for breath.

"I don't have time. I have my projects."

Saying she had urgent business, Roz left me to explore

my office on my own. "I'll come find you in an hour or so and give you a tour of the library."

I stood in the doorway of my office—the house's old pantry just off the kitchen—and processed the news that the library might be scrap lumber before Thanksgiving. Where could I go from here? Returning home was impossible.

A wooden desk filled the wall under a casement window that opened toward the river. Along the opposite wall were filing cabinets, a low bookshelf, and a leather armchair with a side table and ginger jar lamp.

I dropped into the armchair. What a morning. My office door nudged open, and the black cat I'd seen last night slipped through. The tip of one ear was missing, and a pinkish scar shone through the black fur on its edge. He fixed me with eyes the color of rye whiskey.

"Hello, kitty." I dropped a hand for him to smell. "Did I do wrong by answering that ad in the *Library Gazette*? I'm not needed here, but I can't go home."

The cat pawed at the bookshelf, pulling a flyer to the floor. I reached down to put it back and saw it was a schedule of the month's events. The library hosted weekly classes in English as a second language. Probably helpful for the field workers. Thursdays were organ lessons—the library had an organ?—and once a month, the knitting club met in the conservatory. I'd just missed an afternoon tea with "Original poems by Wilfred resident Helen Garlington." The library was a community center, it seemed. I set the flyer on the desk.

"Okay, so they do need me—as an events coordinator, at least. And they probably need help cataloguing and packing up the books for storage once the library is history. Then I'll be homeless, like you."

The cat pointed his head toward the kitchen, where two ceramic bowls on the floor caught my eyes. "Rodney" was painted on one. Apparently the cat belonged to the library.

"Funny little guy. I almost believe you understand me."

The cat stretched, reaching out one paw then the other, and leapt onto the chair's arm. He bumped my shoulder with his head.

In the past twelve hours, everything had changed. I'd fled across the country to a nonexistent town and taken a job in a library that would soon be bulldozed. I was dreaming again, remembering my childhood. And now I'd turned into Dr. Dolittle.

"What's happening to me, Rodney?"

The cat, still purring, rolled to his back. On his lower belly where the fur was thin was a star-shaped birthmark, clear and dark and sharp. Just like mine.

I needed a dose of something normal. Dumping the cat from my lap, I grabbed the desk telephone and dialed Mom, first blocking my number. She answered on the first ring.

"Where are you?" she said after my greeting. "I thought you were in New York."

"I am," I said. "Let me tell you, it's been some vacation."

"How come your phone number doesn't show?"

"It doesn't? That's strange." I focused on keeping my voice indifferent. Mom was unusually adept at sussing out a fib. As a kid, I could never get away with playing with my friends instead of studying for a spelling test. I'd sneak in the back door to get my jump rope and find Mom holding my English notebook and a pencil. "How are things? I miss you."

"I miss you, too, honey. Your father's giving a lecture on Madame Récamier at the junior college next week. He's in the den working on his presentation."

The vision of Dad hunched over his desk with a mug of cold coffee and a dozen open history books strewn around him calmed me. Things were still normal somewhere, at least.

"How's Jean?" I said, asking about my younger sister, Eugénie.

"The same, I expect. She emailed me an article on energy healing. Said it might help your father's knee problem."

Mom's words soothed me more than a tranquilizer might have. I closed my eyes and pictured Sunday dinner, with Toni, Toni's husband, and my baby niece, Letitia, taking over the right side of the table. Mom's hand would be resting on the tray of Letty's high chair. Jean, probably wearing yoga pants straight from work or a 1970s flowered dress, would sit across from them, pointing out the possibility of GMOs in the green beans. My empty seat would be next to hers. Twenty years ago, when Jean was in the same high chair, my grandmother was at the table, too.

"I've been thinking a lot about Grandma lately."

"You have?" Her voice was wary.

"Remember how we used to go out to her cottage during the summer? Whatever happened to her place?"

"Why are you wasting your time on ancient history? You're on vacation, Josie. Go to a show or something."

"Do you have any photos? It would be fun to see what

it looked like again. Remember how she had all those cats? And the garden?"

"That place was a fire hazard. After Mom died, we sold the land. I think they built a housing tract on it. But, like I said, it's your vacation. Get out and enjoy yourself." She paused a moment. "You really are in New York, right?"

"Sure. Of course."

"I just wondered. It seems strange—"

"Thanks, Mom. I'd better go. I have a ticket to a show at the Met." If she had two more minutes, she'd squeeze the truth out of me, and I didn't want her to worry. "I'll check in again soon."

Returning the heavy receiver to its cradle, I felt better. I'd always been told I had an active imagination and was a little too curious for my mother's taste. Roz had said the library's fate wasn't a done deal. I shouldn't jump to conclusions until I heard what the judge had to say. As for the cat, Rodney, he was simply sociable, and his birthmark was a fluke.

I leaned back and knocked a book to the floor. *Folk Witch*. This again? Irritation jabbed at me. Was Roz in on some kind of joke at my expense? When I was a girl, other kids used to call me "witch" because of my messy red hair, and I'd hated it. They'd poked me with stick "magic wands" and made up rhyming spells to taunt me.

Rodney eyed me from the kitchen. With purpose, he dove through his cat door, as if daring me to follow.

Why not? A plaid wool jacket hung behind my office door. It was a few sizes too large, but I slipped the book into its pocket and pushed the sleeves up my forearms. I still had a while before Roz planned to take me through the library.

The air outside smelled of river and cottonwoods. My grandmother used to call them "bam trees," short for "balsam" and their sweet, soft fragrance. Instinctively, I moved to the path behind the library, where I could look down on the town, so close, yet removed.

There was Darla's tavern, its parking lot filling with early lunchers. Across the road was a white wooden church with a square steeple next to the old post office that Roz had told me was now a grocery store. Next to that, a shop. Patty's This-N-That, I think Roz called it.

Behind the tavern stretched a dozen or so mobile homes in tidy rows, many of them lushly gardened. I wondered which trailer was Roz's home.

Rodney turned his head toward me and trotted down the path toward the woods. He seemed to want me to follow him. Was this some kind of game? We'd never had pets when I was growing up. Grandma had kept cats, though. She'd always had an orange tabby named Sir Thomas. She must have had a succession of them, come to think of it. No one cat could live that long.

I followed Rodney along the path, just beyond the library, where we stopped. Rodney's tail flicked in the breeze. Here it was, the perfect spot. I yanked *Folk Witch* from my pocket and hurled it into the air. It circled like a Frisbee and disappeared into the brush. *Take that*.

Rodney meowed from the path's edge. His meow was pure and bell-like, not the husky growl I would have expected. He plunged off the trail after the book. The tall grass turned to blackberry vines before sloping to the river. He jumped onto a stump, and a low grumble bordering on a howl escaped him.

"Rodney? Come, kitty. Don't worry about that silly book. I'll order a new one."

Then I saw it. A bit of black emerged from the under-brush. Fabric. Perhaps an old jacket? A chill prickled my arms.

Attached to the black was a hand. And attached to the hand was a woman's body.

They'd found me.

I lifted a palm to my chest, trying to slow my pounding heart from the outside in. I waded into the brambles with my eyes half-shuttered, as if not seeing the body completely would somehow null its existence.

But oh yes, it existed. Lying half-enveloped by a web of blackberry vines was a woman in her midthirties with sleek black hair pulled into a ponytail. Her eyebrows were precisely plucked, and mascara streaked her cheeks. I noted smudged russet lipstick and diamond stud earrings. She was from a big city, had to be. I forced my gaze lower. Blood stained her silk blouse.

I'd read hundreds of mystery novels—especially golden era detective stories, my favorites—and I'd processed goodness knew how many oral histories dealing with death. None of it prepared me for the smashup of physical calm and emotional freak-out that gripped me.

Be strong, I told myself. Gingerly, I stepped forward, thorns rasping at my calves. "Forgive me," I said as I patted the woman's pockets. Nothing. I unzipped her jacket and reached inside, careful to avoid her wound, and came up dry. No sign of a purse, either.

I backed away. I swear I couldn't feel my feet on the ground.

Whoever this woman was, she wasn't from Wilfred. Her urban grooming nailed it. I'd seen scores of her type plying the Capitol's halls, although more often dressed in business suits than black pants and Gucci loafers. They always had an agenda. They always wanted something. This time, the something was me. I knew it.

A woman had come to kill me, and someone else had gotten to her first. Who? And why?

A better question was, why was I sticking around to find out? In five minutes I could be on my way to the airport. I'd find the caretaker, feed him the popular line "it didn't work out," and hitch a ride out of there. My breathing slowed. Yes. It's not like they needed me, anyway, since the library was due to be razed. I'd call the sheriff from the airport, and he'd take care of identifying the body. After all, even hit people had mothers.

Mind made up, I extricated myself from the brambles and turned down the trail to leave. And ran smack into Roz. Her wide eyes were fixed on the body, and her scream sent the cat streaking through the underbrush.

She flipped open her fan and set it in furious motion. "Oh no. She's dead, isn't she?"

Words stuck in my throat, so I simply nodded.

She made a noise like a strangled badger and popped open her top blouse buttons to get air. "I knew something bad would happen. I just didn't know it would be this bad."

CHAPTER FOUR

At last, my throat loosened enough to let me speak. "Call the police."

"On it." Roz's voice was sure, but her fingers trembled as she stuffed the fan in one pocket and pulled her phone from the other. "Sheriff Dolby, please."

So, that was that. I'd have to tell the sheriff why I'd left D.C., and he'd follow up to confirm it. I'd be outed. I didn't have the money to hide out without a job. I'd be forced to return home and pray for my safety. If it came down to a crook's choice between a billion-dollar contract or my life, I knew I should choose the music I wanted played at my funeral and get it over with.

I pressed my finger to my tingling birthmark and closed my eyes while Roz relayed her message to the sheriff. I opened my eyes to a jarringly peaceful sky and birds chirping.

"He's on his way," Roz said. In a shaky voice, she swore under her breath. "What a freaking disaster. This ruins everything." She grabbed my arm and led me toward the library's side entrance. "Come on. Let's wait inside. We can watch from the window."

We had barely settled at the kitchen table, Roz with her head in her hands and me staring wide-eyed out the window, when the sheriff arrived. He was a big man, football-defensive-line quality, as tall and wide as a door. Eyebrows thick and straight as kissing caterpillars laced his forehead. His star-shaped badge read SHERIFF'S OFFICE on top with WASHINGTON COUNTY on the bottom.

"What's this about a body, Roz?" he said. "I hope this is a joke."

Rodney slinked out from my office and hunkered near the door.

Roz shook her head. "Outside. Toward the woods, down the bluff. You want me to show you?" Her tone of voice said she wanted the sheriff to say no.

"I'll be back in a second. Don't move." The sheriff brushed past me with barely a look.

Roz poured us each a glass of water and slid one across the table. She downed hers in a few nervous gulps. Noticing I was watching her, she said, "What? I was thirsty. You should see me with a gin and tonic." The joke hung uncomfortably in the air. "Sorry. Bad taste."

As promised, the sheriff returned a few minutes later, pocketing his phone. "I'm Bert Dolby," he said and proffered a hand. "You must be the new librarian. You found the body?"

"Josephine Way." I shook his hand. "Yes, I was taking a walk, waiting for Roz." Answer his questions, but tell him no more, I reminded myself.

"When was this?"

"Ten minutes ago. Or so." Ten of the longest minutes in my life.

He looked at me, as if expecting me to say more. When I didn't, he prompted, "I'll get a full statement from you later. Right now, let's hit the highlights. The crime scene investigators won't be here for at least twenty minutes. You got in last night, right?" He nodded at Roz. "You wait outside. We'll talk later." She left.

I nodded and squeezed my hands together. "Lyndon, the caretaker—"

"I know Lyndon," the sheriff said.

"He picked me up at the airport and brought me here. About midnight. I called home"—they'd be able to trace that, so I might as well bring it up—"then went straight to bed."

"How about this morning?"

The sheriff wasn't so bad. Despite his bearlike size, he had a friendly way about him. I wouldn't be surprised if he coached high school sports and had turned a few kids' lives around over the years.

"I came downstairs just before nine, and Roz and Darla—you know Darla, right?"

He nodded. "Of course."

"Roz and Darla were in the kitchen. Here," I said, releasing a hand to wave it over the table. "Darla got called back to her diner, and Roz and I followed a few minutes later. We had breakfast, then returned to the library. I decided to take a walk."

"Okay. Now, slow down, and let's take this step by step. What door did you leave from?"

"That one." I pointed to the kitchen door. "I went toward the river. I wanted to look out over the town."

"Did you hear anything, see anything?"

"Nothing unusual. The cat came with me." As if understanding me, Rodney bumped against my legs. I reached a hand under the table to slide over his soft back.

"And then?"

"After I took in the view for a minute, I noticed the path to the left. Roz and I had already gone the other way, toward the bridge, to the diner."

"So you took the path to the woods."

"Right. I didn't get too far when I saw it." I swallowed. "I mean, her. That's when I saw her hand."

"Go on." His voice softened with encouragement.

"I couldn't believe it was a person. So I waded into the brambles a bit." I met his gaze. "She'd been shot." My throat tightened. I wasn't sure I could choke out another word.

The sheriff seemed to sense it. He leaned back. "That's enough for now. We'll talk more later. Roz?"

"Hmm?" She must have been lingering just beyond the door.

"Ms. Way has had a rough morning. You two keep yourselves company in here while the team and I take care of business outside. The library won't be open today, of course."

"No. It's closed anyway."

"We'll need to talk to you, too. Don't go far." He headed for the kitchen door.

Roz snorted. "As if," she said to his retreating back. She turned to stare at me. "I think this has to be it."

"What?" I said.

"Possibly the worst first day of work in history."

I laughed louder than the comment deserved, then cut

it off when it threatened to devolve into tears. "You have
no idea."

"I might," she said. She seemed to consider telling me
something, then changed her mind. "Come on. While we
wait, I'll show you the library."

"First, let's pay homage to our benefactor."

Roz and I stood in the library's atrium next to the
round table I'd seen from the third floor, my apartment.
In front of us, a double door with stained-glass windows
closed off the foyer. Behind us rose a wide staircase with
newel posts carved from golden oak. Four arched doorways led off the atrium.

"That's her." Roz pointed to a life-sized oil portrait of
a woman hanging over the double doors. "Marilyn Wilfred."

As if a portal to a different time, the portrait was of a
young woman standing in the atrium in which we now
stood. Except instead of shelves of books, a velvet chair
and a stained-glass lampshade showed from the open
arch beyond her. Marilyn Wilfred wore a ruby-toned flap-
per gown and a cloche hat. A gloved hand rested on a
round table—the same table we stood next to now. In the
portrait, the table held a crystal paperweight and a vase of
clematis. Today, a taller vase held branches of oak leaves
vivid with the oranges and golds of autumn.

"She looks friendly," I said.

I had that queer feeling again of hearing—or, really,
feeling—the books talk. They murmured like girls at a
tea party. The trauma of finding the body thinned.

"She was beloved. The rest of the Wilfreds, not so

much. But Auntie Lyn—that's what we called her—was a favorite. Everyone in town turned up for her funeral."

"You were there?"

Roz, still gazing at the portrait, nodded. "She lived a good long time. Died not long after the mill closed in the early nineties."

Marilyn Wilfred almost seemed to smile at me. My heart skipped a beat when I saw the black cat lying at her feet. Except for Rodney's torn ear, it might have been him.

"The black cat hanging around here. Rodney. Who does he belong to?"

"He showed up just last week. Dylan named him and made him a bowl in art class. We already had cat doors from Auntie Lyn's time. Is he bothering you?"

"No. Not at all."

Roz's hands dropped to her sides. "Now for the rest of the tour."

"Okay." I was reluctant to turn away from Marilyn Wilfred's comforting smile.

"You know the kitchen, of course. Let's take the ground floor clockwise. Here"—she pointed to the open arch beyond the service staircase—"is the old dining room. Now it's social sciences. We have a great local history section."

Bookshelves lined the room's damask-papered walls, but a chandelier with glass globes and a marble fireplace made it easy to imagine a polished mahogany table surrounded with chairs.

"Next stop, the sitting room."

We passed through a connecting door to a room mirroring the dining room, but with French doors opening to

a balcony. I moved toward the wooden block of drawers
in its center with brass pulls and numbered labels.

"I can't believe it. A card catalogue. I've never seen
one in real life."

"Yep. No computers here. Auntie Lyn's will said no
changes."

"Except for the 'betterment of Wilfredians,'" I quoted.
"Bringing the library into the age of the Internet would be
a huge benefit to everyone, especially students. The library would have access to all sorts of other collections."

She shrugged. "I'm sure you're right. The last librarian wanted to put some in, but he left before it could happen."

"Why didn't he stay?"

"Didn't work out." She pointed to a desk with a trolley
cart behind it. "Circulation. Magazines and new releases
are over there."

Right inside the front door, the sitting room was well
situated for keeping an eye on patrons coming and going.
What a wonderful place to work on a spring day with the
French doors ajar and the scent of the lawn wafting in.

The thought of outdoors reminded me of this morning's scene by the river and my upcoming interview with
the sheriff. "How well do you know the sheriff?"

"Known him for years. It's a small town, remember.
Why?"

"He's reasonable?"

"Reasonable and good at his job. A third-generation
sheriff and proud of it." Her voice was still calm, but I de-
tected a slight tremor. "He'll get to the bottom of this. I'm
sure."

"Oh." It wasn't what he'd find out about the body that
caused my concern, but what he'd dig up on me.

"You're okay, right?" When I nodded, she said, "Then follow me. Now we're going to what used to be the house's real library. It's just beyond the foyer, so the foreman from the mill could stop by to talk business without bothering the rest of the family."

We crossed the atrium to enter a wood-paneled room with a leather-topped desk as large as a twin bed.

"The first owner's study," I said.

"Right. Thurston Wilfred ruled his empire from here. Now it's children's fiction." She reshelved a Nancy Drew novel. "Not a lot of kids in Wilfred. Young families usually move on to Forest Grove or Portland. Ever since the mill closed, the town's been shrinking."

I made a mental note to lock up the fireplace tools. Pokers and toddlers didn't mix well. My thoughts slipped again to the body outside, and it must have shown on my face.

"Don't think about it. I'm not." Roz's sudden frown betrayed her statement. "Duke and Ilona will have a heyday when they find out."

"What do you mean?"

"A dead body on library grounds? They already complain about graffiti and loiterers. One of their chief arguments for the retreat center—apart from the money—is that it would be safer up here. This clinches it."

We paused in the atrium. From the look on Roz's face, her thoughts were as glum as mine.

"Come on," Roz said finally. "Let's skip the drawing room. You can look at it later. It's literature and arts." She pushed open a glass-paned door. "Here's the best part of the library. The conservatory."

I followed her into a glass-ceilinged room bright with sun and saw what she meant about "the best part of the library." Even with the stark view of leaves drifting off the trees, the conservatory was warm enough that a banana plant flourished in a gargantuan ceramic pot. In case the sun failed, a small tile woodstove sat in the corner with a few split logs in a basket.

Outside, a group of khaki-uniformed people, two carrying metal suitcases, marched down the trail. Lyndon watched from his pile of raked leaves.

Roz pointed to a table and chair in the corner, against a window. "I work here most days. I mean, my other work, not as assistant librarian." She shot me a glance. "Darla says it's okay if I keep things here. It's easier to focus than at home."

"What sorts of projects?"

"Oh, this and that."

She shuffled papers. People here were experts at avoiding questions.

She pointed to the ornate railings ringing the second floor. "Upstairs mirrors the ground floor, except it's all former bedrooms, plus another one over the front vestibule. Five rooms of books. Oh, and a bathroom."

"With a tub?" My apartment's bathroom rated only a shower stall.

Roz nodded. "Folks from the trailer court drop by for baths every once in a while. Mobile homes aren't known for big tubs, and some of Wilfred's residents partake a bit too regularly of Darla's pecan pie."

A thought occurred to me. "You don't keep books in there, do you?" Seeing the casual way the rest of the library was run, I wouldn't have doubted it.

"Only cookbooks."

"But the moisture—"

"No big deal. It's not like they're in pristine condition,

anyway. You should see the grease stains in *Cookies Near and Far*."

I'd never want to change the house's lush-if-worn oriental carpets or nooks with old armchairs, and having a library cat had always been a dream of mine. But, no Internet? Rotary telephones? And books in the bathroom? Too bad I wouldn't be around to take the library to its full potential. That is, if the library even existed beyond next month.

"Speaking of damaged books, I'm afraid I lost *Folk Witch*." Roz didn't need to know about my fit of pique this morning. "I'll pay for a new copy, of course."

"*Folk Witch*? The book at the diner I said I'd reshelve? You must be talking about another book." She lifted a paperback with its all-too-familiar cover from her desk. "It's right here."

CHAPTER FIVE

I spent the next few hours in my apartment unpacking and getting settled.

Little touches throughout the apartment welcomed me. Lavender sachets freshened the linen closet. Baskets of firewood next to the bedroom and living room fireplaces almost made me wish for snow so I could strike up a blaze. Best of all, each room had at least one cozy place to read, with a good lamp and a table to hold a cup of coffee.

I imagined what it would have been like had I known I were staying. Despite the horror of finding a body, Wilfred charmed me. Everyone I'd met had been welcoming and friendly, and even Lyndon, the caretaker, was growing on me. The countryside was gorgeous—so green and full of life—and the air was perfumed with fir, moist soil, and river water. Colors here might have been drawn from a crisper palette than back home.

My little sister, Jean, once told me that people tend to be oriented toward their mind, emotions, or body. She pronounced me a "mind" person and said I didn't care about my surroundings as long as I had a book handy. Somehow in the past day, I'd drifted toward my senses. My sheets had the silken hand of years of washing. I luxuriated in the feel of them on my skin. I couldn't even tell you what my sheets in D.C. were made of. I smelled the warm wood of the house's ancient fir joists. The afternoon was thick with birdsong.

And the house—I loved the house and the fact that it was now a library. Back home, I'd toured a lot of fancy house museums and grand public buildings, but none of them spoke to me the way the Wilfred library did. Was it Wilfred that held the magic, or had I changed somehow?

Yet, I couldn't stay. Even if the library wasn't going to be demolished—and that was a big "if"—the body I'd found would end up in the news, possibly with my name attached, and that would be that. I'd have to leave. I just didn't know when.

I sighed and pushed open the bedroom window's curtains. All morning and most of the afternoon, people came and went up the library's gravel drive. They traipsed through the garden separating the library from Lyndon's cottage to the trail by the river. From what I could make out, most were from the county sheriff's office. A van arrived, and two people hauled off the body, bundled in black plastic, on a gurney.

The sheriff hadn't stuck around for most of these proceedings, but from the reports Darla delivered via Roz's cell phone, he was busy. According to Wilfred's robust grapevine, which seemed to terminate at Darla's diner, the sheriff had been seen in Forest Grove and Gaston knocking on doors. I even learned he'd taken lunch—a microwaved burrito from a convenience store, extra hot sauce—in his cruiser. No one had reported any arrests.

All I could do was watch and wait.

"Ms. Way?" the sheriff said from the kitchen door.

"Josie, please." I set aside a P.G. Wodehouse novel. Normally, I'd have searched the library's shelves for a Ngaio Marsh or Rex Stout mystery I hadn't read recently, but crime novels cut too close to the bone this afternoon.

"It's time for that statement I told you about this morning. Mind if I join you in your office?"

I stayed in the armchair, and Sheriff Dolby overwhelmed the wooden chair at my desk. The office felt half its earlier size.

I fidgeted with the fabric of my skirt. Rodney watched from under the desk. "What do you want to know?"

"Why don't you start at the beginning? Tell me about finding her." His voice was surprisingly gentle for such a big man. I appreciated how he avoided saying "body."

"Like I told you this morning, I just arrived last night."

"To take the librarian position," the sheriff said. "You can skip to this morning."

"Was that when they think it happened?"

"We don't have the medical examiner's final determination, you understand, but she was likely killed sometime last night."

"Before I arrived."

"Yes. Looks that way. Lyndon filled me in on your arrival time."

So, all the time I'd been wandering around upstairs alone last night, she'd been there, a stone's throw from my bedroom. Dead. I pulled in my arms as if being smaller would make the shock smaller, too.

"Well, as I said this morning, Roz was planning to give me a tour of the library, but she had something else to attend to. So I took a walk. I found . . . I found her off the trail. Only a few minutes later, Roz came out, too. We called you right away. Ten-thirty-ish."

"Ten-thirty-seven," he said. "Did you touch anything?"

I bit my lip. "I did touch the body."

His thick eyebrows rose.

"To look for ID. I felt her pants pockets and inside her jacket."

"And?"

I felt certain she'd been sent to silence me, but that's all it was—a feeling. To my surprise, before my eyes flashed the cover of *The Executioner's Song*.

"Nothing. I didn't find anything. No purse, no phone, nothing."

"Do you have any idea who she might be?"

This was the moment. Telling the sheriff my suspicions would expose why I was in Wilfred. My cover would be blown. If the story came out in the newspaper—well, it would be like sending up a flare to my pursuer. I shifted my gaze toward the office window. Should I tell?

The day it had happened, only a week ago, had been drizzly. I'd decided to spend my lunch hour in the library's stacks. I could close my eyes now and see it all.

I'd taken the elevator to the deep subbasement. Most people don't know that below the Library of Congress are layered floor after floor of books. The elevator opened to dark acres of metal shelving. I clicked the light switch on the end of the shelf to my right, knowing its timer would give me just enough time to reach my favorite spot deep among decades-old industry trade publications. No one went there. The year before, when the office upgraded our chairs, I'd moved my old chair down and placed an upturned box next to it. I stashed a book light and a cloth napkin in its recesses.

I unwrapped my egg salad sandwich and took in the comfort of being surrounded by books. Thousands and thousands of books, around me, above me, and below me. They seemed to hum their comfort, like a peculiar Gregorian chant. This was the only place I felt this, and only when I was alone. Until I'd come to Wilfred, that is.

The elevator opened and lights clicked on again and steps came down the central aisle. "Mind if I join you?" It was Anton, my office mate. We'd been hired the same day and had been buddies ever since.

"Take a seat." Anton would have to sit on the floor, but he never minded. He was the sort of guy who made himself comfortable wherever he was.

The lights clicked off. We sat in the dim glow of my book light, me with my sandwich and Anton with a takeout bowl of curry.

Then I heard the voices. Lights flickered on across the main aisle a few shelves closer to the elevator.

"You're sure no one can hear us here?" a man's voice asked.

Another man laughed. "You can't even get cell service

this far down. Look. The *Beer Digest* from 1965. Who's
going to find us here?"

I knew the voice but couldn't place it. It had a slight
Southern accent. I set my sandwich on the crate next to
my chair and clicked off the book light. I looked toward
Anton but couldn't make out his expression in the dark.

"Here's the info. Four million in an offshore account,
as we agreed. The access code is in the envelope," the
first man said.

A crinkle of paper. "Great. I guess that's it."

"No. I need assurance you'll follow through on our
agreement."

"You don't trust me." The man, the one with the
vaguely familiar voice, laughed again. "Not that you
could prove anything. But you don't need to worry. We
have solid cooperation in the Pentagon's procurement office, I've seen to that. The senator will sign whatever I
recommend. The contract belongs to Bondwell."

The senator. Senator Markham. Now it came to me.
The voice I heard was Senator Markham's chief of staff,
Richard White. Markham was chair of the defense autho-
rizations. Bondwell was a major aeronautics company.
The elevator dinged, and after muttered good-byes, the
stacks were quiet once again.

It took Anton and me only a few minutes to decide we
had to report what we'd heard. By the close of the day,
FBI agents were taking our statements. Anton had vanished the very next morning. He hadn't shown up for
work, and no one could find him. My supervisor granted
my request for leave, thinking I simply needed a few
weeks of vacation to recuperate. Instead, I'd fled.

"Earth to Josie," the sheriff said. I wasn't in D.C. anymore. Now I was all the way across the country, in rural Oregon. Rodney watched me, his pupils mere slits. When the sheriff spoke, the cat's gaze shifted to him. "Did you find anything that might indicate who the victim is?"

My hands were shaking. I tucked them under my thighs. "No. Nothing. I have no idea who she is. Why would I?"

CHAPTER SIX

By nightfall, the library's grounds were quiet. The sheriff and his colleagues were gone, except for the deputy Sheriff Dolby had thoughtfully posted at the top of the road.

I still didn't feel completely safe. Thanks to the house's floor plan with the floor-to-ceiling atrium, my apartment was open to the library below. However, the solid oak door at the top of the service staircase ensured my privacy, and the apartment was high enough that I couldn't be seen unless I leaned over the railings. I tested the door. The dead bolt was solid. Another plus, a cat door let Rodney come and go.

Only one mystery remained in the apartment, and that was the padlocked door at the end of the hall, to the left of the service staircase. The door must lead to the tower extending over the vestibule. In that case, it made sense to lock people out. A fall that far could kill.

In every room I went, Rodney was somewhere nearby—in an armchair, at the foot of the bed, under the kitchen table. I was getting attached to the little guy.

I changed into a cotton nightgown, wrapped a warm chenille robe around me, and left a pile of bobby pins next to the bathroom sink. If I could, I'd sleep. I turned down the blankets on my bed, then realized one vital element was missing: a novel. I'd finished the Margaret Millar mystery I'd brought on the plane, and I'd had my fill of P.G. Wodehouse for the day. Heck, I lived in a library now. Finding something to read would not be a problem. I was halfway to the door when Rodney meowed from the bed.

"What, kitten?"

He padded to the head of the bed and rubbed his nose on the bedside table. There, next to the lamp, was one of my favorite novels, *Pride and Prejudice*. Who was leaving books out for me? I'd ask Roz in the morning. She didn't have to go to this trouble.

I slipped under the covers. Jane Austen had seen me through many a crisis. Her stories held no more surprises—I could recite some passages by heart—but the soothing story of friendship, family, threatened love, and, finally, justice was better than a massage and a hot bath for restoring my equilibrium.

I snuggled in, smoothing the quilt over my chest, and opened the book two-thirds through, looking for the part where Elizabeth's aunt and uncle take her to Pemberley. Rodney settled next to my shoulder and purred. Loudly.

So loudly that I placed a finger on the page and closed the book.

"I'm going to have to get earplugs, if you keep this up."

Rodney raised his chin, and for a split second, colors flattened. I had the bizarre sensation of staring at the ceiling, up where Rodney's gaze was. My body gently vibrated. As if I were purring. In a flash, everything was normal again. I caught my breath. What had just happened? The day's stress had clearly been too much for me. I shut my eyes and opened them. My vision was fine. Weird.

Rodney inhaled, boosting his purr another few decibels, and rolled to his back, exposing a luscious belly—and his birthmark. I knew better than to fall for the furry booby trap of a cat's belly, but I examined the birthmark more closely. It was a star, like mine, with the top point stretched further than the four other points. Also just like mine.

I rubbed my eyes and returned to my book. Elizabeth and her aunt and uncle's carriage was pulling into Pemberley, and Elizabeth remembered her difficult last words with Darcy. She longed to see him, yet dreaded running into him. I turned the page.

The words were gobbledygook. They might have been the fake language designers use to fill pages in sample brochures. I flipped ahead. All the book's pages were the same. What was this? Some kind of freaky printing error?

I closed the book and stared, perplexed, at the twining morning glories on the wallpaper. I'd been a librarian in one capacity or another for a full five years. Tens of thousands of books had crossed my desk, especially at the Library of Congress, where I'd catalogued scores of them every day. In all that time, I'd never seen this sort of printing calamity. I was surprised one of the former librarians hadn't noticed it earlier and pulled the novel out of circulation.

The hum of the two floors of books below me sweetened into a lullaby. "Come choose something else," they seemed to say. "Come find another story."

Rodney jumped from the bed and stood at the door.

"Oh, all right." I threw back the covers and reached for my bathrobe. What was one bad book? Worlds of them lay sleeping below me.

I stood in the hall and leaned over the railing to take in the dark library below. The building was entirely silent. Even the murmuring books had shushed. Libraries were supposed to be quiet, but during a working day, layers of sound filled them, and that's how I liked it. Patrons asked for recommendations and flipped through books. Computer keys clacked. Librarians delivered information on how to nurse foster kittens or what the average winter snowfall is in Duluth or, more often, where to find the restrooms. Libraries were hives of activity, and as so, they were noisy.

Not the Wilfred library tonight. Moonlight splashed through the skylight and cast diamond-shaped shadows on the parquet floor. Besides the occasional whoosh of a breeze through the trees, and the creak of old timber, I couldn't hear a thing. I reminded myself that I didn't need to worry. Sheriff Dolby had posted someone at the top of the road. No one would be able to drive up or even take the path from town without being stopped.

I pulled my robe closer and took the stairs to the ground floor. Literature was in the old drawing room, I remembered. There was enough moonlight that I didn't need to turn on an overhead lamp. I'd easily be able to find a thriller or maybe a good family saga to ease me to sleep.

Or another Jane Austen, a voice seemed to say. *Persuasion*.

I did adore *Persuasion*. Poor Anne, in love with Captain Wentworth, yet he ignored her, until that delicious scene in the drawing room in Bath. Austen. She'd be shelved at the end, near the fireplace. I crossed the wood floor until I reached the Persian carpet—strange as it was to have oriental carpets in a library, I liked it. I passed the shelves and let a hand run along books' spines, and my fingers tingled as the volumes vibrated with story.

I turned the corner and stopped cold. In the armchair between the fireplace and the window was a man. I stepped back and grasped the edge of the bookshelf. The man was still, and his eyes were shut. I held my breath until I saw the gentle rise of his chest. He was sleeping. But he wasn't one of the sheriff's deputies, was he?

He didn't look it. He might have been a ghost. He wore the type of simple wool pants and rag wool sweater that have been in fashion for a hundred years. His loafers were tumbled next to the chair, leaving him in socks, one of which had a hole at the toe. He was probably seven or eight years older than I with soft brown hair that receded from his temples. Three volumes of Hardy Boys novels rested on the chair's arm, and *The Clue of the Screeching Owl* lay open over a knee.

All at once, his eyes snapped open. I grabbed the spine of a fat Anthony Trollope novel and held it like a cudgel. We stared at each other, neither of us moving.

His lips turned downward slightly, but when he spoke,

his voice was rich with warmth. "You must be the new librarian."

"Who are you?" I said, barely letting him finish his sentence.

"Thurston Wilfred."

My grip on the novel tightened. "That's a good one. He's dead."

"The fifth. Thurston Wilfred the fifth. They call me Sam. I'm your neighbor, at Big House. You can put down the book. It's okay."

I became conscious of the disaster of red curls fluffing over my shoulders and my bathrobe with its kitschy pink chenille flowers. I stood straighter. "How do I know you're who you say you are?"

"I guess you don't know."

"And even if you are, what gives you the right to come barging in here after hours? There's a sheriff's deputy outside, you know. I could have you arrested."

"I know. I talked to him when I arrived."

The Trollope novel—*The Eustace Diamonds*, I noted, one of my favorites—almost seemed to slip back into the shelf by itself.

Sam let out his breath. "I'm sorry to frighten you. The deputy told me about this morning. That must have been a shock."

"Finding a dead woman? Yeah, I'd say so."

He ignored my sarcasm. "If it helps, nothing like this has happened before in Wilfred. At least, not as far as I know. You'll be safe."

It occurred to me that although I'd found the body, it was only a stone's throw from the Big House. "Do you have any idea who she was or how she got there?"

"Me? No." Strangely, he almost smiled. At least, his mouth did.

"I guess we're both a little edgy," I conceded.

"When I got back into town this afternoon, I couldn't help coming here. The library has always been one of my favorite places. I loved being surrounded by books. Auntie Lyn used to let me come in when it closed and eat cookies and read. Right here."

He wore a slight frown, but his voice was warm and his eyes soft. If not for the downward turn of his lips, I'd have thought he was happy. Unexpectedly so. I looked at him a moment longer. I told myself it was because the light was so dim. He looked at me, too.

Then he sneezed. Rodney rubbed against the toe peeking from his sock. "Excuse me," he said. "I'm allergic to cats."

I returned to full attention and put a hand on a chenille-draped hip. "Yes, I'm the new librarian. Josephine Way. If you don't mind, the library is closed after hours to anyone except staff. How did you get in, anyway?"

He held out a key. "We've always kept a key. You know, as part of the family."

I snatched it from his palm and slipped it into my bathrobe's pocket. "The library is closed."

He rose, and I backed out of his way. "I understand," he said.

"I appreciate that you're comfortable here, but we can't have patrons coming and going whenever they feel like it."

"Understood."

"The library opens at ten tomorrow morning," I added.

"It's nice to meet you. We'll undoubtedly be seeing each other again. Good night."

I let him out the front and bolted the door. Something momentous had happened, but I didn't know what it was.

I leaned against the door frame. One thing was curious, though. I'd seen a light at Big House last night, late. Yet he'd said he'd arrived just this afternoon.

CHAPTER SEVEN

I awoke the next morning feeling both apprehension and excitement. This was it. For the first time, I'd be running my own library. I saw myself as a combination administrator and matchmaker, bringing people and books together for what might be long, happy relationships. What could be better than that?

Rodney jumped from the bed and stretched on the chair by the window before vigorously cleaning his face. All night he'd slept cuddled against my shoulder, as if to give me comfort and courage.

As I prepared for the day, I was still dizzy from dreaming. Where had it all come from? I'd always been a decent sleeper. When Anton had come in to work with a double espresso and complained of insomnia, I listened patiently, but without understanding. For me, going to bed was easy. Bath, a few chapters of something from my pile of vintage mystery novels, then a stretch of unbroken sleep.

Since I'd been in Wilfred, all that had changed. Not only was I dreaming, it was as if every dream I'd been meant to have over the years were lined up and coming at me triple-time. I'd awake from one dream, Rodney purring next to my ear, then fall asleep into another.

The dream that stayed with me through all of this was the one I'd also had the night before, of standing in my grandmother's moonlit garden in my nightgown, holding a glass of pungent liquid, feeling dread and resignation.

At last, dressed and fortified with a hot breakfast of poached eggs and toast, I went downstairs. Rodney followed me and took a right to the kitchen and his cat door to the garden.

A second after the cat door flapped, the kitchen door opened to Roz. She shed her coat and checked that the coffeepot was burbling. "Dylan's coming right behind me on his bicycle."

"The intern, right?" I said.

A moment later, a freckled blond dressed in too-short stovepipe trousers with a matching vest and wingtip shoes joined us. His cheeks were ruddy from pedaling up the hill. He set his bicycle helmet on the counter.

"Dylan Tohler, ma'am." He thrust out a hand.

"You can call me Josie." I pointed to the carnation in his buttonhole. "I like your style."

"My grandpa left me these clothes. I figure they suit the setting."

"Ready for your debut?" Roz asked me.

"I guess so," I said.

"You'd better be, because there's a line waiting to get in. Everyone wants to see the new librarian and finder of dead bodies."

I'd known Roz less than three days, but something about her already felt like family. "Then let's do it." I stepped ahead of Roz to cross the atrium and propped open the foyer's inner door. At the front, I threw open the bolt and heaved the brass handle.

Half a dozen people waited outside in the drizzly fall morning, and another few were coming up the path from town. My breath quickened. I couldn't wait to get started. Despite the gesture to enter, the patrons waited in the foyer to be introduced.

"You must be the new librarian." A woman with short gray hair and binoculars dangling around her neck beamed at me. Her T-shirt read BIRDERS DO IT IN THE BUSH. "Ruth Littlewood. Lifelong Wilfredian and library devotee."

"It's nice to meet you. I bet you have great suggestions for our natural history collection."

The next patron introduced himself and, as if to stretch conversation, asked about books on gardening.

"*Growing Vegetables in Cascadia* is one you might want to check out." A jolt went through me. Where had that title come from? As far as I knew, I'd never even heard of the book. I must have seen it, and its title had stuck in my mind. Then, surprising me further, I said, "Upstairs, back bedroom. You'll find it on the shelf nearest the closet."

"I hear your welcome in Wilfred wasn't as, um, friendly as it might have been," he added.

"Hmm?" I was still stunned at my sudden knowledge of local gardening.

"He means the dead girl in the bushes," the man behind him said. He stuck out a hand. "Craig Burdock." He craned his head. "I haven't been to the library in ages. Nice digs." He drew a strand of his long hair behind his ears, and his eyes grazed my figure. "If I'd have known how attractive it was in here, I'd have come sooner."

Although I hated to make generalizations about readers, Craig Burdock didn't look like he spent a lot of time with books. He had shaggy hair and tight jeans and, curiously, wore moccasins without socks, despite the crisp morning. Two books titles leapt to mind: a biography of Al Capone and *Studies in Juvenile Delinquency*.

"Can I help you?" I asked in my most professional voice.

"Yeah, you sure could."

"With a book?" I added.

"I'm looking for love poetry."

I should have laughed, but there was something riveting about his velvety brown eyes. This guy had deadly charisma. "You might like Lord Byron. Poetry's back there." I waved toward the house's old drawing room.

"Craig?" A woman in a bathrobe stood frozen inside the door. She had a purple towel in one hand and a basket holding a bar of soap and a loofah sponge in the other. Trailing her on a dirty satin ribbon was a blond terrier mutt.

Craig Burdock's expression wavered before settling on a smile. "Hey, Lalena. Maybe I'll see you later?"

"Maybe you'll see me in hell." She turned to me, purposefully ignoring Burdock, who slouched off to poetry. "Welcome to Wilfred. I'm Lalena Dolby."

"Josie Way," I said, extending a hand.

"I'm here for a bath. I hope that's okay. Some of us

from the trailer park come up sometimes. Did Bert tell you about me?"

"You mean Sheriff Dolby?"

"My brother. Well, my half brother. My mom named us after Donovan songs. Bert was named after 'Bert's Blues.' 'Lalena' for me. Obviously."

"Obviously."

"Later she was on to Neil Diamond. I might have been named 'Sweet Caroline.' Who knows?"

"Or 'Cracklin' Rosie,'" I said, dredging the title up from Dad's collection of LPs. "Bert's quite a bit older than you, isn't he?"

"Fifteen years. Like a father, in some ways. It didn't surprise me at all when he went to work for the county sheriff. Dad was a sheriff, too, and so was Grandpa. It's the family business." She continued toward the stairs, then stopped and turned. "You don't have a departed loved one, do you?"

"What?" I stepped back.

"You know, a loved one I can connect you to."

"No. I mean, none I need to chat with," I said, thinking of the body in the bushes.

"I do tarot, palm readings, and communication with the dead. Come see me, if you want, but not before ten in the morning."

"Okay." I felt a little discombobulated.

For almost an hour I stood just inside the door greeting patrons. After shaking my hand, a few Wilfredians said things like, "Sorry about your experience. We're a good town, and I hope you'll enjoy it here," giving me meaningful looks. Roz kept passing through the hall and waving her hands as if to say, "Busy!"

Only one person asked specifically about the body, a

ten-year-old who probably plagued her teacher with off-topic questions. She paused chewing her gum long enough to say, "Someone plugged a stranger out back, huh?" I directed her toward the children's section and *Harriet the Spy*.

In fact, I was a well of book recommendations, and I loved it. Patrons probably more interested in checking out the new librarian approached me and asked something offhand, like where *War and Peace* was shelved. I'd find myself jotting down the name of another novel for them, and, in one case, recommending a do-it-yourself manual on installing brake shoes.

Where did it come from? It was like I was plugged in to a cosmic book catalogue, and each of my suggestions was an arrow striking a bull's-eye. It was exhilarating. This was what I was meant to do. This was why I loved books so much.

At last, the stream of looky-loos abated, and, almost giddy, I made my way back to my office.

"I haven't checked out so many books in—well, ever. Murder sure boosts circulation," Roz said.

Lyndon came through the back door with an armload of dahlias. Roz swiveled to watch him, and he seemed to feel the need to say something. "Flowers. For the atrium."

"Did you arrange the branches there now? They're beautiful," I said.

He grunted and filled a vase from the kitchen faucet.

"Lyndon is very talented with plants and flowers," Roz said with pride.

Without looking at her, Lyndon passed through to the library.

Roz sighed. "I'll get the circulation desk. I only work half a day, so you might want to eat lunch now."

"Good idea." I turned toward my desk, then caught Roz just as she left. "Oh, in this morning's craziness, I forgot to tell you that I left a copy of *Pride and Prejudice* on your desk last night. Could you pull it from circulation? There's some kind of printing error with the last half, and it's completely unintelligible."

"Figures," Roz said. I prepared myself for her inevitable downer statement. "I suppose we'll have to go over every single book that comes in."

I spent the next half hour with a sandwich in my office. I looked over the circulation records and library events and couldn't help making notes for improvement. I felt a high that whooshed through my veins and flowered in ideas and energy. I wouldn't be around to see any of the projects through, but the library needed a computerized system to check out books and track inventory. As far as I could tell, no one had been issued a library card in years, and books were lent with a simple notation of name and date in a ledger. Also, cookbooks should definitely be moved out of the bathroom.

Such a shame I'd be leaving so soon. There was so much I could do here.

"Yoo-hoo." Roz stuck her head into the office. "Is this the book you were talking about?" She lifted the volume of *Pride and Prejudice*.

"That's it."

"Looks fine to me." She set the book on the desk and ruffled its pages. "See?"

I pulled it closer and flipped to the passage I'd read last night. I turned the page. The text read without a hitch.

CHAPTER EIGHT

I was in the sitting room tidying the circulation desk when Sam crossed the yard from Big House. The sun picked up strands of premature gray in his hair. He glanced up and I hurriedly busied myself with the pencil holder. Some part of me had been waiting for his return.

"Ms. Way?" he said from the arched entrance to the hall.

I turned and faked surprise at seeing him. "Did you come back for your Hardy Boys novel?"

"No, I actually came to apologize." Now just the desk was between us. "When I got home, I realized what a shock it must have been for you to find a stranger here after hours. Especially given what had happened that morning."

"You're right." In the light of day, Sam should have

looked like any other library patron. He should be less intriguing. I firmed up my voice. "I didn't like it."

"I could tell. I'm sorry." That strange look of dissatisfaction settled over his mouth again, but you couldn't see it in his eyes. "I have a bad habit of falling asleep too easily, especially when I'm content. I've always loved this library, and it had been a long day—"

"That's okay," I said, suddenly unwilling to see him uncomfortable.

"Thanks. I can't afford to alienate anyone else in this town. Friends?"

"Friends." I shook his hand.

I wasn't sure what else to say. I didn't see any reason he should stick around, but I wasn't ready for him to leave yet, either.

"Hello, Roz," he said. "Long time, no see."

Roz was standing in the entrance to Thurston Wilfred's old office watching us. "Not since I last babysat you, Sammy. Couldn't have been more than a few days before your family skipped town."

His frown deepened. "Still the same dour attitude?"

"Ha," she said. "You know it. And I see you still look mad when you're happy." She nodded at me. "Watch out if he smiles. Then you're in for it." She leaned against the arch and crossed her arms over her chest. "What brings you back to town?"

"Just feeling homesick."

"You moved to Los Angeles, right?"

"Right."

"Mother still alive?"

"She sends her love."

Roz snorted. "She was smart to stay away. I can't

imagine you've had an enthusiastic welcome in Wilfred, either."

He twirled a pencil in one hand. "I guess I understand," he said finally. "I was only eight when the mill shut down, you know. It's been twenty-five years."

"People don't forget."

There was a sadness in Sam. I felt it. Despite the easy waves of book recommendations I'd made over the day, I couldn't think of anything to offer or say. I grabbed the Hardy Boys mystery he'd been reading last night and pressed it into his hands.

"Come back anytime," I said.

"Thanks, Josie. I will."

In the reflection off the open French doors to the hall, I watched him cross the now-sun-dappled grounds to his house. *Thanks, Josie*, he'd said. My breath caught. I'd never told him my nickname.

I followed Roz to the conservatory. "Did you tell Sam about me?"

She raised an eyebrow. "No. That's the first I've seen of him in years. Why?"

Something about the night before felt too intimate to talk about. I changed the subject. "What happened with Sam's family, anyway? Why is everyone so hostile to him?"

Roz sat at her desk. Besides an older couple browsing popular fiction, the library was quiet. Beyond the glass walls, Lyndon was raking leaves. She turned to me, reluctantly, I thought, and closed her laptop before I got a look at her mysterious project.

"What does it matter? You two seem to get along fine. Why wreck it?" she said.

If there was something to wreck, I wanted to know about it. "You've made lots of disparaging comments about the Wilfreds. Everyone has. I figure as long as I'm here, I ought to know some of the history. Is there more than what you've already told me?"

Roz pointed to a chair. I sat. "It's like this," she said. "As I told you yesterday, the Wilfred mill is the whole reason the town exists. A couple hundred people worked there, and the town was set up to support them—us. Dad worked marking lumber."

"Okay." So far, pretty straightforward.

"The last year the mill was open, a union organizer came to town, and a lot of the guys thought he had good ideas about raising their wages and fixing up company housing."

"There was company housing?"

"Where the trailer court is. The houses weren't bad, but they're in the bend of the river and tended to flood in rainy years. We've put the trailers up on cinder blocks just in case."

"So, the mill didn't go union, and people resent that?"

"It wasn't that."

Roz kept glancing over my shoulder. I was against the wall, so she couldn't be watching for patrons. I turned and realized she was watching Lyndon's reflection in the conservatory's glass panes.

Roz noticed that I caught her and quickly added, "The mill shut down with no warning, in the middle of the night, and the Wilfreds skipped town."

"No warning at all?"

"None. Like most of the mills around here, it was getting harder to find good timber to harvest. But it wasn't like the Wilfreds were going bankrupt. One day, the mill was running as usual, and the next day the place was gone. As in, burned to the ground. Christmas was right around the corner, too."

"Whoa." No wonder people were still angry.

"All that's left is the mill pond and the concrete shell of the stacking house. The Wilfreds pay Lyndon to keep an eye on Big House, but they never said anything about coming back." She leaned back and folded her arms. "Now Sam shows up. There are a lot of old scores to settle."

"Is there a theory about why the mill shut down so suddenly? Maybe some kind of double books or insurance fraud or something?" Since my experience in the Library of Congress stacks, I wouldn't put it by anyone to steal.

Roz shook her head. "Most folks figure the Wilfreds saw the writing on the wall with the union and didn't want to deal with it."

"A harsh way to go out of business."

Roz turned back to her computer. "No kidding."

Six o'clock. Time to close the library.

It had been a good day—maybe not exactly what I'd pictured as a kid when I dreamed of running a library—but in many ways better. Among the Wilfredians who simply wanted to check out a murder scene, I'd met some real book lovers, and I'd made some reading recommendations that had surprised even me. Who knew I'd suggest a book on raising Pomeranians to a woman browsing the self-help section? I never would have guessed I'd press Raymond Chandler's *The Long Goodbye* into the hands of a man looking for a how-to book on repairing lawn mowers. I had a gift for this. An uncanny gift. Heck, a kind of magic. I didn't want it to end.

All around me, books seemed to sigh in contentment. They felt happy for a day's work well done. Or maybe that was me.

As I unlocked the book return box on the front porch, a white Mercedes pulled in front of the library and killed its engine. A blonde who might have been anywhere from thirty to fifty years old stepped from the car in heels I recognized from the Neiman Marcus catalogue Anton used to peruse during coffee breaks. Manolo Blahnik, last spring's collection. I hoped she'd bought the boots on the facing page. Nights were getting chilly.

"I'm just closing up," I told her.

She joined me on the porch and placed a hand on the brass doorknob. "I'm Ilona Buckwalter," she said, as if that exempted her from the rules.

Ilona. The name was familiar, but I couldn't quite make the connection. "I'm new here," I said. "I haven't met everyone yet."

Ilona pushed her way inside, and I followed. She took in the hall, her gaze resting briefly on the staircase's newel posts, then the light fixtures. "You're the new librarian, huh? I'm sorry you won't have a job much longer. I'm sure the job market is solid for librarians. In the meantime, Darla was smart to bring you on. We'll need someone to clear this place out." From her tone, it was clear she didn't know and didn't care about the library employment situation.

"I was just about to close," I repeated. "We'll be open tomorrow at ten."

Ilona's heels clicked across the floor as she touched a brass wall sconce and headed for the dining room's marble fireplace. "It's not my fault I'm late. It's that stupid Sheriff Dolby and his damn speed trap."

Good for him. My smile loosened to a neutral position when she turned to me. "Nonetheless, I have paperwork to do."

"I'm a trustee. You work for me." She smiled and shut it off instantly. "Surely a few more minutes won't hurt."

Now I remembered. Ilona was the trustee managing the library's sale. I knew from an internship and working at the university that trustees were a big deal in the library world. They decided budgets and hired the head librarians. In turn, librarians compiled reports and generally tried to prove their worth.

Ilona's heels clicked on the parquet floor as she passed to the parlor. "We'll keep the books, of course. You'll have to find a place to store them. I'll salvage some of the fixtures. The new owners might want to use them in the retreat center. Bring a bit of Wilfred's history to it." She ran a hand over the mantel's filigree. "I might keep this one for myself."

Her presumptuousness was getting on my nerves. Not to mention her lack of respect for my time. I glanced up at Marilyn Wilfred's portrait. *Give me patience*, I asked her. I swear she lifted an eyebrow.

"You're sure the library will be demolished? You know it's an active crime scene. Someone was murdered."

I'd intended the words to shock her, but from her expression, I might have been offering her baked Brie and chardonnay.

"Oh, that's not a problem. The body was found outside. The sheriff says it won't slow the plans at all."

"Sheriff Dolby?" I asked.

She snorted, an inelegant noise that didn't jibe with her diamond studs and perfectly sculpted nose. "As if. No, I mean the sheriff of Washington County. The real one. He says they're finished with the crime scene now. No problem at all."

"What about the legal challenge Darla filed?" I said.

"The judge will throw that out. It's simply a matter of days."

"You can't be sure of it—"

"Why not? Marilyn Wilfred's will was clear. The sale of the library is for everyone's best. We need the jobs the retreat center will bring. It will rejuvenate the entire town. We all know it. My study proves it. The trustees voted in its favor, didn't we?"

"Not everyone," I couldn't help adding.

"I haven't seen any testimony filed against the sale."

"But there is the suit to stop it."

"And a countersuit to drop the first suit," she snapped. She moved on to Thurston Wilfred's old office.

I clenched my fingers and released them. It didn't seem fair that such a self-centered person as Ilona Buck-walter would profit from the library's demolition. She didn't care about Wilfred, that was plain. She wanted the real estate commission that funded her Botox shots. It wasn't fair.

It wasn't fair. Those were the words that had gone through my mind when I'd overheard the senator's aide mentioning the offshore account the bribe would be deposited in. Those were the words that got me into trouble every time.

Ilona turned to face me full-on. The woman I saw might have been the sister of the one who'd imperiously strode in earlier. Her expression had softened, and her eyes pleaded with me. "I sound awful, don't I? Could we sit down? Just for a moment. I know you're closing."

With surprise, I took one of the armchairs near the fireplace. She took the other and relaxed, her head lolling against the chair's back. Now she was no longer the wealthy socialite. She might have even been from Wilfred itself, but in fancier clothes. Viewed from the side, her nose wasn't as ready to be pictured on a Roman coin. Small lines underlay her eyes and striped her forehead. She set her purse on the ground. Rodney appeared from nowhere to sniff at it.

"How long have you been in Wilfred?" she asked.

"This is my third day. I came in from"—I almost said "Washington, D.C.," but corrected myself at the last second—"Maryland."

"So you don't know why the retreat center is so important." She sat up. "I'm a local girl, from Gaston, up the highway. It's awful, what happened when the mill shut down. It was a smack in the face, let me tell you."

I nodded, thinking of Sam. Out of the corner of my eye, I caught Rodney testing the strap of Ilona's purse in his teeth. I opened my mouth to chastise him, and he raised his head and stared at me. I returned my attention to Ilona.

"The timber economy is gone now. Half the town's residents—those who stayed, that is—are on food stamps. Wilfred's in a sweet location, though. Between the coast and wine country, and the Kirby River is beautiful. There's a chance for the town to grow and reestablish itself."

"People do hate change," I said. Now that Ilona was acting human, I found myself more sympathetic to her cause.

"They do. I understand that. We weren't mill workers,

but my father took off when I was a kid, leaving me and Mom to figure out how to get by with not much more than an ancient Pontiac and Mom's shorthand skills. It wasn't easy."

I eyed her diamond rings. "You've come a long way."

"Have you ever heard about shrimp?"

"Shrimp?"

Rodney seemed surprised at the change in conversation, too, and raised his head.

"Yes, shrimp. Their bodies grow, but the shells don't. So, as they get bigger, they have to shed their old shells while they wait for the new ones to grow. Meanwhile, they're completely vulnerable. It can't be easy. Imagine. They're tender. They're simply pulpy bodies resting on the ocean floor, easy pickings for any bigger fish that comes along. But it's necessary, or they'll die. It's a risk they have to take."

I had the image of Darla, Lyndon, and Sheriff Dolby as pinkish blobs with shrimp tails. "I see what you mean."

"I'm not going to lie. It's not easy. People—some people, not everyone—have fought me every step of the way. But Wilfred needs to grow a new shell." She stood and smoothed her skirt. "There's one other thing that bothers me."

"What's that?"

"The body you found." She shook her head. "It's too quiet up here. For years, kids have been coming to hang out and do who knows what, then we find someone murdered in the bushes. With a retreat center, there will be people here all the time. It will be so much safer."

I reluctantly agreed she had a point. Other than Lyndon, who seemed to stay holed up in his cabin when he wasn't working, the library's grounds would be deserted and tempting for anyone intent on secret meetings or other trouble.

"Thank you for letting me stay late," Ilona said.

"I'll see you out."

She reached for her handbag. "Where's my purse?"

"Rodney!" I said. Without our knowing, Rodney had pulled Ilona's bag halfway across the room. A lipstick rolled from its depths. "Let me pick it up for you."

"No, I'll get it. Ow!" Ilona slipped her foot out of her sandal and rubbed a toe. "Where did that come from?"

It was *The Eustace Diamonds* again, this time lying corner-out on the floor. "I'm sorry. I have no idea what it's doing there. It belongs across the hall in fiction."

She returned her foot to her shoe and limped to the door. "I'll leave you to clean up, then. And I'll undoubtedly see you around. I'm staying nearby to keep an eye on things. After the other night's murder . . ." She shook her head.

I watched the car disappear through the trees. Lyndon had pulled the curtains on his cottage windows, and yellow light escaped through a crack on one side. Beyond his house and a thin veil of trees, Big House loomed.

A light was on there, too, but the curtains were not drawn. Across the garden, Sam's silhouette faced me, then turned away.

CHAPTER NINE

At last, the library was completely quiet for the first time all day. Ilona's visit had left me wondering if perhaps I was wrong to want the library to survive. Now it was just me. Well, me and Rodney.

Rodney trotted purposefully toward the kitchen, pausing at the entrance to make sure I was following. In the kitchen, he pointed his chin at his empty bowl. I quickly remedied that and refreshed his water, too.

Moonlight illuminated my office. It was time to touch base with my sister. I was so far away from home—farther than I'd ever traveled—and talking with someone I knew loved me was irresistible. I wouldn't tell her about the body I'd found or about the library's imminent demise. I simply wanted her to know I was safe and to hear her voice. Plus, I wanted to get her opinion on my almost-magical skill with books.

I turned on the ginger jar lamp, transforming my office into a cozy den with a puddle of light on the desk and Rodney, hunger satisfied, purring at my side. Whoever had put an armchair in here had been a genius. I dialed Toni's number, taking care to block mine.

"Josie! I'm so glad you called."

I sat straighter. It was more than sisterly love that had prompted the urgency in this greeting. "What's wrong?"

"I don't want to alarm you."

I knew that tone of voice. It was the voice physicians used to tell patients about the results of medical tests that hadn't come out well. I'd heard it last before Grandma died. The doctor had joined us in the waiting room with a puzzled look but a matter-of-fact tone. "Mrs. Ainsley is very healthy on many levels. At her request, we tested her pancreas. I'm afraid I have some bad news." When she'd died, my childhood had gone with her.

"Tell me, Toni," I begged my sister now on the phone.

"Are you sure you're safe, I mean, wherever you are?"

I clutched the heavy handset. "I'm fine." Outside, the fir trees whooshed in a wind that seemed to have come from out of nowhere. Lyndon had said a storm might be blowing in. "Spit it out."

"Someone broke into your apartment today."

"What?" At my exclamation, Rodney leapt from my lap to the desk and lowered to his haunches.

"Your landlord called. Remember, I'm your emergency contact. She said one of your neighbors reported that your door was ajar. She checked it out, and the lock had been broken. She called you, then called me when you didn't answer."

My breath froze in my lungs. Just what I'd feared.

Whatever had happened to Anton could have happened to me.

I pictured my apartment's beige couch, the television, and buff cotton rug over the apartment's wall-to-wall Berber carpet. I'd never before thought of it as bland, but now it struck me how devoid of character it was. Basically, my apartment's only life came from the bookshelves lining the walls.

The intruder couldn't have found anything at my apartment that would lead them to me. Or did they?

"I left my phone at home on the counter, charging," I said suddenly. I'd thought that was smart. No one could track me by my phone's GPS, but I was now aware of what it meant. If I were in New York, as I'd told them at work, or anywhere, really, I would have taken my phone with me. It wouldn't take Sherlock Holmes to deduce I didn't want to be found.

"So, they know," I said.

We both let that sink in.

"No one can find me," I added. "So they know I'm in hiding. Big deal. I'm in the middle of nowhere. Really. There's drama here—"

"What kind of drama?"

"It has nothing to do with me. Honest. Just small-town stuff."

"So you're in a small town?"

"Forget I said that. Anyhow, I'm safe." For as long as it lasted. Another month. Maybe. Would that be long enough for the FBI to gather the evidence they needed to shut down the sweetheart deal? "Did they take anything?"

"Not that I could tell. That's what worries me the most. Take care of yourself, Josie."

I plucked the phone's coiled cord. "I will. Remember, that's why I left. You'll cover for me with Mom, right?"

Toni groaned. "She's been fussing about you, by the way. She wants to know why you won't answer your phone."

"Tell her you've talked to me, that I'm having a good time and keeping busy." Keeping busy finding bodies, but she didn't need to know that. Truth was, I had had one of the best days in my professional career. I'd found what I was meant to do. When I returned home, I vowed to find a position that let me spend time with patrons.

"All right," Toni said. "I'd better go. The baby is waking up."

"Kiss her for me. And don't worry about the break-in. I'm completely safe where I am."

As I hung up, I had one comforting thought. If the break-in took place today, the stranger I'd found yesterday couldn't have been sent from Bondwell or the senator's office. They didn't know where I was. Yet.

I paced my apartment, opening the refrigerator and shutting it, picking up the copy of *Folk Witch* that plagued me, then tossing it aside. The night stretched ahead, and I didn't want to stay in the library alone. I bundled up in a coat and scarf and took the trail across the river to Darla's diner. I couldn't help but glance toward Big House. Its curtains were closed.

The night air was moist with the dark smell of the river, and the breeze that had picked up earlier shook the trees and blew my curls around my face.

Ten minutes later, I was at the diner. The parking lot was packed. Ilona's Mercedes straddled two spots. I pushed open the front door to garlic-scented warmth and a livelier crowd than I'd have expected on a weeknight. Once again, I was struck by how different life was here than in D.C. The counter was shoulder-to-shoulder with flannel-shirted diners, and Willie Nelson played on the jukebox. Through the arch connecting the diner to the tavern, Ilona's ivory suit lit up the dark. She was flanked by two men in plaid shirts and baseball caps, and she held a wineglass.

"Josie." Roz gestured from the corner we'd occupied at breakfast my first morning. "Come sit with me, if you want."

"It's busy," I said, draping my coat over my chair and taking in the aroma of french fries and something spicy in a tomato sauce.

Roz leaned forward so I could better hear her. "It's the murder. Kind of like a natural disaster. People want to hang out together."

"I guess that's why I'm here, too. Plus, I'm hungry."

She caught my glance at her plate. "It's spaghetti night. All you can eat, plus meatballs. One of Darla's rare breaks from Southern food." Roz's seat faced the door. She waved, and I turned to see the sheriff amble over.

"Mind if I join you?" he asked. He'd changed out of uniform and wore a pocket T-shirt and jeans with a hand-tooled leather belt. He was still a big guy, but he was a lot less foreboding in street clothes.

"I'm glad to see you," I said. "Anything new to report? Anything you can tell us, anyway?"

"We've ID'd the body. You girls found her. I feel you ought to know."

"Lips are sealed," Roz said, mimicking a zipping motion.

"Mine, too." A pinprick of worry stirred in my gut, as I remembered the break-in at my apartment in D.C. "Was she—was she local?"

"I can't tell you that. Next of kin hasn't been notified."

"It's just that she didn't look local," I said. "Compared with what I see here—"

"Not everyone here is a farmer," Roz said. "Or a blue-collar worker. There's a college in Forest Grove, you know."

"All right," I said. "No offense meant. I just—wondered."

The sheriff's gaze rested on me a moment longer than necessary. "Don't you worry," he said with purpose.

"How about the murderer?" Roz asked. "Any leads there?"

The sheriff's face relaxed. "I feel fairly confident we'll be making an arrest soon. That's all I'll tell you."

Both Roz and I stared at him, hoping to elicit more information, but he leaned back and kept silent.

"I met Ilona Buckwalter today. Just before I came down here," I said.

"No kidding. She tell you I gave her a ticket?"

The sheriff's lips only twitched, but Roz burst into full-on laughter. It was a treat to see after her Eeyore behavior earlier. "What'd she say? She try to get you to buy her a drink?" Then, to me, "That's her schtick. She brags she never buys her own drinks."

"She seems to be doing all right tonight." I gestured toward the tavern.

Roz's smile vanished. "Does Darla know she's here?"

"Ilona told me she's staying nearby until business is settled with the library."

"At the Raincloud Farm Guesthouse," the sheriff said. "She bragged about it to me, too."

"Fancy," Roz said. Then, for my benefit, "On one of the winery properties. Verandas, cathedral ceilings, wood-fired hot tub. I hear it's a minimum of three hundred dollars a night. Lord, she's irritating." Roz was now back to full cranky mode.

"I can see why she might grate on you," I said, remembering Ilona listing the parts of the library she planned to salvage for personal use. "I was put off by her at first, too. She's not bad, though. I mean, how else will Wilfred ever get on its feet?"

Roz eyed me warily. "You don't like the library?"

"It's not that. I love the library." This was a fact. Saying good-bye wouldn't be easy. "Maybe it's time for Wilfred to move on. Think about its future, not mourn the past."

"What about saving the library keeps Wilfred in the past?" Roz's eyes narrowed slightly.

"It's just that . . . have you ever heard the story of how a shrimp grows?"

Roz snorted, and her eyes snapped wide. "You've been talking to Ilona, all right, and she fed you the shrimp story, didn't she? You know, how a shrimp needs to shed its shell before it can get bigger?"

Shoot. I didn't respond, but I guess my expression said it all. I was a sucker.

"Don't feel bad," Roz said. "There's no one here who hasn't heard her preach at least once about the brave shrimp. One time—"

The sheriff stood and pushed his chair under the table. "This is my cue to leave. Roz, Josie, I'll be seeing you around. My takeout order should be just about ready."

"She's a fraud, Josie." Roz slid a fan from her purse and flipped it open. "Always has been."

"How do you know?"

"She goes around talking about the jobs the retreat center will bring Wilfred, but she's already solicited bids from a demo crew from California. Not here."

"How do you know?"

Roz stopped fanning herself and examined the fan's tip. Finally, she set it down. "She might have left her briefcase in the kitchen while she was in the restroom."

And Roz had perused its contents. I raised an eyebrow.

"Oh, don't get so high and mighty," she said. "I was only thinking about Wilfred."

"Sorry I've left you waiting." Darla was at our table holding a pad. She drew a pen from behind her ear. "We're slammed tonight. Having the spaghetti?"

"Yes, please," I said.

An arpeggio of laughter rang from the tavern. Ilona emerged, dangling her key chain and waving at someone on a bar stool. It was too dark to make out who it was.

"You settle up?" Darla said, not overly kindly.

"Oh, the boys took care of it for me. It's been years since I've had to buy a drink," Ilona said and turned as she pushed open the front door. "*A bientôt*."

Darla turned to Roz and me. "What?"

"It means 'see you soon,'" I explained. "My dad teaches French history."

"Not that," Darla said. "We're not idiots, you know. I mean, what does she mean she'll see us soon?"

"She's staying nearby," Roz said.

Darla swore under her breath. "There goes any semblance of peace in Wilfred." She stomped toward the kitchen.

"Everyone here seems to be either Team Library or

Team Retreat Center. Tell me more about it. Which trustees agreed to sell the library?"

"There are five trustees. Besides Darla, you've got Lyndon. Marilyn was thoughtful enough to make sure the caretaker was always involved. For the past twenty years, it's been Lyndon." Roz seemed to have to force her attention back to the subject at hand. "Then there's Duke McConway. That's him in the tavern."

"Sitting with Ilona?" Through the arch, I saw a baseball cap and bit of plaid shirt stretched over a generous belly. His hand-tooled belt had popped its silver rivets here and there.

"That's him," Roz said, curling her lip.

"Tell me more."

"He lives in the Magnolia Rolling Estates—just behind my trailer, in fact. Used to be a forklift driver, a good one, to hear him tell it. Then he repaired coin-operated telephones. I guess you know how that went."

I nodded.

"Now he does odd jobs at some of the farms in the valley. His hobby is ballroom dancing."

"As in foxtrot and two-step?" I couldn't have heard right.

"He's pretty good, too. For such a big guy, he's light on his feet. Personality-wise, though, he's no Fred Astaire. Playing tunes with his armpit is more his speed."

"Okay, so that's Darla, Lyndon, and Duke." I counted them off my fingers. "I assume Darla and Lyndon were pro-library. How did Duke vote?"

"For the retreat center, of course. He's counting on a plum forklift driving job. You see him kissing up to Ilona."

"Two more trustees left," I said, my blood pressure rising. "Ilona is the fourth, of course." I shook my head. "Who's the fifth trustee?"

"That seat belongs to the Wilfred family."

"So, it's vacant," I said.

"Mostly. For years the votes had been unanimous. We didn't need the Wilfred family vote. This time Ilona made sure the vote came in, and she made sure it was the vote she wanted."

"Sam." I was surprised I'd actually spoken his name. "Don't tell me Sam voted for it."

"He did. His was the vote that cleared the way for the retreat center."

"He loves the library."

Roz pursed her lips. "Or not."

"He came by the first night he was in town. He told me he feels happy there." I was having a hard time taking all this in. My ears began to ring. *It's not fair*, I thought.

I had a hunch Roz would reach for her fan, and she didn't disappoint.

Darla slid oval platters heaped with spaghetti in front of us and hurried away. There was no way I'd be able to eat all that. I speared a meatball.

Roz paused, hand on her fan. "You're planning to leave Wilfred, aren't you?"

I'd just had one of the most rewarding days I'd ever experienced as a librarian. Somehow, I'd seemed to wake up. I saw the world more clearly, felt it more deeply. Strange, nearly magical, things were happening, but they felt so normal. Whether it was Oregon's country air or the shock of finding a body—or something else I didn't understand—I couldn't ignore it.

Ilona didn't care about the library. All she cared about was her commission, and she'd lie and cajole to get it.

Thinking of how I'd swallowed the shrimp story whole, I felt my face burn. It wasn't as if I had anything to go home for, anyway. My apartment had been broken into, and Anton had disappeared. Going home meant putting my family at risk. But where else could I escape?

No. It wasn't right that Ilona would steal the library from Wilfred and lie about what would replace it. *Not fair*. I set down my fork. The ringing in my ears had intensified into a tidal wave of crashing sound. My finger reached under my collar for my shoulder and touched my birthmark.

I knew what I had to do. The rush of noise halted.

"I'm staying right here."

CHAPTER TEN

I was in my office before the sun rose, rooting through the library's records and taking notes. Thunder rumbled across the valley, but my office was a warm cocoon. I tapped my pen on my notebook. Rain pelted outside, streaking my window and matching my mood.

"What are you doing here so early?" Roz's voice startled me. Today she wore a polka-dotted blouse that accentuated her round face, and she'd made an attempt at lipstick. Its dusky rose was already wearing at the center.

"I couldn't sleep. I have an idea for stopping the library's sale, and I wanted to get started on it."

Roz dropped into the armchair. "Yeah?"

"Ilona submitted a report showing that selling the library would benefit Wilfred financially, right?"

She nodded. "If you want to call a self-interested pitch at stuffing her own wallet a report, then, sure."

"Well, what if we gave the judge our own report showing how important the library is? I bet I could pull together something convincing about the difference having a library has made. I've done research reports for members of Congress."

I looked away. I hadn't meant to drop in the last bit. I didn't want to be traced back to my old job.

"What can we say that the judge doesn't already know? I mean, it's clear what we do here." She frowned. "No, I really don't think it would help."

"You'd be surprised. Look at what I've dug up so far." I waved toward the mess of papers stacked on my desk.

Past librarians had been good about saving mimeographed schedules of library events, and I'd found records going back to World War II. On some, the blue ink had faded beyond legibility, but I had plenty to work with. Over the years, the library had hosted Esperanto classes, fly-tying workshops, Bible studies, a Golden Age mystery book club (I wished I could have been at that one), a military vehicle club, Polish cooking demonstrations, a haiku club, and even a square dancing meetup, although I wasn't sure how they pulled that off. Some of the librarians had saved sign-in sheets, giving me an estimate of how many patrons had been served.

Circulation records were good, too, despite the lack of a digital system. Except for a stretch in the early 1970s, past librarians had prepared quarterly reports, first for Marilyn Wilfred, then for the trustees, on the number of books lent and community members served.

"We can tell him a lot. For instance, did you know that last year alone the library sponsored seventy-eight meetings and twenty-five study groups? We lent more than two thousand books. Plus, think of the résumés drafted, people who have learned English, students tutored—all of that."

"I suppose it couldn't hurt to put something together. Although I bet it's too late."

"Maybe it is," I said, not taking Roz's downer attitude personally. "But maybe it's not. We won't know unless we try. Why not text Darla and ask?"

"I'll call." Roz stood, tucking her laptop under an arm. "Darla's not a texter. I'll see if she's willing to get in touch with the judge's office."

Around me, the library seemed to sigh with relief, but maybe it was the autumn wind. While Roz called Darla, I grabbed my coffee cup and stepped out the kitchen's side door, handily protected by an overhang, to watch the rain melt into the lawn. I couldn't help checking Big House for lights. Sam. I hugged my cardigan closer. I couldn't believe he'd voted to demolish the library.

Roz was soon standing next to me. "A cold rain means curtains to the garden. I bet we have frost soon. You can kiss the dahlias good-bye."

Count on Roz for the cheerful outlook. "Maybe your hot flashes won't bother you so much in the cold."

"Ha. As if. Anyway, Darla says she'll call the judge's office as soon as they open."

"Fingers crossed," I said.

By noon, I was elbow-deep in papers, with a box near the door rapidly filling with recycling.

"What happened here?" Roz asked. We'd agreed she would handle the patrons this morning while I pulled to-gether information to support the library.

"Except for the trustees' reports"—I patted a stack of

binders—"the files are a mess. There's a lot of good information, but it's randomly filed. I thought I'd do some
organizing. What kind of librarians did you guys hire?" I
said. "This is so not librarian. Our code is all about organization."

From the bottom of one filing cabinet's drawer I lifted
a pair of used pantyhose in orange-brown and dropped it
into the trash. Its package had probably labeled it "sun-
tan." No sun I knew could make that kind of tan.

"Strictly speaking, the two hired over the past year
weren't proper librarians. I think Trudy studied hair-
styling, but she was waiting for a chair to free up at her
cousin's salon. I don't know what Justin's story was. I
never saw him much, to tell the truth. You were the first
one we found through the *Library Gazette*. Darla's idea."

"I'm not surprised." My thoughts turned to the card
catalogue. I hadn't even had the chance to dig into that
yet. I had to wonder if it even kept to alphabetical order.

"Can I have this?" Roz lifted from the pile a keychain
featuring a hula dancer in a grass skirt.

"Take it."

"What are you looking for, anyway?" Roz said.

"The library's bylaws. You said there was a copy in
my office."

"Right here." Roz pulled a yellowed file folder from
the stack at the desk's far rear. "That's it. Marilyn's will
should be with it. Dylan's coming in at one. Stay with the
report."

The tap of Roz's footsteps disappeared into the hall as
I settled in with the folder. I started with Marilyn Wilfred's will.

Given the old-fashioned state of the library, I'd half-

expected a vellum document dripping with fountain pen
ink, but her will was neatly printed and notarized. I
glanced at its date. She would have been ninety when the
will was drawn up.

After a few minutes of scanning, I understood the
will's main provisions. Marilyn Wilfred had left her
house—long since converted into a library—to the town
of Wilfred, along with a trust to maintain it. Lyndon, as
long as he lived, received a salary and use of the caretaker's cottage to maintain the house and grounds. He
would have been a young man when Marilyn drew up the
will. She'd chosen well.

That was pretty much it. A provision in the will re-
ferred to the library's bylaws. If those were violated without correction within three months, the library and trust
would be liquidated and dispersed to Marilyn's living relations.

Including Sam, I thought. Interesting.

Next, the library's bylaws. The pages were carbon
copies faded in spots. I ran my fingers over the ridges of
the notary's seal.

The bylaws were older than Marilyn Wilfred's will.
They'd been drawn up in the early 1950s and amended
when her will was written. Two full pages described the
library and its grounds, including the caretaker's cottage.
Another page listed the library's assets, including "Thurston Wilfred's original desk" and of course, books. As Roz
had told me, the bylaws mandated five trustees, including
a member of the Wilfred family and a representative of
the caretaker.

Here was the section that provided for the library's existence as long as it was for the "betterment of Wilfred-

ians." The bylaws didn't define what "betterment" meant, leaving lots of latitude for the trustees. Perhaps too much. The arguments I'd already heard flitted through my mind. The library was a community center, an anchor of Wilfred's history, a source of information and training. Yet, if the library were demolished, the retreat center that replaced it could recharge the town's economy.

I set down the folder. When it came to heart or wallet, which was more important? All around me, the library's walls whispered for their survival. Yes, a community had to bend with the times, but it shouldn't leave its past behind. Of course I had personal reasons for defending the library's survival.

Back to the documents. In another clause, the bylaws laid out that if the library were destroyed through "fire or other means," any monetary proceeds, plus the trust, would be applied toward the establishment of a new library. This must be what Darla was referring to when she said a new library would be built if this one sold. Where and when was anyone's guess. Odds were high that Ilona would find a way to profit from that, too.

Twenty minutes in, I found the provision I was looking for. "Trustees shall serve with the welfare of Wilfred's residents as their primary concern. At no point shall a trustee direct the library's policies or resources for personal gain." Then, further down, "Violations of these provisions will result in the trustee's removal."

That was it, then. Ilona could argue that selling the library would benefit Wilfred, as long as another library was planned. If she—or another trustee—were desperate enough for the library's sale to break the law, the project was not for Wilfred's benefit. It was personal. And if I could prove that, the trustees' decision could be over-turned.

As for the argument that the library's grounds had become a draw for troublemakers—and worse—hopefully the sheriff's investigation would prove differently.

It was a beginning.

CHAPTER ELEVEN

Midday, Roz stuck her head into my office, where I was sorting circulation records. Apparently no one had ever bothered to collect fines for overdue books, even though the library's policy asked a modest five cents a day.

I closed the laptop. "Have you heard anything from Darla yet about whether the judge will accept our report?"

"Not yet. I'm sure he has a full docket. Crime is so bad around here. The Wilkinsons' tractor was stolen, graffiti at the high school—"

"A corpse in the bushes."

"Oh yeah," Roz said, her voice dropping. "There's that."

We both let that one sit a moment.

"I'm knocking off work," Roz said finally. "I'll be in

the conservatory for a few hours working on my project—"

There was the mysterious project again.

"—then I'll stop by my place for dinner. I'll be back for the knitting club at six." She leaned against the door frame. "I can introduce you around."

"That's all right," I said. "Stay home. I can handle a few knitters."

"Ha. That's what the last librarian said. These knitters shouldn't be carrying pointy steel objects. You'll see." Her phone chimed. "Darla."

I waited impatiently while Roz answered with a series of grunts, then, "You're kidding."

The second she pressed OFF, I said, "Was it about the judge? What did he say?"

"Not the judge. The murder. The word at the diner is that the sheriff arrested someone."

My hands flew to my armrests, knocking a pen from the desk. Rodney appeared from nowhere to bat it toward the corner. "You're kidding."

"No. He just took in Craig Burdock."

"Burdock?" I said. "I remember him. Tight jeans, shaggy hair, nineteenth-century poets?" I squinted. "He didn't look like a murderer."

"They never do," Roz said in her typical downer tone. "You know, 'he kept to himself, a quiet guy.' Although I guess no one would say that about Craig."

"I mean, I could see him pocketing cigarettes and breaking hearts, but killing someone?"

"Yeah," Roz agreed. "Sheriff Dolby takes his position seriously, though. He doesn't mess around. If he arrested Craig, he had good reason for it."

As clearly as though I were holding the book in my

hand, I saw the cover of Joseph Conrad's *The Secret Agent*. Someone was still after me. It was still possible the murderer had thought the victim was me. Should I have told the sheriff my story?

"Sheriff Dolby can't have investigated a lot of murder cases, not in Wilfred," I said.

"It's family honor with him. He's not the type to be impulsive about making an arrest. Some folks might say he's too slow, in fact. One year, we had a terrible problem with graffiti and everyone knew the kid who did it. Bert wouldn't lay one finger on him until Patty had photographs of the kid tagging her store." She shook her head. "No, if he arrested Craig, he has solid evidence."

Doubt niggled at me. "We still don't know who the victim was."

"Not yet. We'll hear the whole story before long."

Roz wandered off. I emerged from my office and stretched. The library's records—such as they were— were now sorted into piles, and I had a good idea of the information I had to work with. I made my way to the circulation desk in the house's old sitting room. The library wasn't as busy as yesterday, but Roz's grumbling about the "freak show" in popular fiction told me it had been busier than usual.

A young woman with a toddler on her hip dropped a paperback into the returns box. "Thank you for your recommendation. I devoured it cover to cover last night after I put Kimberley to bed." She patted the little girl, who was sucking two fingers. "What else should I read?"

There had been so many patrons the day before, I hardly remembered what I'd recommended. I edged to the returns box and caught sight of a bare-chested man in a kilt. Romance. The woman and now her daughter looked at me expectantly.

"You might enjoy Eliza Chatterley Windsor's work," I said. My eyes widened. I'd never even heard that name, but there it came, straight out of my mouth. How was I doing this?

Roz was instantly at my side. "No, you wouldn't."

"I thought you were in the conservatory."

"I came back to get my sweater." Then, to the patron, "Wouldn't you rather read something more literary?"

The patron looked from Roz to me and back to Roz. "Why? Josie was spot-on with yesterday's suggestion. I want the Eliza Whatever-Her-Name-Is."

"Chatterley Windsor," Roz said. "Eliza Chatterley Windsor. Unfortunately, they're all checked out at the moment. Let me show you where James Joyce is shelved. You—"

"Eliza Chatterley Windsor is right here." I cast Roz a *what's your deal?* look and pulled a fat paperback from the new releases shelf. "Her latest. *The Billionaire's Babe.*" How I was coming up with all this, I had no idea, but I liked it.

Roz stuck out her lower lip, a real feat given her slight overbite. "Fine." Then, to me, "You have another customer."

It was the man I'd recommended the gardening book to. "I just want to thank you. I'm returning this, because I'm buying my own copy. I was up half the night planning a vegetable garden and most of the morning getting the rototiller in working order."

"I'm glad you found it useful."

"Useful? I'll tell you how useful it's been. If things go

well, I'll have enough spring greens to sell my overflow to the grocery. Maybe even take them to the farmer's market in Forest Grove. My wife says she hasn't seen me so happy in years."

This was astonishing. Maybe a job at the Library of Congress had prestige, but this? This was a thousand times better. I didn't know why I'd ever doubted myself. Watching people mosey from room to room in the old mansion, plucking a book here and there from the shelves and dropping into armchairs to read a chapter—well, this was heaven. I swear, even the books seemed satisfied to share their stories and give up their information.

Then I remembered. My days here were numbered— the same number as the days left to the library. I almost heard the volumes near me sigh. The *Oxford Dictionary* on the stand in the corner let out a gentlemanly moan.

I was headed to literature to check on Dylan when Lalena stopped me. She had her dog with her, trotting on his satin ribbon, but this time she'd left her bathrobe and towel at home.

"Hi, Josie. The Eiffel Tower history was fascinating. I came back to see if you have any novels set there. Maybe a mystery?"

Secret of the Blue Lily. I was getting used to my book matchmaking skills now. "I can recommend a great one about a perfume shop in Paris. Let me show you."

The last time I'd seen Lalena, she'd practically run up the stairs to get away from Craig Burdock. Murder suspect Craig Burdock, I amended. Lalena followed me to popular fiction. The book I was looking for nearly glowed from the shelf. I handed it to her. Other than

Dylan sorting novels on the other side of the room, we were alone.

"I heard about your brother arresting Craig Burdock for murder."

She halted. "Craig? Bert arrested Craig?"

"You didn't know? I'm sorry, I—"

"Don't apologize." She looked dazed.

"That's what the grapevine says, anyway."

"No." She shook her head. "He didn't do it. Impossible."

"Is that something you know, or information you're getting from the beyond?"

"I know Craig. He's not that kind of person. We were lovers." She dropped to an armchair. Her dog jumped in her lap, and she absently rested a hand on his head. "Craig? Really?"

"I could be wrong," I said. "It's secondhand info. Maybe third hand."

"No. It couldn't be him. I mean . . ." Her voice softened, and she stared somewhere in the distance beyond me. "He was so kind. When Aunt Ginny died, he helped me sort through her stuff before I moved into the trailer. We spent three solid days working, and he never complained a moment. Sure, he took a few things to sell, but I told him it was okay."

"You aren't still going out with him, are you?"

She grimaced. "No. He was playing around with some dental assistant in Forest Grove. He might not be reliable in the boyfriend department, but that doesn't mean he's a murderer."

"Your brother wouldn't have arrested him without evidence," I said. "Roz says he's a good sheriff."

"He is," she said quickly.

"Then there must—"

"He's a good sheriff and a good brother."

"What's that supposed to mean?" *That he arrests men for murder if they cheat on his sister?*

"No. No, it couldn't be Craig. He was so loving with Sailor. He'd never kill someone. It's not part of his code."

"His code?"

"Hmm," she said without answering my question. She stood. "Well, I'd better get home. I have an appointment to contact Patty's dead mother at two." She picked up the dog's ribbon-leash. "Come on, Sailor."

CHAPTER TWELVE

That evening, five women, a man, and a boy took seats in the library's conservatory. Each toted bundles bursting with yarn, and each eyed me suspiciously. The rain had stopped, and night draped the room's glass walls like black velvet, absorbing light from the table lamps dotted among the orchids and banana trees. Say what you want about Lyndon's demeanor, he was a kick-butt gardener.

I took a second look at the man. Wasn't he one of the library's trustees? I'd only seen him at Darla's, from the rear, but his Tweedledum figure was hard to miss.

"Duke McConway," he said. "Trustee. Pleased to meet you at last, Josie."

"And a knitter," I said.

Duke's thinning hair was brilliantined into a modified pompadour. He gave me a shrewd smile.

"I keep myself busy. In the telephone booth repair business, I got good with my fingers."

"So, you're the new librarian, eh?" a plump woman in a purple velour tracksuit said.

"Not for long," said another woman, older, sorting a tangle of oatmeal yarn. "If you ask me, they had no business hiring another librarian. I suppose they didn't even tell you the library was history?"

"Good riddance, too," a third woman added. She'd claimed the seat closest to the radiator. "This town needs the jobs."

"Who cares? I'm moving to New York," the boy said. His bag was especially large and bulged with gold-threaded yarn.

"I'm glad to see you're enjoying the library now," I couldn't help but point out. "It's a great meeting place for groups like yours."

"When the library shuts down, we can meet in the back room of Patty's This-N-That," the woman in purple said.

"Not me," oatmeal yarn woman said. "I poked my head back there last week, and it was full of scissors. Little copper ones, some with brass handles, strange iron scissors—"

"Patty sells whatever she likes," Roz told me. "It changes according to her mood. The only thing they have in common is that they're useless."

"Scissors are useful," the oatmeal yarn woman said, using hers to cut a snarl from her skein.

"Remember when Patty was into bells?" Duke said. "She hung them out front. Within a week, folks had petitioned Darla to demand she take them down. No one could sleep, thanks to the racket."

I'd read a lot of novels, and whoever said that "truth is stranger than fiction" might have spent time in Wilfred.

"Well, whatever," the woman in purple said. "It's pleasant meeting here, no doubt, but it will be even more pleasant to see this town prosperous again. Get the kids staying here to work for a change." She sighed. "I miss Preston Jr."

"And no more murders in the bushes," Duke pointed out. "With a retreat, the place will be busy. Kids like Craig Burdock won't be loitering about, shooting visitors."

"You really believe that?" said a woman with maroon-dyed hair that matched her sweater. "I don't see it. It's a setup, if you ask me."

"Why?" I asked.

"Craig's always been all talk, no action. The kid's fundamentally lazy."

I hadn't seen Rodney all day, but now here he was, his gaze fixed on a ball of coral yarn in the basket of the knitter near the radiator. Remembering how he took off with Ilona's purse, I kept an eye on him. "Why would someone set him up?"

"Who knows?" the woman in the maroon sweater responded. "He's gotten himself on the wrong side of lots of folks."

"You're saying he ticked off someone enough that they'd go and kill a stranger and pin it on Craig? I don't think so," Duke said as he pulled a half-finished tea cozy from his bag.

"If we had jobs here, boys like Craig wouldn't be getting in trouble," a tall, thin woman said.

The ball of coral yarn jiggled as its owner pulled a

skein from her tote. Rodney's haunches rocked from side to side. He was preparing for a strike.

Don't you dare, I warned him silently.

"I'm just saying there are other folks in Wilfred more likely than Craig to off someone."

I was just about to ask, "Like who?" when Rodney went for the kill. I was a second too late. By the time I'd reached him, he was belly up in the tote of yarn, with a coral strand in his mouth and his feet kicking variegated green.

"Rodney!" I yelled as the owner of the coral yarn neatly extracted the cat from her bag and handed him to me. "I'm so sorry."

"Been fostering kittens for years now," she said. "I should have seen that coming."

"We'll get him out of here. Enjoy this week's knitting club." Roz put a hand on my elbow and guided me, Rodney slung over my shoulder, toward the hall. "Coffee's in the urn. In an hour and a half we'll be back to clean up." Then to me, "Come on."

Roz led me to the kitchen. Rodney went straight to his dish to crunch kibble.

"Have you had dinner yet?" Roz asked.

"No. I thought I'd eat last night's leftovers."

"Darla always makes us something for knitting circle night as a consolation." She tilted her head sideways toward the conservatory. "They're sharks."

"They're okay," I said with hesitation.

"Sharks. Marsha Boyes has been working on the same sweater since 1976. She comes here only to tear into Wilfred's residents. If you had stayed a few minutes longer, the knitters would have had you in tears. Either that, or reaching for Lyndon's pruning shears in defense," Roz said. "No mercy, that crowd."

"They seemed convinced that Craig isn't guilty," I said. "Except Duke, that is."

Darla's gumbo steamed as Roz dished it into bowls. "I have to admit I agree with them. I just don't see it. As for Duke, he'd believe anything that besmirches the library."

The image of an old hardback of Zola's writings flashed through my brain, with *J'Accuse . . . !* highlighted. Wasn't it a letter about a man who'd been wrongfully sentenced? Strange. When I returned my attention to dinner, I noticed Roz staring at me.

"What's with you, anyway?" she said. "You're so jumpy."

"Think about it. You'd be jumpy, too, after finding a dead woman in the bushes." I stared back at her, hoping she'd buy my story.

She kept her eyes on me. "I was there. That's not what I'm talking about. You don't seem afraid, just surprised. And wary."

"I guess I'm still adjusting. It's been a lot to take in."

"You're not hiding anything from me, are you?"

I forced a smile. "Hiding? Oh no. I just—I don't want the library to go away, that's all."

Roz seemed to accept this explanation. Her gaze passed over the kitchen's casement windows, its pendant light fixtures, the old six-burner stove, and rested on the doorway with its view of books. "I know. The retreat center could be built somewhere else. Heck, I'd give up my space at the Magnolia Estates, if they wanted to use that. But no, it had to be above the river. Had to be fancy."

"Had to be out of the flood plain, is more like it," I guessed.

Roz's phone chimed. "Darla," she said and answered.

I put down my fork. With all the action lately, Darla's call could be about anything. I hoped it would be good news from the judge.

Roz hung up. "Darla says the judge will accept our report on the library."

"That's great news."

"Except that we have to have it to him by close of business tomorrow."

It was past midnight when I made my rounds of the library, double-checking that doors and windows were locked. I'd made a good start on the report after the knitters left. If I rose early, I should be able to finish it in time to deliver it to the judge's chambers by five o'clock. That is, as long as no last-minute emergencies got in the way.

Rodney followed me upstairs. The night had cooled, but my rooms were warm and smelled of old wooden beams and the bowl of apples Lyndon had left for me in the kitchen. Before closing my bedroom curtains, I pulled up the window and took a few draughts of moist autumn air.

Lyndon's cottage below was dark. I imagined him in bed dreaming of compost and lawn mower parts. Beyond him, a light was on at Big House, and the strains of a soprano filtered through the trees. Opera. Sam listened to opera. Another sound joined the music: the *whoo-whoo* of an owl.

I shut the window and turned toward my bedroom. I never would have chosen the room's faded floral wallpaper and ornate Victorian furniture, but, surprisingly, I liked them. I liked knowing they had a history, and I loved running my fingers over the hand-chiseled detail. They couldn't have been more different from the clean-lined furnishings I had at home. As soon as I returned to D.C., I was going to offload my bland couch and hit the antiques stores.

This was only one way Wilfred had changed me. So much had surprised me during the four days I'd been here. It was as if I'd lived in a filtered dome that grayed out my environment and emotions. Now the dome had lifted. Colors were more vibrant, and I was quicker to laughter—and anger. The very air smelled richer. And my dreams, all my crazy dreams.

Something unusual was definitely happening. How much of it was me, and how much was Wilfred? It felt almost—magic.

On a whim, I said aloud, "Books." Rodney jumped on the bed and sat, alert. I breathed in deeply. "Books. Tell me how to train a Chihuahua."

Chihuahuas: The Big Book on a Little Dog, third edition.

A chill prickled the backs of my arms. "Books," my voice faltered a bit, "what are the plots of Mozart's operas?" It might have been *Don Giovanni* I'd heard through the bedroom window.

Opera through the Ages, back shelf in the drawing room. *A Cambridge Companion to Opera*. On loan to Big House.

I barely had time to catch my breath when another title slipped into my mind. *Folk Witch*.

Whoa. I fought to steady my breath, and my finger went to my shoulder, where my birthmark tingled. I fell to the bed next to Rodney. He was purring, eyes half closed.

When my pulse calmed, I sat up. Time to try something else. My brush sat on the old dresser with its cheval mirror. "Hairbrush, move to the right." I closed my eyes. I didn't want to see. After a moment, I opened them. The brush hadn't budged. This time, I kept my eyes open. "Move, hairbrush." Nothing.

So, my weird power was reduced to a supernatural card catalogue?

Not that that was so bad. Below me, books held the world's knowledge and imagination—oceans of it. Even a few feet of shelf told stories of generations of love, war, comedy, and tragedy. People were lost at sea, flew to the moon, crossed the Sahara in caravans, and dawdled in Queen Elizabeth's court. They grew wiser—or not. They survived—or not. The experience a single page could communicate awed me.

All that energy. My body felt warm with it now. I held out a hand. It tingled. I rested it, palm down, on the quilt and yanked it back when the heat grew too intense. The quilt's cotton smelled as if it had just been ironed. Rodney squeezed under my hand and pressed himself against it. He flopped next to me and licked a paw.

I couldn't ignore it. Since I'd come to Wilfred, something strange had happened to me. Strange, and scary. And wonderful. I had power I'd never felt before.

But what good was this power if it couldn't help find a murderer? Enough doubt had been cast on Craig Burdock that I wasn't entirely sure of his guilt. Real power would lead me to the truth. The ability to match a reader with the book she needed was nothing compared to saving lives— right now, my own.

And the library. Laying facts before a judge was a start to saving the library, but magic to open minds would be so much more useful.

"Books," I said, "what will happen to the Wilfred library?"

This time nothing came.

CHAPTER THIRTEEN

The next morning I was putting the finishing touches on circulation figures for the report when Roz burst into my office.

"It's Lyndon," she gasped.

"Hold on. Catch your breath."

"The sheriff." Roz leaned against the door frame and patted her pockets, probably for her fan. She came up empty. "The sheriff's questioning Lyndon. Come and see for yourself."

I followed Roz to the conservatory. She pointed between potted banana trees. "There."

A mist had risen from the river and lay in a haze over the stretch of garden between the library and the trail toward the woods. The sheriff, about Lyndon's height but twice as wide, stood legs slightly apart, nodding his head in response to something Lyndon was saying. The sheriff pointed toward the river. Lyndon shook his head, dropping his rake and adding hand gestures that clearly said, "No way."

"He thinks Lyndon did it," Roz said. "But he couldn't have. This is a disaster."

"I thought he arrested Craig Burdock."

"I did, too!" She twisted her plump fingers together.

"Then why is it a disaster? You said Sheriff Dolby is fair. He'll figure out that Lyndon was driving me from the Portland airport when the stranger was killed."

Roz groaned and sank to her desk chair. "It doesn't look good. I mean, who has the strongest motive for keeping the library going? Lyndon. Without the library, he doesn't have a place to live. Or a job."

"How does shooting a stranger help keep the library alive?"

"Maybe he thought Ilona sent her to vandalize the grounds. I don't know." She let out a mew.

"Still, remember the timing. If he wasn't here, he couldn't have done it. Besides, the sheriff already has his suspect in jail."

This seemed to have no effect on Roz. She fidgeted with a drawer pull on her desk. Everything here was tidied up and locked away. What had she been doing in the conservatory, anyway? She was supposed to be out front at the circulation desk.

"I bet the sheriff has to talk to everyone. To cross them off the list," I said. And certainly to Lyndon. Roz was right—he had a solid motive.

"Josie . . ."

"Yes?"

"He left Wilfred right after lunch. I saw him."

"He didn't need to leave town that early. The airport is only a few hours away."

"I know."

"Well," I said, casting about for something reassuring, "If he wasn't in Wilfred all afternoon and evening, he definitely couldn't have shot anyone. He'll just have to tell the sheriff where he was."

"You see, maybe he didn't go anywhere," Roz said. "Maybe he made it look like he was leaving, but he stayed behind."

"Oh." She didn't have to lay out the rest of the scenario.

"Not that he would—or did. But the sheriff might think so."

"This sounds thin. I'm sure Lyndon will tell the sheriff where he was, and that will be that." Crows cawed in the distance, and at last, the sun began to burn through the cloud cover and illuminate the conservatory's windows. "I think I saw some returned books to process up front."

Roz seemed to snap to. "I was just—I just stopped by the conservatory to make sure the knitters had cleaned up. And then I saw Lyndon." Slowly, she rose to her feet. "Plus, we have to get ready for the quarterly trustees' meeting."

The sheriff and Lyndon were walking toward the caretaker's cottage, Lyndon leading the way and the sheriff following purposefully. The rake lay forgotten in a pile of leaves.

"Trustees' meeting? I didn't see it on the calendar." I still needed to finish the report laying out the library's value to Wilfred.

"Tomorrow night. It was cancelled due to all the in-fighting, but Ilona decided at the last minute that they should hold it anyway. Darla told me this morning at the diner. We have to put together a quarterly report, and they'll take care of the rest." As she spoke, Roz gazed mournfully toward Lyndon's back.

"Thanks to all the work I've done for the judge, a quarterly report will be no problem." When she didn't respond, I added, "I'm sorry. This is hard on everyone. Remember, I promised. I'll do whatever I can to help sort this out." Starting with a talk with the sheriff.

I left Roz in the conservatory and went to the kitchen, where I could keep watch on Lyndon's cottage. It didn't take long—only about ten minutes. Lyndon emerged right behind the sheriff and made as if to return to the pile of leaves. I had a hand on the door handle when the sheriff, instead of continuing toward his car, circled the cottage and continued to Big House. He was going to talk to Sam.

Why? Sam wasn't even here when the woman was killed. Or was he? I remembered the light in the upstairs window the night I'd arrived.

Well, I'd catch up with the sheriff at some point. Meanwhile, I stopped by my office to grab my cardigan, and I went to find Lyndon.

Lyndon heaped leaves into two open-topped cages in a flower bed running alongside the house.

"Are you going to burn them?" I asked.

"Nope. Compost." He continued forking leaves in the bins without looking at me.

Despite the sun beginning to pierce the clouds, it was chilly without a coat. I hugged my arms. "I saw you talking with the sheriff."

"Yep."

I hadn't known Lyndon long, but I'd known him long enough to suspect it would be easier to squeeze lattes from river rock than get him to talk.

"Roz was worried about you," I said offhand. "We saw—"

"Roz was?" He leaned the pitchfork against the compost bin.

"Yes. She worries the sheriff might suspect you. Apparently, she couldn't find you the afternoon before the stranger was shot."

"I went into town to pick you up. She knows that. So does the sheriff." He returned to his pitchfork.

"After lunch? My plane didn't even get in until nine-thirty that night."

"Maybe I had other business in Portland."

A girlfriend. Lyndon must have a girlfriend. I watched him shovel, a hank of greasy hair falling over his forehead. He hadn't shaved, and his plaid jacket was neatly mended but not meant for show. No, no girlfriend, I decided. Lyndon was practically feral. It had to be something else.

"Does the sheriff know where you were?" I said. "It would clear you right away if you had a proven alibi."

He didn't even raise his head from his task. "How do you know what he asked me about, anyway? Maybe he wanted tips on planting bulbs."

"Okay." I put my hands up. "I give up. I wanted to know if the sheriff was making any progress, that's all. I thought he'd already made an arrest, then he was questioning you—"

"Craig Burdock didn't do it," Lyndon said.

I waited for him to say more. He stuck the pitchfork into the ground and faced me full-on. "I've known him since he was born, and don't get me wrong, he's no angel, but he's not a murderer. Not even close."

"Maybe if he were provoked?"

"No," he said firmly. "I told the sheriff so."

"Then you're a possible suspect, especially if you won't say where you were that afternoon."

"I was at a meeting," he said quietly.

"A what?"

"A meeting. Private. I went into Portland early to go to a meeting. That's all I'm going to say."

A meeting. Why would he be so secretive about that? "Fine. I'm sorry for prying. I—"

"There's a lot you don't know. If you really want to get to the bottom of this, you should be talking to someone else. Or leave it to the sheriff. It's his job." One of his eyelids twitched. He wouldn't look me in the face.

I'd never heard Lyndon angry. I'd never seen him express any emotion, really. His floral arrangements might be tender, but he had the demeanor of a baked potato.

"Anyone in particular I should talk to?" I ventured.

"If you don't mind, this compost isn't going to turn itself."

The sheriff was waiting for me in the atrium. "Mind if we talk in your office?" he said.

"That's fine," I said.

In my office, I gestured to the sheriff to take the arm-chair this time to better hold his bulk, and I took the chair at my desk.

"I thought I'd give you an update," he said.

"Thank you. The rumor mill has been working twenty-four-seven."

"You've probably heard we made an arrest."

I nodded once. "Craig Burdock. People are shocked. They say he doesn't have it in him to kill someone."

"Isn't that what they always say?" The chair that seemed so roomy when I sat in it was full arm-to-arm with the sheriff. I wondered if he had a special source for furniture at home, or if he simply suffered chairs and ta-bles that didn't suit his giant's frame.

"True. But you'd think it would show somewhere. Somehow."

"Maybe if he were the calculating type. Not Craig. I can't see him planning something like this, but in the heat of the moment, who knows?"

"You're pretty sure about it, then?" The cover of *The Fugitive* flitted through my mind.

"Oh, definitely. Burdock has a record as long as your arm. That's not even counting what's in his sealed juve-nile files."

"Violent crimes?"

He shrugged. "Mostly petty stuff. Shoplifting, tres-passing. He was working up to bigger things, though. The sheriff in Forest Grove bagged him for breaking and en-tering last year. Tried to rob the Thousand Subs deli. Not only did the security camera catch him, everything was locked up for the night. Even the cold cuts. Couldn't have made it out with so much as a slice of bologna." He shook his head. "Never was the brightest bulb."

"Murder isn't petty theft or breaking and entering," I pointed out.

"Craig had dreams of being a big-time crook. Talk to anyone, and they'll tell you. He could spend hours at the tavern preaching about how society was stupid to stick to a regime of law and order, and all it took was the guts to break the rules to get ahead." Disgust was clear in the sheriff's voice.

"You must have some kind of proof," I said. "I just can't help but wonder if it's a setup."

He steepled his hands over his belly. "What do you mean?"

"Someone might have framed Craig. Maybe planted evidence, or—"

"What gives you that idea?"

"I haven't heard a single person say Craig would kill someone. Plus, there's more." I leaned forward. I didn't want to say it, but the truth had to come out. "The night I arrived, I saw a light at Big House. I think Sam arrived a day earlier than he lets on."

The sheriff's demeanor remained unchanged. "I know all about Sam, and he's no worry to you." He stood.

"You're sure? Why would he lie about when he came to town?"

"I told you. Sam's accounted for."

I couldn't relax. It was all too easy. "You're still questioning people, though. Lyndon, for instance. You must not be completely sure about Craig." I didn't like speaking to the sheriff while he towered above me, so I stood, too.

"Procedure. We had ample evidence to book Burdock, but we need to cover all our bases. Besides, folks like

Lyndon might have information we can use to seal the case."

I couldn't fault his reasoning. "Ilona Buckwalter says troublemakers have been hanging out on the library's grounds for years."

He sighed. "True enough, although it's usually just kids taking a bottle into the woods. Count on Ilona to use it as an argument in her favor." He must have noticed my frown, because he added, "I'm sorry you stumbled into all this. I admit Darla might have been a bit misleading in offering you the job."

He placed a hand on my shoulder. It was surprisingly light, given its size. "Don't worry. It will all come out all right in the end. I can't tell you everything I know, but I want to give you some assurance."

"Thank you." I moved to open the door, then dropped my hand. "Oh, before you go, what about the victim? You told me earlier that you'd identified her."

"It's no secret now. Her prints were in the FBI's data-base. Her name's January Stephens. She has a short—but serious—record. A professional. Craig was likely trying to get a spot in her organization."

"A professional what?"

The sheriff's hand replaced mine on the doorknob, and he pushed the door open. Roz loitered suspiciously close, pretending to examine the contents of the silverware drawer.

"What they call a 'fixer.' Isn't that interesting?"

CHAPTER FOURTEEN

"A fixer? What's that?" I asked, dreading the response.

"A fixer is someone an organization sends to solve problems that can't be settled legally," Sheriff Dolby said.

Uh-oh. "Like what?"

His boots creaked as he leaned on one hip. "Say a CEO has a sideline of embezzling, and he's on the verge of being busted. He hires a fixer to solve the situation with bribery, maybe. Blackmail works, too. Sometimes even murder."

I cringed. I didn't want to do it, but I couldn't hide any longer. I was withholding evidence. Plus, it wasn't about just me. Craig's future was on the line. Maybe he was a troublemaker and a lousy boyfriend, but that didn't mean he deserved to spend his life in prison.

"I have something to tell you." The words came out like pulled teeth.

The sheriff looked at me, then glanced toward the kitchen. "Roz?"

"What?" Roz said. "I was looking for grapefruit spoons, that's all."

"Trying to listen in is more like it. Let's take a walk, Josie. We'll go somewhere private. Grab your jacket," Sheriff Dolby said.

I shrugged on the plaid jacket from my office and followed him out to the path along the Kirby River. The sheriff set a meandering pace. A breeze rustled the leaves still clinging to the cottonwood trees. Woodsmoke drifting up from someone's woodstove in the trailer park spiked the air with the smell of autumn.

"What do you have to tell me?" he said.

Here it was. The moment when my anonymity and safety—such as it was—would come to an end. "She was here for me. January Stephens."

"For you? And why would that be?" Although the sheriff couldn't have even been my father's age, he sounded like a grandfather quizzing his granddaughter on her homework.

"Because there's an assassin after me." As soon as the words left my mouth, I realized how ridiculous they sounded.

"Ms. Way, Josie, you're telling me someone wants to kill you? I can hardly believe that."

He took the news surprisingly well. I glanced up to a calm face. Not bored, but not excited. He didn't believe me.

"I'm telling you the truth." Telling the truth and possibly laying a fast track to the cemetery. "I came to Wilfred to hide. I used to work at the Library of Congress. Actually, I still work there. They think I'm on vacation."

"Yet you took the job of Wilfred's librarian."

"I know. I would have stayed, too—at least awhile."

"Hmm," he said with put-on seriousness. "So, you're a librarian with a killer on her tail. Maybe you'd better start at the beginning."

"You don't believe me," I said, anger rising. "I'm trying to tell you something difficult."

"I'm sorry. Please. Continue."

I studied his expression again. He was listening. "A little over a week ago, I was with a colleague, and we overheard a congressional staffer making a sweetheart deal with a lobbyist from Bondwell Corporation."

"Bondwell. That's aeronautics, right?"

"Right." At last, he was taking me seriously. "We reported it. It was a big deal. It flew up the chain of command, and by the next day the FBI was involved."

"How does this put your life at risk?"

"My colleague—the one who overheard the conversation with me? He disappeared the morning after the investigation went public."

The sheriff's footsteps crunched on the gravel path. We came to the embankment where I'd found the body. The brambles were flattened in some areas and completely cut away in others. The sheriff's office must have taken them to examine for hair and fibers—or maybe they'd simply been in the way. The main thing was that there was no dead woman.

"You were threatened?" the sheriff asked.

"No. But after Anton disappeared, I was afraid—I was afraid the same thing would happen to me. So I took the library job here. I'd seen the ad in the *Library Gazette*."

Anton had read it aloud to me the day before, and we'd laughed. Who'd take a job in some backward hamlet in Oregon?

"Who knows you're here? I mean, besides us."

"No one. Not even my family. I told everyone I was going to Manhattan on vacation."

"That's a long vacation."

"I'd planned to turn it into medical leave. I just needed to hide until the case was settled or went to court."

The sheriff gave a wry smile. "To think Darla was so worked up that she hired you without telling you the library was on the chopping block. And you weren't planning to stick around, anyway." He stuffed both hands in his pockets. "Please, go on."

"That's the whole story. I told my boss and family I was going on vacation, but I came here instead. I left my phone at home so I couldn't be tracked, and I withdrew money from my savings account." Thank goodness for the tiny inheritance from my grandmother.

"So, no knows you're here."

"Not a soul. I've called home so no one worries, but I blocked the phone number." The library's trustees had purchased my plane ticket. I hadn't used a credit card.

"But you think the victim was sent here to kill you?"

The covers of two of my favorite vintage crime novels, *Headed for a Hearse* and *Death Walks on Cat Feet*, flashed through my brain. "Yes."

The sheriff stopped and turned to the view of town. A thin trail of smoke rose from a chimney beyond the grocery store. Autumn was hard upon us. At home, Mom would be filling the big bowl on the sideboard with quinces, and Jean would be making teas with cardamom and cinnamon.

"Josie, I don't want to dismiss your story. I'm sure you have lots of reasons to worry about folks being unhappy with your discoveries in Washington."

"You don't think the body has anything to do with it?"

"No. No, I don't. We have firm evidence against Craig."

"I can't believe it." I'd been so sure. It was gut-level knowledge.

"For one, whoever killed her was already in Wilfred. There's only one road into town, and I was at the speed trap all evening. I saw everyone passing through."

"At some point you had to look at your phone or take dinner. You couldn't have watched the road every single minute," I said.

"Craig was seen heading toward the library on foot."

"Crossing the river?" I asked.

"Not quite, but on his way."

There was more, I knew. I waited.

"Also, we found a handgun at Craig's."

I faced Sheriff Dolby. "A handgun—you mean *the* handgun?"

"We're still evaluating it, but it looks conclusive. It was a weapon with a silencer, not something you find every day. Its identifying info was wiped."

"How did he get a gun like that?"

"I doubt it was his. It likely belonged to the victim. They got into an argument, Craig grabbed the weapon, and that was that."

I let that sink in. The facts were irrefutable, but they still didn't sit right. "Could it be a setup? I mean, maybe someone's framing him."

The sheriff gave me a *"where did you come from?"* look and ignored my question. "Also, I should tell you that as a matter of policy, I ran your information through our databases. I've known about you and your allegations about Bondwell and Senator Markham's aide for a few days now."

"Oh." I was momentarily tongue-tied. We'd come to where the trail entered the woods. I couldn't see far with the thick canopy shrouding the daylight. "You didn't say anything."

"I figured you had your reasons for keeping your silence. If the department gets notice there's a search for you, or if you give me any reason to question your safety, I'll have to notify the FBI. Until then, we'll let things stay as they are."

Mute, I nodded.

"So, no crazy risks, and no messing in the murder investigation. Understood?"

The forlorn cover of *Postscript to Nightmare* seared itself in my brain. I nodded once again.

Both relieved and disturbed, I returned to my office. I needed a moment to come down from the drama surrounding my confession to the sheriff. I glanced at the clock. Roz would be here for another hour. Before she went home, I needed to finish the report supporting the library.

I'd accumulated a lot of good information. I could enumerate numbers of books lent, events held, requests for information answered—at least, I could for most years and could extrapolate others. What I couldn't do was respond to the argument that the library's property was a breeding ground for trouble. Not with a murder to explain away.

If Craig Burdock really did turn out to be the murderer, it would only lend credence to what people had said: Troublemakers cross the river to the library's grounds. Replace the library with a facility with lots of visitors and even security guards, and the troublemakers would move on.

It was a tough argument to refute, and I wouldn't try. Instead, I'd lay out how the library had served the town. I opened my laptop, and Rodney leapt into my lap. He butted his head against my chin.

"Sweet kitty," I said. His responding purr was loud enough to draw my attention. "What? You want something, don't you?"

He stepped onto the desk, purring with enough ferocity that he had to open his mouth.

"Is it this?" I picked up a copy of *Murder on the Orient Express*. I hadn't set it on my desk, but I was starting to get used to books appearing randomly.

Rodney melted on the desk and plopped to his side. He licked a paw.

"You like it that I found this book. Okay."

Of course I'd read *Murder on the Orient Express*. In my teens I'd flown through Agatha Christie's mysteries. Hercule Poirot was a thorough investigator. In this novel, he'd questioned each suspect twice. The paperback tingled with energy. It wanted me to investigate the murder.

"You're joking," I said aloud. In response, the book warmed in my hands. I dropped it on my desk and stared.

I forced myself to breathe evenly. Something very strange was happening between books and me. It felt almost—magical. There was that word again. I'd always loved books, but never before had books been alive for me. At least, not beyond the printed page. And they certainly hadn't materialized like this.

Something was going on here, and it wasn't clear to me. Not yet. The change from my old life to this one had shaken something loose. *Something*. Whatever that was. Now *Murder on the Orient Express* had presented itself. Why?

The book wanted me to channel Poirot. It wasn't satisfied with the sheriff's determination that Craig Burdock had killed the woman I'd found, and it wanted me to find the real murderer. Find the real murderer, and the library's grounds would be less of a threat to Wilfred, bolstering the argument that the library was beneficial to the town. Keep the library, and I could stay on, undetected— as long as the sheriff didn't give me away. An innocent man didn't stay in jail. And the books would be happy.

"Okay," I said aloud. Rodney raised his head. I closed the laptop and pulled a notepad and pen in front of me. "*Motive*," I jotted.

Two main motives came to mind. First, the murderer could have thought the victim was me. Chilling, but possible. Both of us were women, city dwellers, and strangers to Wilfred. In that case, the motive was to eliminate evidence that could be used in a trial against Bondwell and Richard White. The murderer would be someone from out of town. No way Bondwell would hire a rookie like Craig to go after me.

The sheriff was convinced this wasn't the case, though. Remembering this, my shoulders relaxed. He said that no one could have entered town at that time. He was at the speed trap and saw everyone coming and going.

Okay, motive number two: the sheriff's premise that Craig wanted to join a criminal gang, and that his discussion with a professional criminal went south, leading Craig to kill her. The sheriff had found the murder weapon in Craig's apartment. If this is the way the crime went, the sheriff was on task to solve it.

Then of course the murder could have happened for any number of other reasons. Maybe a homicidal stranger was living in the woods and somehow lured out-of-towners to the library and knocked them off. Maybe the victim killed herself, and Craig found her gun and walked off with it. Maybe one of Craig's ex-girlfriends caught him in the act with the stranger and framed him.

Besides that, anyone intent on the library's sale had a motive to make the library's ground feel like a dangerous place. I shook my head. Murder was extreme, even for someone as fervent on turning a buck as Ilona.

I stared at my list, Rodney purring from my lap. What next? I'd work backward and eliminate the primary suspect. Yes.

The first step was to figure out if Craig was truly the murderer.

CHAPTER FIFTEEN

It was barely noon. I wanted to spend a few minutes following up on a hunch. I told Roz I'd be away from the library for a few minutes and grabbed my coat.

Lalena Dolby's trailer wasn't hard to find. A plywood sign shaped like a hand hung from the mailbox post announcing PALM READINGS, APPLY WITHIN.

Most of the dozen or so mobile homes in the Magnolia Rolling Estates were squat doublewides with porches and clipped evergreen shrubs. Not Lalena's. She lived in a pink singlewide that must have rolled off the assembly line when sedans had fins. Tubs of pink roses surrounded it, and a wind chime sounded low notes from the breeze off the river. Like its neighbors, this trailer perched on a four-foot-high foundation of cinder blocks. From the stoop, I could barely make out the library's top windows through the trees on the bluff across the river.

I knocked, and a dog barked inside. The door opened to Lalena wrapped in a ruffled robe holding half of a peanut butter and jelly sandwich. She must have been expecting someone else, because her face fell. "Sailor, no barkies. Hi, Josie. Can I help you?"

"Could I talk with you for a few minutes?"

She eyed me warily. "Why? I turned in all my books on time. The New Orleans book on hoodoo, I swear it was already damaged. Someone else must have dropped it in the bathtub."

"It's not that. I wanted to ask you about Craig Burdock."

She seemed to think it over while she swallowed a mouthful of sandwich. "Okay, come in. Don't mind the dog. He won't bite."

I followed her to a linoleum-topped kitchen table, her buff-colored terrier trotting after us. The rest of Lalena's sandwich and a jelly jar of yellow liquid sat next to a romance novel. The kitchen was as pink as the trailer's exterior—pink stove, pink refrigerator, and pink countertops. A lamp with a base shaped like a sad clown lit the table.

"Sit down, please. What do you want to know?" she asked, taking the seat across from me.

"It's adorable in here," I said.

"Is it?" She looked lazily around the kitchen. "I hate pink."

"Oh. But—"

"This was Aunt Ginny's place. She left it to me when she died. I haven't had the chance to do much more than hang my sign out front."

"It's so cozy, though."

"It's such a hick trailer. In a hick town. I need to go somewhere else, at least for a vacation. Somewhere like—"

"Paris," I said, remembering the history of the Eiffel Tower she'd checked out at my recommendation. "Have you been there?"

"No. Probably never will." She drained her tumbler and rose. "Want some?" She refilled her glass from a box of wine in the refrigerator.

"No, thanks. This is my lunch hour at the library."

"I don't usually drink in the middle of the day." She examined the glass's straw-hued liquid. "Not bad for box wine. I'm just so . . ." She set down the tumbler. "You didn't come to hear my troubles, though. You said you want to know about Craig? Maybe you'd rather have my psychic impressions of the library's future."

"You really think the retreat center is a done deal?"

"People sure seem to think so. Folks in the diner talk about how things will change. The Rudds might move to Forest Grove and rent their farmhouse to tourists. And Sam Wilfred came back to get in on the action."

That got my attention. "What does he have to do with it?"

"Big House still belongs to his family. It's a nice place. Great view. Sam will make a lot of money renting it out once the center is up and running."

Oh. So that's why he was here. That's why he voted for the complex. All his talk of happy memories of the library couldn't compete with lining his pockets. The thought grated on me.

Lalena eyed me, one brow lifted. "I'm getting a psychic flash. That's what you really wanted to talk about. Sam and the library."

"No. That's not it." I hastily redirected the conversation. "Your brother suspects Craig is the murderer, but you told me it couldn't be true. Why not? I got the impression it was about more than his love of animals."

Lalena got up and dumped her tumbler's contents down the sink. She filled her glass with water and took a few swallows before returning to the table.

"Craig and I dated for a few months. You haven't been here long, but Craig doesn't have the reputation as the best boyfriend on the planet."

No surprise there.

"Underneath all his hustle is a sweet guy, though. I know it. I see it. He acts like the big gangster because he's insecure. He's not a murderer."

"Do you have evidence he couldn't have killed anyone, or is it just your instinct?"

"'Just' my instinct? That's how I make my living, you know." Her dog put his front legs on hers. She lifted him onto her lap.

I wavered between questioning her further about Craig or following this thread. I decided to plunge in. "What's it like?"

"What's what like?"

"Being psychic."

"What do you mean?"

"Well, you have unusual abilities. It must have been scary to realize you could do things other people couldn't. That you knew the future."

She shrugged. "When you have the gift, you have it."

"It didn't freak you out?"

"What the—?" Something behind me had snagged Lalena's attention. I turned to find Rodney clinging to the window screen, his belly splayed to show his star-shaped birthmark, and his golden eyes boring in at us. Somehow he'd managed to scale the side of the trailer. Sailor yapped from Lalena's lap.

"Rodney!" I said. "Get down."

He turned his head to me, then leapt from the window and disappeared from view, leaving claw marks in the screen.

Lalena dumped the dog off her lap and shouted, "Okay, so I'm not psychic. I don't need to be. I tell people things, and they see what they need to see."

"What do you mean?"

"It's like this." She slid a deck of tarot cards from the counter. "Give me an issue. Tell me something you're concerned about."

"Well, the library, for one."

She handed me the deck. "Shuffle. Go ahead."

I had a friend in college who read tarot cards, and I'd seen her deck, heard her talk about arcana and the Celtic cross and things like that, but I'd never handled tarot cards. This deck was big in my hands but worn enough to shuffle easily. I'd expected to feel some sort of tingle like I did with books, but they might have been playing cards for all the energy they communicated.

"Is that enough?"

"Frankly, it doesn't matter. Okay, now cut the deck and turn over the bottom half. Don't worry about it. Whatever card is up will be fine."

I cut the deck and flipped up the bottom half as instructed. The card showed a man in a broad hat standing in front of a table holding a pentacle, a sword, and a goblet. He hoisted some kind of stick in one hand. "What's that?"

"The Magician."

I felt as if I'd grabbed an electric fence. I dropped my hands to my lap. "Oh."

Lalena didn't seem to notice my shock. "It means you have the tools at your disposal to solve the problem. Really, though, you could have chosen any card, and it would give you the answer you want. Like this." She pulled a card with a man seemingly penned in by pentacles. "Four of Pentacles. Stay the course, it says, and protect yourself. Or this." She pulled a card with a crowned woman holding a sword. "Queen of Swords. Use your brain."

"But I chose the Magician."

"Right." She gathered up the cards and tied them into a square of velvet. "Magic is really nothing but you seeing what you need to see—or want to see. It's confirmation bias."

"So . . ." I looked at the boomerangs in the pattern of the linoleum tabletop. "So, you don't think people can have magical abilities, like, say"—I forced a laugh—"being able to recommend the perfect book to someone?"

"You think you're magic? I really did love that book on the Eiffel Tower," she said. "But, no. You're simply a good librarian. You've probably absorbed a lot that you're not aware of. There are people who are freakishly good at remembering numbers and dates. Maybe you're one of those, except with titles."

"What about knowing who's going to call, guessing the next song on the radio—things like that?" I asked.

"Coincidence. Take the phone calls. How many people call you regularly, anyway? Chances are high you're going to know when you're due to hear from a friend." Lalena glanced up at the sound of a car crunching gravel, creeping down the road forming the trailer park's spine. "That'll be Mrs. Garlington for her weekly appointment."

"So, you're not psychic?" I said.

"Keep your voice down." She tightened the knot on the deck of tarot cards. "Not more than anyone else. People give off all sorts of clues with how they act, what they respond to. Mrs. Garlington, for instance"—she nodded toward the driveway, where a car door thunked shut—"she wants to complain about her son and hear how much he loves her. I can do that, and she'll walk out of here happy."

I stood. "I'll let you get to business, then. You really don't know more about Craig Burdock—where he was the night of the murder, for instance?"

"No. I haven't seen Craig in weeks. Not after what he did to me with the dental assistant." She hesitated a moment, as if unsure whether to speak. "You need to talk to Duke."

"The library trustee?"

She nodded. "He lives across the drive. The night of the murder I saw him leave on foot carrying a canvas bag."

"Did you see where he went?"

"No, but it wasn't to Darla's. He turned right at the highway, not left, like he was headed to the library."

The dog barked at the doorbell. Lalena crossed the

trailer's tiny living room in a few steps to open the door to Mrs. Garlington.

I had no choice but to leave. I turned to say good-bye and stopped short. Sailor was lying by the pink sofa happily chewing on something. I stepped closer. In the dog's mouth was Craig Burdock's fringed moccasin. The moccasin I'd seen him wearing two days earlier.

CHAPTER SIXTEEN

Craig Burdock been wearing those moccasins when I saw him at the library. Clearly, Lalena had spent time with him lately—after he was at the library, but before he was arrested the next day. Why had she lied? It could something as innocent as she was embarrassed that she had been seeing him again. Or she could be protecting him. She was certainly eager to toss blame Duke's way.

And the talk about magic. Even if Lalena were right and I had some sort of superpower remembering book titles, that wouldn't explain the books that appeared by my bedside each night. Or the copy of *Pride and Prejudice* with scrambled text. I remembered back to my flight from D.C. to Portland. Could I have bumped my head when I was so suddenly ill?

Right now, my grumbling stomach reminded me that I

had more pressing matters: lunch. The entrance to the Magnolia Rolling Estates let out down the block from Darla's tavern. I'd get a sandwich to go and take it to the library, where Roz would be ready for her own lunch.

The diner was quiet. Darla wiped down a counter, and through the cutaway to the kitchen, the cook was chopping onions, likely prepping a gumbo or jambalaya for dinner. Someone sat at the counter sipping a Coke. His bulk spread over the stool, his elbows were planted wide, and if I wasn't mistaken, his sweater was hand-knit. Duke McConway. *Kismet.* Two thoughts leapt to my mind: Lalena's claim that Duke was on a mysterious errand by foot the night of the murder and *Amphibious Vehicles of the D-Day Landing.*

"Josie, hon." Darla tossed her cloth into a bucket and wiped her hands. "What'll you have?"

"Something I can eat at my desk, please," I said. "How about a grilled cheese?"

"I'll duck into the kitchen and get it started. Marty's busy with dinner prep."

That left me alone with Duke. He swiveled on the stool and took a long draw through his soda straw. "You finish your report for the judge yet?"

"Word sure gets around quickly." His tone irritated me. In the old days, I would have smiled politely and said no. The Wilfred me wasn't as docile.

"I don't see why you're wasting your time. Point one, it's the trustees who decide what's good for this town. Point two, anyone with half a brain knows Wilfred needs commerce, not an ancient house sitting on a plot of land breeding trouble."

"Where were you that night, anyway?"

"Ha. That's a good one."

Not the response I'd expected. "I'm serious. You were seen out on foot that night."

"Are you accusing me? Because, if so, come out with it." He punctuated his comment by hoovering his straw through the dregs of his soda. "You aren't the sheriff."

"The sheriff isn't the only person who cares what happens up there," I said. "I found the body. I live there."

"Not for long."

Darla returned to the counter. "Josiekins, you need protein. You're getting hangry. Duke here has his objectionable qualities, but—"

"Hey, Darla."

"Let me finish. He may not be a perfect gentleman, but he doesn't go around shooting strangers and tossing them in the bushes, do you?" She winked at me.

I got it. Good cop, bad cop. "You protest a little too much, Mr. McConway. Did you tell Sheriff Dolby you were up there that night?"

"Who said I was?" He was standing now, shifting from cowboy boot to polished cowboy boot. The few silver rivets still left on his belt glittered. "What gives you the right to come into town, not even having roots here, and make accusations?"

"You should know you can't do anything here without someone seeing you."

I'd gone too far. Beads of sweat popped on Duke's forehead. He was holding his temper, but just barely.

Darla saw it coming, too. "Josie, now, you don't know Duke like I do. He's not that kind of man."

"I'm tired of all this insinuation," Duke said. "The sooner that library is history, the better. It's tearing up the town. Even you, Darla. I never thought I'd see the day. What I do, and when, is my own business."

What had I gotten myself into? "I never meant to—"

"You want to know what everyone was doing the night you arrived? Ask Darla here where she was. You just might find the answers illuminating, especially for a library trustee." With that, he slammed money on the counter and whisked past me, a buffalo on Fred Astaire's feet.

Darla's face blanched. She busied herself at the cash register, neatly smoothing Duke's bills and avoiding my eyes. She had something to hide, too, it was clear. What was it?

Could she and Duke—? No. Couldn't be.

"I'm sorry. I blew it," I said.

Darla's phone rang, and she fished it from her apron with relief. "Hello? Judge Valade?"

"Grilled cheese to go." The cook handed me a foil-wrapped sandwich.

I took the sandwich without letting my gaze leave Darla.

"Hmm," she said. "Okay." Pause. "Okay." Pause. "Right, well, good-bye."

"What did he say?" I couldn't ask fast enough.

"They moved up the deadline. The judge is leaving early today, and you'll have to have the report to him by three." She looked at the clock above the counter, a black cat whose eyes shifted from side to side with each swing of his pendulum tail. "It's already past one."

Roz was waiting at the library's front door when I returned. "What took you so long?"

"I went to the tavern for a sandwich and was, um, way-laid." I unwrapped the scarf from my neck and slipped off my coat. "Do you think you could stay this afternoon? The judge is going out of town and upped the deadline. I have to get it in by three this afternoon."

"Oh, I would, but I can't. I'm on deadline. I'm going to work on my project at home this afternoon. I have to finish it." She heaved a sigh. "I'm sorry. I knew it."

"Knew what?"

"Why even hold out hope?" Her voice rose in a flash of anger. "It never pays. The library is kaput. The judge won't even give us until the end of the day to get in our report. That doesn't bode well for his reading it."

"What is this project, anyway?" I said. I guess I was getting used to her negative ways, because her rant didn't faze me.

"Nothing," she said automatically. "Dylan is in the kitchen. Get him to watch the circulation desk. He'll love it." A moment later, she was out the door.

Roz was right—Dylan was thrilled to lord over the circulation desk. I told him I'd be in my office, but my door would be open, and to let me know if anything challenging came up. He said he'd make me proud, and as I headed toward my office, I heard him say, "Welcome, fellow Wilfredian, to our humble library."

"I've known you since you were in diapers, Dylan." Mrs. Garlington had sheet music tucked under an arm and sounded upbeat. Lalena must have delivered on her psychic reading. "Don't give me any of that hogwash."

Rodney was napping in my office armchair, but that was all right. I needed to focus at the desk. The report's shape was already laid out. All I had to do was to fill in some of the facts—and find a way to get around the argument that the library's grounds attracted troublemakers. I glanced at my watch. It was too late to interview the sheriff, but I could go through the local newspapers and look at crime reports. Say, five years' worth. This would be the last bit of bolstering the report would need.

I took my notebook to the old dining room and found bound copies of the *Forest Grove News-Times*, which looked to be the nearest newspaper to Wilfred. The paper was a weekly, which would, fortunately, make my work faster. I lugged volumes for the past five years to the worktable. Bound newspapers. I shook my head. This library needed updating in a serious way.

Pen in hand, I got to work. Wilfred had suffered very little crime, and none of it would have made the fine print in Washington, D.C. Someone had been periodically taking eggs from a sidewalk stand and not leaving money; a propane tank was stolen off a truck parked in the church parking lot; a drunk driver was detained.

The library's grounds didn't get off scot-free. The police had caught kids from Gaston trying to break into Big House. Vagrants camped along the river path over the summer. One article in particular caught my eye. The Save Wilfred's Youth group was founded just a few months ago. At the top of their agenda was to keep teenagers away from the library grounds after hours.

Then I heard it. There was no other way to describe the sound: The books were grumbling. They grumbled in bass, in soprano, in short chuffs, and in long moans. This couldn't be explained by a good memory for titles. This was something else entirely.

"Ms. Way?" Dylan stood in the doorway.

"Yes?" It was hard to focus on him with the chorus of books demanding my attention.

"I was thinking of adding a 'Dylan's Favorite Graphic Novels' section to the card catalogue. What do you think?"

"I—uh—that sounds fine." Whatever the noise was, it clearly didn't bother Dylan.

He squinted. "Are you listening to me?"

"Can you hear that?" I said.

"Hear what?"

I was going to sound like a crazy person. I took a breath and tried again. "Tell me what you hear."

He was game. The arm holding the clipboard dropped to his side. He closed his eyes. "I hear the wind in the oaks outside."

He was right. All around us leaves swished and fell to the ground. Lyndon would have his work raking cut out for him tomorrow. "What else?"

"Someone upstairs is walking. Maybe checking out the local history section."

Again, nailed it. The organ wheezed into the "Pepper Pot Polka," rattling the windows. Not even the books' grumbling could overcome that.

"I also hear Mrs. Garlington practicing for the Grange Hall dance," he said. He removed a set of earplugs from his blazer's inside pocket. "Want a pair?"

I had to laugh. "Say, do you know anything about the Save Wilfred's Youth group?"

"I've seen their posters at school. Why?"

"Who started the group? Any idea?"

"You should know. A couple of them are library trustees. Duke McConway and another lady."

"Blond? Looks like she's from the city?"

"That's her." He screwed in the earplugs. "I'll be in circulation if you need me to listen to anything else for you."

"Make sure you take those out before you talk to patrons," I said.

Duke and Ilona. I bet they started the group with the sole aim of making the library look bad. Before I left, I went to the window and looked down over the garden, past the caretaker's cottage to Big House.

Sam was at the edge of the garden, facing the library. He seemed strangely alone and small among the giant trees. An imaginary finger brushed my neck, and I shivered.

What did Sam have to do with all this? He was involved. I was sure. But I didn't know how.

CHAPTER SEVENTEEN

At last, the report was finished and tidily formatted with a table of contents and a cover I'd fashioned from office supplies left over from the disco era. Hopefully, the judge liked glitter purple. A digital copy was ready to be emailed. I had half an hour to spare.

I grabbed the phone. "Darla, this is Josie. Can you review the library report quickly before I send it out?"

"Honey," she said, "I trust you. Roz said you've done good things."

"You're sure?" I asked. "You don't want to look it over?" I appreciated her trust but was surprised she'd let it go without at least a quick scan.

"Positive. Send it to Judge Valade with my blessing."

The thing was, I wasn't sure how to get it to the judge. The library didn't have an Internet connection, and I didn't

even have my cell phone to set up a hot spot. Nor did I
have a car.

I grabbed the report and was making my way to Lyndon's cottage to beg a ride into town when the front door
opened with a creak. From the *rat-a-tat-tat* of heels, I
knew it was Ilona Buckwalter before I even turned
around. Dylan had left an hour ago. I had to make this
quick.

"You really should do something about that front
door," she said. "It sticks. Not that it will matter much
longer, anyway."

The library didn't want her here. A low grumble, almost a growl, rose throughout its rooms. "Can I help
you?"

"I understand you're putting together some kind of report for the judge, trying to convince him that Wilfred
needs the library." Today Ilona wore a "duchess at the
hunting lodge" outfit in green and blue plaid with high-
heeled leather boots. Miniature foxhound earrings with
emerald eyes jiggled as she walked.

"Of course I am." I held my laptop like a baby. "The
judge should have all the information before making a
decision on whether or not to throw out Darla's appeal."

"He has all the information he needs." She looked at
me as if I were barely smart enough to spell my own
name.

"Then you won't mind if I add my two cents." The
books' grumbling had started up again.

"I know you put a lot of work into that report, but I
understand the judge has already made up his mind. I
wouldn't be surprised if we have a decision within the
next couple of days."

I refused to be swayed. "How did you know about my report, anyway?"

Ilona ignored me. She was too busy digging through her purse for her ringing phone. She tapped its screen, then dropped it back into her bag.

"Sam told me."

My expression must have given me away. I'd seen him only a few hours ago looking up at the library. What did he know about the report? I supposed Darla might have told him. Or Duke.

Judging from her smug expression, she was enjoying my surprise. "We keep in touch, you know. Old friends."

No matter how much Ilona irritated me, and despite her role as a trustee, I was still the librarian here. I mustered my dignity. "Thank you for checking on me. If you don't mind, I'm busy right now."

She eyed my laptop. Her cackle was as sharp as a gun's retort. "That's the report, isn't it?"

"I'll be going now." I made for the side door through the kitchen.

"Wait. How are you going to get it to the judge's office? You don't have Internet service." She stepped forward. Now that she was closer, I made out tiny rifles lying at the dogs' feet on her earrings. "Why don't you let me drive you?"

Oh no. No way was I getting in her Mercedes to be waylaid who knew where. "No, thank you."

Her expression softened, and she stepped back. "Honey, you're in a tough spot. You've spent hours putting together a report the judge won't look at for two minutes. I hate to think of all that wasted effort."

"Thank you for your concern." I had my hand on the doorknob. I wasn't falling for Ilona's charm this time.

"Darla hired you. Now you find out you won't have a job. I told her we shouldn't do it, we should just leave the library open part-time with Roz. She wouldn't listen."

"All water under the bridge now. So, if you don't mind—"

"Darla's the one you should be questioning. Think about it." She tucked a platinum-blond hank of hair, stiff with styling gel, behind an ear. "She hired you and had you come all the way across the country, and she didn't tell you the job might not last. That's wrong."

"She's fighting so hard to save the library."

"Darla?" She said it so loudly that I jumped back. "She wants the new retreat center more than anyone."

"That's impossible. She's printed notes on the bottom of the menus and everything. She loves the library."

"Really? And how many books has she checked out lately? Huh? In fact, have you ever seen her with a novel?"

True, Darla hadn't been one of the library's patrons since I'd been in Wilfred, but that didn't mean she'd never used it. I was just about to tell Ilona so, when she jabbed a pink frosted fingernail into the air.

"She wants it both ways," Ilona said. "She wants people in Wilfred convinced she cares about the library. Really, though, she's a businesswoman. Think about it. With the retreat center, business at her diner will triple. She owns the plot of land behind the Magnolia Rolling Estates, and she can build guesthouses there. Her voice would matter in the county a lot more than it does now."

The truth in Ilona's words didn't match what I'd seen of Darla's desire to keep the library alive, but it did stir my interest. However, I had no time to think about it now.

"Ilona, the library is closing early today. We'll see you

soon. Good-bye." Only fifteen minutes until the judge's office closed. Maybe I could find an Internet connection in town. If I ran, I could be at the diner in five minutes. I was ready to knock on a stranger's door, if necessary.

"As a library trustee, I feel awful about having you come all the way across the country for a job that's so short term." She pulled an envelope from her purse's side pocket. "I have a check here, made out to you. It's enough money for you to live for a few months, if you're frugal."

I felt the doorknob turn under my hand, and I yanked my fingers away. In walked Sam Wilfred. He looked at me, then Ilona, his mouth going from frown to smile. Hadn't Roz said he frowned when he was happy?

"Ilona was just leaving." I ignored the envelope in her outstretched hand until she shoved it back in her purse.

"You won't get this offer again," she said, patting her purse's side pocket.

Any twinge of regret I might have felt was killed by her sheer odiousness. "Good-bye. Come again." *Not*, I added silently.

"I'll see you at the trustees' meeting tomorrow night." She reluctantly left through the open door. I closed it behind her and turned to Sam. "Do you have a cell phone with you?"

"Of course." His frown deepened.

Sam had voted for the retreat center, but I didn't have time to go elsewhere. "I need a wi-fi hot spot. Right now."

If he was puzzled, he didn't show it. "Got it."

CHAPTER EIGHTEEN

While the English as a second language class started in the conservatory, I settled into my office chair. It was already dark. Laughter and bits of stilted English came from the conservatory. The students—mostly farmworkers, judging from their sun-poached skin and roughened hands—had settled around the central table, lamplight reflecting on the room's glass panels. Kevin, the grocer and English teacher, had handed around assignment sheets. Besides this group, the library was empty, lights turned off in every room except my office.

The report had made it safely to the judge's chambers. After I emailed it, I called to double-check that it was received, and I put the hard copy in the mail. All there was to do was to wait.

Now would be the perfect time to call my sister. Dinner should be over, the baby in bed. I dialed 1-1-6-7 on the old rotary phone to block the caller ID and finished with Toni's number. I pictured a pulse of light racing over thousands of miles of telephone line, ricocheting off exchanges to sound at Toni's house in Silver Spring, with the crickets chirping and fireflies drawing circles in the night.

"Josie?" she said.

My whole body swelled with happiness to hear her voice. "Toni. How are you? How's the baby?"

"Never mind that. It's been two days. I was worried."

"How's my apartment? Anything else from the FBI?" I kept my voice low.

"No. Nothing. I just checked with the landlord today. How are things on your end?"

"I'm safe, if that's what you mean. There are complications—"

"Complications?"

"Nothing having to do with Bondwell or Richard White. But unless something changes, I might have to leave here soon."

"Come home," Toni said.

"I can't. You know that."

Rodney, ever the master of surprise appearances, was rubbing his chin against my chair. Seemingly weightless, he leapt into my lap. My birthmark sparked.

"Tell me," Toni commanded. "You don't have to tell me where you are, but tell me what's happening."

I contemplated this. Maybe I could tell her just a bit. She couldn't trace me to Wilfred.

"Okay. I took a job at an obscure library. The next day I found out that the library is probably going to be demolished within the month. That is, if a couple of the library trustees have their way." Toni didn't need to hear about the body I'd found in the bushes, although I longed to tell her.

"What? Why would the library's own trustees want to tear it down?"

"One of them's a real estate agent, and she makes a bundle if she can sell the land for a retreat center." I let out a sigh. "It's not fair."

"I know that tone of voice. Trouble."

"People here love the library. It's a community center. The trustees—the ones who want the sale, that is—say there's a lot of criminal activity here, but it's not true. The pro-library trustees have sued the others to stop the demolition, and the first trustees have petitioned the judge to throw the suit out of court. I just sent the judge a report in support of the library."

"Criminal activity? Oh, Josie. I'd feel so much better if you'd tell me where you are. What if something happens? How would we ever find you?"

"It's better like this." Rodney bumped his head against the phone's receiver. I dropped a hand to scratch him between the ears. "You can help me another way, though. As a physician."

"How?" she said almost before I'd finished my sentence. "Are you feeling all right?"

"It's a little difficult. You see, I—"

"Spit it out."

"I'm starting to wonder if there's something weird with my brain." I'd wanted to talk this over with her the last time I'd called, but news of the break-in at my apartment had cut it short.

The line was silent. Rodney's purr vibrated against my torso.

"What do you mean? I haven't noticed anything unusual. I mean, other than disappearing like you did."

"I told you I'd been dreaming again, right? Well, I also have a strange relationship with the books here."

A relieved laugh escaped Toni. "You've always had a strange relationship with books. A dedicated relationship, anyway. You were the only kid I knew who preferred books about dolls to the dolls themselves."

"That's not what I mean." How to explain it? "It's like the books talk to me. Books I swear I haven't ever seen tell me what shelf they're on. You know how I worked in cataloguing?"

"Sure. You always wanted to work with readers instead."

"It turns out I'm a freaking genius at it. For instance, right now I want to recommend a book to you."

"Okay." I knew that voice. She was humoring me.

"*Mrs. Beeton's Book of Household Management.* Page sixty-two, how to remove fruit stains from cotton."

"Whoa." Rodney's purr obscured everything but Toni's voice through the wire. "I was eating yogurt and jelly this afternoon and got apricot jam on my scrubs. I was just wondering how I was going to get it out."

"See? Isn't that weird? How was I supposed to know that? Plus, I've never heard of the Mrs. Beeton book. But I bet you anything I was right. I don't know what's wrong with me." Or what's right with me. My voice broke. Rodney buried his head in my cardigan.

"Don't be upset, Josie." When we were girls, Toni was the one who would pull me up when I fell off my bike. Even though she was only a few years older than I, she soothed me like a parent. "Maybe it's the stress."

Leaves, driven by a soft wind, shushed against the glass, and the casement window rattled. The moon would be creeping higher, I knew, and soon stars I'd never seen through the smog out east would pierce the night.

"No. It's more than that. I'm not even telling you some of the creepier things. I've had actual books appear at my bed-side. No one else could have put them there." Now I really did feel like a child. I wanted to have a three-handkerchief humdinger of a cry. I hadn't felt this way since I was a kid.

"I've never talked to anyone about this before, but I want to tell you something," Toni said.

I sniffed and reached for a tissue. "Just a sec." I blew my nose and deftly tossed the tissue into the wastebasket. Rodney let me jiggle his head as I did so and kept close to me. "Okay."

"Remember how much time Grandma spent in the gar-den?"

"Yes." An odd turn of conversation.

"I think she was a witch."

This should have shocked me. I should have shouted, "What?" But strangely, I wasn't surprised. It didn't take more than a moment to recover and say, "Oh."

"Remember that book she kept in the kitchen?"

"The big leather one? The one with the papers and dried flowers sticking out of it?" The book, fatter than the cookbook Grandma made her casseroles from, occupied the kitchen's top shelf where we girls couldn't get at it. As a book lover, I'd always been fascinated by it. I even asked Mom where it went after Grandma died, and she'd acted like she hadn't heard me.

"Yeah. That one. I think it was her grimoire—her witch's diary."

Get the book. This book is yours. I squeezed my eyes shut against the voices. Rodney gave my wrist a single lick.

"But Grandma went to church every Sunday," I said. "How could she be a witch?"

Toni sighed. "I don't know, but I'll tell you this. One night—I must have been only ten or so—we were staying the night at Grandma's, and I woke up."

As Toni talked, I felt the warmth of Grandma's house again, with cats popping in and out of the cat door, bunches of dried herbs hanging in the kitchen, and a stack of quilts in the living room, waiting to be pulled up for story time. Grandma had always laid us out in the living room in sleeping bags. Sometimes Jean, the baby, snuck out and crawled into bed with her.

"Yes?"

"I went to the kitchen for a drink of water, and I saw Grandma in the garden. The moon was bright, must have been full. She was out there picking plants, and I swear I saw her lips moving, but there was no one around. She'd stop and listen, then talk. The strangest thing."

Thinking of Roz, I said, "Maybe she had hot flashes and couldn't sleep."

"The next day she was bottling up plants in liquid and labeling them for the neighbors. Remember how the minister's wife used to come for a tincture when she had allergies?"

I did remember. She hadn't been the only one, either. The farmer down the road had used to brag he'd grown a full head of hair after a course of Grandma's compresses. The first grade teacher had come to her for help stopping an outbreak of chicken pox. At Grandma's funeral, a neighbor even whispered she'd been responsible for bringing home her wayward husband.

"I thought—I don't know—I guess I thought she simply knew a lot about folk remedies." I leaned back in my chair. "I was talking to someone here today about magic. She thinks magic is simply people seeing what they want to see."

"Some of it might be. In medicine we studied the placebo effect. I guess that's a sort of magic."

"This is more, though. I know it." I sighed. "Since I've been here, I keep having the same dream. I'm a little girl, and I'm standing in a garden at night. Kind of like what you describe with Grandma. Mom's there, too."

"What happens?"

"It's starry, and the air smells like lavender and grass. Grandma looks like she doesn't like it, but she hands me a book. *Grimm's Fairy Tales*. I remember the blue cover with the castle on it."

"You always did love that book. Sometimes I wonder if you love books more than real life, to tell the truth."

Not anymore, I thought. Now life was almost unbearably vivid. "Toni—"

"Never mind. What happens next?"

"Then I feel the air sucked out of my body—a big whoosh and a snap." I sat up. This was almost like the feeling I'd had on the plane to Portland.

"Then what?"

"Then everything goes dark."

We were both quiet for a moment.

Toni was first to speak. "I'm going to talk to Mom about this. She's not telling us everything about Grandma."

I heard the faraway sound of the baby crying. "You've got to go."

"Yes. There's just one more thing."

A prickling settled over me, starting at my throat and washing down my body. "What?"

"It's something I noticed once and brought up with Mom. She told me it was nothing and asked me not to say anything."

"What, Toni?"

"Grandma had a birthmark on her shoulder, just like you. A witch's mark."

CHAPTER NINETEEN

"What are you saying?" My hands had gone cold, and Rodney was purring loudly enough to obscure the conversation from the class in the conservatory. "You're a doctor. You believe in science, remember?" Despite my words, I wanted her to tell me more.

"Just a sec." Toni must have put her hand over the receiver, because her voice was muffled as she called out to her husband. "There. Bill's taking care of the baby. Anyway, you wouldn't have called unless you wanted to know something like this. Admit it."

Rodney nosed his head under my free hand and stared into my eyes. In the space of a second, I was in his body, seeing myself, legs tucked under me on the armchair, holding my phone. Then I was me again. Whoa.

"Josie? Are you still there?"

I caught my breath. "I'm here. I don't know what to

make of the whole thing. Books talking to me, dreams. The colors outside even seem more vivid. I've never seen greener trees and a bluer sky, even when it's overcast. Food even tastes better. At first I thought it was the landscape, but—" I almost gave myself away. "It's no secret that I've always loved books. Obviously. So, why now? Why do I have these weird abilities now?"

"It probably isn't all that weird, if we only understood it. Grandma probably learned a lot about the healing properties of plants, that's all. Some folk magic was mixed in, and she got the idea she had to collect them by a full moon."

"That explains her, not me."

Toni cleared her throat. "Listen. You asked me if I thought you showed signs of mental illness. Witchy things aside, you're under a lot of stress, right?"

I couldn't argue with that. "True."

"You're in a new environment surrounded by new people and a new job."

"That's true, too." She didn't have to tell me the rest. I knew. I'd been telling it to myself for days now. She'd tell me I was tired, distracted, and, therefore, experienced odd things.

"And maybe you have some psychic ability."

"What?"

"Think about it. Jean and I have a bit, too. Remember when Jean sprained her ankle and you dropped your book at home and ran to the playground to find her?"

I did remember. "You were at debate club."

"I felt it, too, and excused myself to call Mom. And you know how we can never buy each other birthday gifts without the other sister knowing what it is?"

I laughed. "True." When I was in second grade, Toni

had given me a doll only to discover I'd already fashioned a makeshift house for her in the corner of my bedroom.

Toni's voice grew solemn. "It's something deeper with you, though. Grandma coddled you and Mom worried over you. They knew you were special."

Was Toni jealous? She was the smart one, the accomplished one. She won the science fair at school and a full scholarship to college. In school, I squirreled myself away in a corner of the library. I'd have much rather spent my days with Trixie Belden than quadratic equations.

"I don't get it," I said. Voices in the central hall told me the English class was getting out. "I'd better go now. Thank you, Toni-tone," I said, using a childhood nickname. "You've given me a lot to think about."

"Call again soon, okay?"

I was sad to hear the receiver's *thunk* into its cradle, cutting my connection with Toni and my old life. Yet Wilfred had given me something that felt even truer to who I was.

Later, once the library was closed up for the night, I went upstairs and made myself a mug of herbal tea. While the tea steeped, I leaned over the railing to look into the dark hall surrounded by rooms of books. Marilyn Wilfred seemed to smile benevolently at me.

The muted shushing of thousands of stories softened the air. Here and there, I picked it out. "Witch," a shelf of books whispered. "Witch," the shelf across the hall answered. Now a room of shelves whispered in concert. "Witch."

"Stop it!" I yelled. The rooms silenced. My pulse thudded in my ears.

Once my breathing returned to normal, I took the tea

to my bedroom. My hands shook as I set it on the side table next to the chair by the window. Could it be true, everything Toni had told me? In my work with the Folk-life collection, I'd come across oral histories of so-called witches. They were valued and feared in their rural communities. But that was nearly a century ago.

I glanced over to see what the library had chosen for me to read that night. *Romp with a Billionaire*, a romance by Eliza Chatterley Windsor. What? Not the kind of reading I'd choose for myself, but books had their reasons.

This new normal was really strange.

The next morning, I opened my eyes to a calm, orderly bedroom—a librarian's bedroom, not a witch's. I hadn't dreamt. It was as if my brain had shorted out, and all I could do was sleep and hope it repaired itself.

Rodney yawned, stretched on the quilt at the foot of the bed, then padded up to head-butt my chin. All this business about being a witch? Hysteria. Sure, I might have a touch of intuition where books were concerned. Only natural. I also had a vivid imagination, and I'm no dummy. Here, in Wilfred—a new town, a new job, and let's not forget the possibility of someone sent to silence me—my head was working in overdrive. That's all.

My feet hit the chilly floor and sought slippers. Besides, say I was a witch. Wouldn't I be able to detect a murderer and power him straight to jail? Couldn't I simply cast a spell and—poof!—the library would be saved?

I pushed back the curtains. The sun poured over the lawn, sparking the dew into a thousand diamonds.

I picked up the romance novel to return downstairs.

Last night I hadn't read more than a few pages before I fell asleep.

There was no romance novel on the nightstand now. In its place was an old pal, *Folk Witch*. I turned it in my hands, then tucked it in my pocket. This time, I planned to read it.

CHAPTER TWENTY

For breakfast, I walked down the hill to Darla's diner. The ground was moist, and pine needles stuck to my clogs.

I was going to have to stop these meals out. The wad of cash I'd brought to Wilfred was dwindling. Darla had told me to expect a paycheck at the month's end, but I'd need that money to fund my next hideout—that is, if the retreat center became a reality.

But I knew I could find one thing at the diner for sure, and that was Darla. If Craig Burdock had been mistakenly arrested, the real murderer was still at large. Ilona had been quick to point a finger at Darla. Darla was faking her interest in the library, she'd said. Darla was after the cash the retreat center's visitors would bring to town.

It was true that Darla's old sedan could use an upgrade, and she was ambitious. Maybe not as ambitious as Ilona, or not in the same way, but she wanted a lot in her life. I'd flipped through circulation records, and Ilona was right—I didn't find anything checked out to Darla. Roz had told me the library subscribed to *Southern Dame* for her, but I couldn't find evidence she'd looked at a single issue.

The diner was warm and busy, with grits on nearly every table. I took the spot at the end of the counter I was beginning to think of as mine. Without speaking, Darla pulled a mug from under the counter—the same mug I'd drunk from my first day—and filled it with coffee.

"I heard you got the report in on time," she said.

"I did. There's a copy waiting for you at the library. I'm on pins and needles waiting to know what the judge thinks. How'd you hear?"

She handed me a menu. "Sam was here last night asking about you."

My face warmed. "Me? He asked about me?"

"Well, not outright, but feeling it out. Hungry this morning?"

"What do you mean?" I said. "About Sam, that is."

"If you have an appetite, I recommend the Russian omelet. You won't need lunch." I nodded, and she took my menu. "Asked a few things—how we'd heard from you, why you chose Wilfred, you know." She put her hands on her hips. "I don't trust him."

Before I could follow up, Darla grabbed an armload of platters from the kitchen and slipped from behind the counter. She returned in seconds and refilled my cup.

"I'm not the only one, either," she said, picking up her conversation where she'd left it and simultaneously tearing an order slip from her pad and sliding it to the cook. "His family shuts down the mill and takes off in the middle of the night. Oh sure, we saw him from time to time when he came to visit his aunt, but the Wilfreds didn't give a damn about what happened in town. If it weren't for Marilyn, he'd have been run out. Now he shows up out of the blue."

"He was just a kid."

"Maybe he was then, but he wasn't a kid when he voted to demolish the library."

I couldn't argue with that. Still, Sam didn't seem like someone who would sell out his hometown and his aunt's legacy. "Some people might be suspicious of you," I ventured. "I mean, where were you the night the intruder was shot?"

Slowly, Darla turned away from the kitchen and faced me. "What are you getting at?"

"Some people might say—not me, but I'm putting it out there—some people might say you'd gain a lot if the retreat center goes in. Business here would really pick up. You could expand. Maybe Wilfred could regain its incorporation. You could run for mayor."

She busied herself preparing checks as if I'd simply mentioned that the sun was out and wasn't that nice. "You've been talking to Ilona, haven't you?" She didn't wait for my reply. "As it happens, I was here during the day and went home that evening to watch TV. Marty held down the fort at the tavern. I told it all to the sheriff. You satisfied?"

She left to take orders to the dining room and returned moments later with a stack of dirty plates, which she deftly dumped into a tub. The cook rang his bell, and at the ding, Darla slid a plate with a whopper omelet in front of me. I prodded it with my fork. This thing was as big as a baby.

"You've definitely fought for the library," I said.

"For sure."

"We've never talked about why you love it so much. Are you a big reader?" I let my mind go blank. Not a single book recommendation surfaced for her.

Darla avoided my eyes and pulled close saltshakers to fill. "There's something attractive about that man, I admit, and he's asking after you. If you're smart, you'll mind my words and stay away from him." She lifted an eyebrow. "Sam, I mean. He hasn't been bothering you, has he?"

I wanted to follow up on Darla's connection to the library, but this distraction about Sam was too tempting not to follow.

"I've seen him around once or twice, just in passing. Bother me, though? No. He's too old for me, anyway," I said. "If that's what you mean."

"Too old? You're, what, twenty-five? Sam's not even ten years older. Why, my second husband, Marcus, was seventeen years older than me." Her face took on a faraway look. "Don't knock it 'til you've tried it." She returned to reality and patted the counter in front of me. "Still, not Sam. He's not being completely honest."

"What do you mean? Do you know something?"

Darla leaned forward. "Sam says he only showed up in town a few days ago." She looked up the counter to make sure no one was listening. "Not true. I saw him in Forest Grove the night before. Who's to say he's not the one who shot her?"

"I thought you said you were home watching TV the night January Stephens died."

She straightened and looked me square in the eyes. "I was. Most of the night, that is."

"Most of the night," I repeated.

"Eat up," she said and turned away.

At noon, I went to find Roz. She might have some insight on Darla's connection to the library. Plus, I wanted an idea of what to expect at the trustees' meeting the next evening. Thanks to all the work I'd done for the judge, I had solid quarterly statistics. Although it gave me pause, Ilona seemed to be planning the logistical part of it. What would they want from me?

Roz was in the conservatory, holding her mysterious project against her chest and staring out the window. I followed her gaze to see Lyndon planting what looked like tulip bulbs in the bed fronting the path along the bluff.

"He's an optimist," I said.

Roz's expression was uncharacteristically dreamy. She caught me watching her, and her gaze hardened. "He just goes and goes. He's always been that way. Ever since high school."

"You've known him a long time, then."

"We dated briefly in our senior year, if you can believe that." She barked a short laugh and studied her fingernails.

I glanced at her, then at Lyndon's tall form bending over the ground. "I wonder where he'd be without his cottage."

"Homeless."

She held plain manila folders, unlabeled, nothing to

indicate what was inside. "Well, if the library's sale goes through, you'll have the chance to work on your project full-time. Whatever it is."

"I'm not going to tell you about my project," she snapped.

"All right, all right." We fell to watching Lyndon work. "I don't suppose there's a spot for him at the Magnolia?"

Sheriff Dolby strolled by the conservatory, his shoulders almost cartoonishly wide. Lyndon stood as he approached. A sound like a kitten's mew escaped Roz.

"I've got to go," she said and was out the door before I could ask about Darla or the trustees' meeting.

It didn't take a witch to see that Roz had the scorching hots for Lyndon. I wondered if she'd had a thing for him since high school. All those years.

My own love life had been quiet. Okay, nearly nonexistent. I'd watched Toni meet her husband and fall goofily in love, and one guy or another was always after Jean, but I observed from behind a book. I figured I'd meet a kind, practical man at some point and settle down, but I wasn't in a rush.

Now Toni's words last night came back. "Sometimes I wonder if you love books more than real life," she'd said.

On its heels, the image of Sam's slender form walking across the garden came to mind, but it was chased by the knowledge that he'd voted for the library's demolition and stood to profit, just like his family had before him. Soak Wilfred for what it was worth and move on.

Outside, Lyndon nodded at something the sheriff said. The sheriff gestured toward the library, then to the cottage. Lyndon nodded again.

I absently placed a hand on Roz's desk and felt a murmur below its oak top. I drew back my hand. Only books did that to me.

The Duke's Temptation. The title slid neatly into my brain. Could it be—?

I went next door to popular fiction and found the book inched farther out than the others on the shelf. The cover featured a man in an unbuttoned shirt with floppy poet's sleeves and abs like corrugated steel. Who knew dukes kept full-service gyms in their castles? I opened the book a third of the way through.

Lyndon, Duke of Forster, strode into the stable and—

I gasped and turned again to the cover. *The Duke's Temptation*, written by Eliza Chatterley Windsor. Wasn't she the author of the romance that had appeared beside my bed upstairs? The one about the billionaire? I pulled it from the shelf and read its back cover. "Forster Lyndon was the toast of New York society . . ." I crossed the hall to the card catalogue and flipped until I found Eliza Chatterley Windsor.

Twelve books, all romances. All featuring some version of the library's caretaker, from Amish farmer Forest L. Den to the Marquis de Forstaire, hero of the French revolution.

Roz wrote romance novels—that was her project. Roz was in love.

CHAPTER TWENTY-ONE

That evening when the library closed, I made a decision. Lyndon was across the garden locking up his tools. He was pulling off his gloves when I arrived, breathless, at the shed. Beyond him lay his cottage, and beyond that was Big House, a faint light in the kitchen window. I pulled my gaze away.

"Lyndon, I wonder if you'd have a cup of coffee with me in the library's kitchen?"

"Yes, ma'am. Everything all right?"

The sparse lawn felt cold under my feet. "Things are fine. I just wanted to talk with you about—everything." There were no classes in the library tonight. We'd have privacy.

Less than a week ago, Lyndon had been a creepy man of few words who might have emerged from one of Mabel Seeley's gothic mysteries. Now I saw him as someone hardworking—and loved. He smelled of soil and river air. He was a part of Wilfred's fabric.

A few minutes later, Lyndon joined me in the library's atrium. The books around us hummed and sighed—they were content. Before following me to the kitchen, Lyndon straightened the urn of dahlias on the table below the cupola. He pulled out a branch of leaves that were starting to curl, and he pinched a drooping blossom from its stem.

"Coffee?" I asked.

"Water's fine, ma'am." He settled his lanky frame onto a chair, like a spider would take a tuffet. "Is it about Ilona's meeting tomorrow?"

I poured us both glasses of water. "No, and please call me Josie. This 'ma'am' business makes me nervous." He was old enough to be an uncle. If anything, I should be calling him "sir." "Besides, as a trustee, it's your meeting, too."

"I guess."

"I wanted to talk with you about a few things. For instance, what will you do if your cottage is sold with the library?"

"I'll work it out. I suppose someone needs a handyman." His thick eyebrows drew together. "That's not why you asked to see me, is it? Because I hardly think you're in a better situation than I am."

"I can't argue with that." I rolled my tumbler between my palms. "If it were up to me, I'd stay in Wilfred." He didn't need to know about the vipers' nest that awaited me in D.C.

"And?"

"And I want to do what I can to see that the library isn't demolished. As far as I can tell, the only thing that will stop that is if the judge rules to hear Darla's case against the trustees. If he does, the key will be proving that the library grounds don't foster crime. Like murder."

At the mention of the body, both of us swiveled toward the window facing the river. Lyndon shook his head.

"The sheriff will take care of that," he said. "Known him all my life. He's an honorable man."

"I saw him questioning you again."

Rodney leapt onto the chair next to me and nosed his way into my lap.

"I swear, that cat never took a hankering to anyone the way he seems to like you."

I kissed the top of Rodney's head. Whatever happened to the library, he'd be coming with me. Somehow I doubted he'd like life much in a one-bedroom apartment in a D.C. suburb, but we were bonded.

"Does Sheriff Dolby really think you're guilty? You were with me most of the evening."

"Nah. Dolby thinks I might have spotted the gent before I left to pick you up at the airport. That's all."

This was one of the longest sentences I'd heard him speak. Imagining Lyndon and Roz together was to picture a kitchen full of Roz's downbeat chatter and Lyndon's occasional nods. Somehow, it wasn't as crazy as it sounded.

"The sheriff doesn't believe that now, does he?" I asked. "You said you were somewhere else all day. You told him, right?"

Lyndon glanced around the room as if he were afraid someone would overhear us. "I didn't tell him about that."

"Why?"

"None of his business."

"But it is his business. It's all of our business." I leaned forward, squeezing Rodney from my lap. He jumped to the floor and trotted toward his dish. "Someone was murdered."

Lyndon folded his arms over his chest and wouldn't look at me. He stared at the ceiling, then the refrigerator, with its weekly list of activities pinned by a heart-shaped magnet, to the faucet. "Tap needs fixed. I'll change those washers." He placed his hands on his armrests in preparation to rise.

"Lyndon!" I pounded my fist on the table. "You want to go to jail because you're stubborn about where you were?" I lowered my voice. "Maybe no one can verify that you were there?"

"Oh no. There were plenty of other folks with me."

"I don't understand." I leveled my gaze at him. "Those people know where you were. Why can't the sheriff know?" Then it occurred to me. He was embarrassed. Lyndon had been at some sort of twelve-step meeting, and he didn't want word to get out.

He pushed his untouched water away. "All right, I'll tell you, because you're a stranger here. But it goes no further."

"Sure. Don't worry. My great-uncle was a problem drinker," I offered.

Lyndon raised an eyebrow. "Huh?"

"Go on. Tell me."

"I was getting an award from the northwest chapter of the National Ikebana Society."

That stopped me cold. "What?"

"I study ikebana."

"You've got to be kidding," I said. At the same time, I could see it.

"I've always had a knack with flowers and plants.

Auntie Lyn got me started with a book on ikebana, actually."

Blue room, shelf near the window, my brain supplied. "You mean, you're too embarrassed about the award to admit it? Embarrassed because it has to do with floral arrangements?"

He looked at his hands.

"You've got to be kidding."

"It don't matter," he said. "I told the sheriff something better, something that proves I couldn't have done it."

I waited for his response while Rodney nipped at the heel of my shoe.

"I've never shot a gun. Don't know how."

"I thought hunting was a rite of passage out here."

He shrugged. "Everyone in town knows. I just had to remind Dolby." He lowered his gaze again. "In fact, I'm vegan. Don't approve of violence against people or animals."

I let the words soak in. Vegan. Ikebana master. Pacifist. For a few seconds, I wondered if Roz had cast her affections in an unproductive direction but decided she still had a chance.

"Lyndon?"

"Ma'am—I mean, Josie."

"Have you read *Fifty Florists Who Changed Bouquets Forever*?"

Despite Lyndon having cleared himself to the sheriff—or so he said—he didn't seem particularly happy. Given his standard demeanor, I couldn't tell if it was his usual gruffness that clouded his mood or something else. Maybe I could draw him out.

I caught him as he returned to the vase of flowers in the atrium. Splashes of ruby and cobalt light fell from the cupola's stained glass. Lyndon's constant fooling with the vase made more sense now.

"Little did I know our flowers were designed by a nationally recognized expert."

He didn't respond, but I caught a quiver of a smile. Just because he'd cleared himself didn't mean he couldn't help point the way to the murderer.

"Lyndon, what do you think of Sam Wilfred?" My heart beat in double-time when I said his name.

"Sam? Why? What do you want to know?"

"I mean, with the murder and with Sam showing up unexpectedly—could there be a link?"

"Nah." He pulled out a branch of leaves and reinserted it at a sharper angle, transforming the bouquet's shape from loose to elegant.

"Why not? He voted to sell the library. Maybe he wanted to throw shade on the library's grounds."

"Not the type." Lyndon turned away from the vase to face me. "He was just a kid when his family shut down the mill, you know."

"What do you mean by 'not the type'?"

"Haven't you talked to him?"

"Sure, but—"

"Then you know. He's a watcher, not a meddler. Even as a boy he could sit on Big House's porch and stare over the bluff for hours. He knew who'd been at the tavern and who got a new vehicle and when the snowdrops would be coming up. Loved the library, too. Always had a stack of Hardy Boys mysteries next to him."

"Then why did he agree to sell it?"

"I said he wasn't a murderer. Didn't say I could read

his mind. Now, if you don't mind, I'd better get back to my cottage. I have a batch of cashew cheese in the food processor."

He strode toward the library's front door, unusual for him. He liked to keep to the tradesmen's entrance at the side. I thought I'd try one more time.

"Lyndon."

He sighed and faced me. "Yes?"

"I know the library's fate bothers you. But is there something else?"

He pulled at a button on his plaid shirt, as if to see if it were loose. Finally, he said, "You're Roz's friend, right?"

"Sure," I said quickly. As quickly as I could about a woman I'd met less than a week earlier.

"I've seen her looking out the conservatory window."

"Yes . . ." My shoulders relaxed.

"Kind of intently, like she was looking for something. You don't think she has something to hide, do you?"

"Oh, I wouldn't worry about that." I pictured Lyndon as the Marquis de Forstaire, in a powdered wig, wielding a sword. "She has an active imagination. That's all."

CHAPTER TWENTY-TWO

Last night's rain had left the grounds moist but the sky clear. A trail of smoke rose from Lyndon's cottage. Behind it, Big House was dark. If Sam was home, I couldn't tell.

Sheriff Dolby was the library's first customer. "Morning, Josie. Coffee ready yet?"

"Just about."

I was learning that Wilfredians counted on coffee with their reading, and, second to Darla's, the library was their preferred caffeination location. I'd thought Darla would have been mad at how much coffee patrons drank here instead of at her café. Then I learned she supplied the coffee, for free. She had a strong tie to the library. What it was exactly, I had no idea.

"I wanted to let you know I'm cutting back on the extra patrols I'd assigned to the library," the sheriff said.

"Now that Craig's under arrest, you're fine. Besides, Lyndon and Sam are right nearby."

"You're sure Craig is the murderer?"

"Absolutely. I know you don't believe me. I understand why you might be anxious, given your situation."

The coffeepot beeped, and I poured each of us a cup. I pushed the sheriff's across the table to him. "I suppose everyone in town has asked each other where they were that night. For instance"—I stirred my coffee in a deliberately offhand way—"where were you?"

He gave me an inscrutable look. "At the speed trap, as usual."

"All night?"

"Sure." His face cracked into a grin. "Caught Darla barreling past, hell-bent-for-leather. Wait until she sees the ticket that's showing up in her mailbox."

"But she said she was—" At the sheriff's sudden freeze, I bit off the sentence.

"You're asking questions? Asking where people were?"

I studied my coffee cup. "Like you said, I'm here alone. It's only natural I want to know who I should keep an eye on."

"You have particular suspicions?" The chair creaked under his weight. "Josie, if you know anything, you need to tell me." The joking country boy was gone. Here was the sheriff, serious and measured.

"I don't know what to think," I answered. "First, Darla tells me she was home, but now it seems she was out at least part of the evening. Why does she care so much about the library, anyway?"

"I have Darla accounted for. Who else?"

"Ilona, of course. She has the most obvious motivation. Cash. The river trail already has the reputation of attracting trouble. A dead body? What judge wouldn't rule for the retreat center after that?" On a whim, I added, "I could even see her enlisting Duke's help. They've already started a bogus youth crime prevention group."

"Josie, I appreciate all the thinking you've given this, and we're definitely gathering loose ends—some of which you've mentioned. But you need to keep out."

"I can't help but be concerned." Suddenly, the coffee didn't taste so good. I put down my mug. "What if the murderer thought the victim was me?"

"You've brought this up before. You really think so?"

"I already told you why I'm here. I can't help but wonder. And from everything I've heard, it just doesn't seem like Craig Burdock is the type to shoot someone and leave her in the bushes."

"Who have you been talking to?"

"Your sister, for one. She doesn't think he'd be up for more than joyriding in a stranger's car."

Sheriff Dolby shook his head. "They dated, you know. She's biased. I wouldn't rely on what she has to say."

"Roz and Lyndon are skeptical, too. Lyndon says until the murder, Craig hadn't been to the library since he was in high school. Apparently libraries aren't a big attraction for him."

"The river trail might be, though," the sheriff pointed out. "It's just the sort of place that draws troublemakers. Lyndon coops himself up in his cottage after hours. He'd have no idea who's hanging out here."

"I don't know. After listening to everyone, I guess I just want to be sure."

"You have a specific idea of the murderer, then? Someone you haven't already mentioned?"

I took a deep breath. "Yes. I can't tell you exactly why, just that I don't think he's being honest, and—"

"Who, Josie?"

I didn't want to say his name. Still, here was the sheriff, and it was murder we were talking about. "I can't figure it out exactly, but I don't trust him."

"Who?"

"Sam."

"No. You've got that wrong." The words came fast and sure. "We talked about this. Let it go."

"I can't let it go. Look at the timing of his visit," I said. "He hasn't been in town for years, then suddenly he shows up on the same day the body was found."

"Coincidence," the sheriff said, maybe a little too quickly.

"He hangs around. I see him everywhere. I even think he's been walking the grounds at night."

"A fellow's entitled to do a little walking at night. I don't see a problem with that."

"But he doesn't even use a flashlight. What's that about?"

The sheriff tucked a thumb into his belt. "He knows this land better than he knows his right hand. He used to play here all the time as a kid, along with some of the other boys from the mill families. Hide-and-seek after dark. Big House isn't very welcoming, really. Not a place for kids to play—his mother made sure of that." He shook his head. "You should see the front room. Dolled up like a showplace."

"He's been asking around about me, too, according to Darla."

"Is that so?" The sheriff looked at me in a way that implied what Darla had told me—that he was interested in me romantically.

"You know what I mean."

"That he's planning to seduce you and slip you a poisoned library card?"

I folded my arms. "No, that's not what I mean."

The sheriff chuckled. "Relax. I was just having some fun. You can forget about Sam. It wasn't him. I'm positive."

I took a deep breath. "Sam arrived the day I found the body, right? Or, at least, that's what he says."

"And?"

"I saw a light on in Big House the night I came to town. The night before Sam said he'd come to Wilfred." I paused to give the sheriff the chance to respond, but he didn't take the bait. "He wasn't telling the truth."

"You'd been traveling for hours. Light is tricky. You were tired and saw your own bedroom lights reflected across the way."

It wasn't that. I knew it. I waited for Sheriff Dolby to say more. This was a big ploy I'd read in vintage detective novels. The detective waits for the subject to rush to fill the silence with some juicy nugget of information.

It didn't work this time. The sheriff picked up his hat and was at the kitchen door in an instant.

"See you, Josie. Like I said, don't worry that we won't have an officer on the grounds. You're perfectly safe."

I thought of my chart upstairs of suspects and time-tables. One person I hadn't included was the sheriff.

CHAPTER TWENTY-THREE

Even from my third-floor apartment, the books' grumbling was impossible to ignore. I didn't blame them. I'd be grumbling, too, if I didn't have to keep up some pretense of professionalism.

Tonight was the library trustees' quarterly meeting. I'd prepared handouts summarizing circulation and patronage, then figured out minutes ago it wasn't going to be that kind of meeting. Ilona had set up a portable screen in the atrium next to a tabletop display of the proposed retreat center. Platters of cold cuts and cheese covered the kitchen table—I'd been successful, at least, in keeping food away from books. She'd even enlisted Duke's help to tie a half-dozen Mylar balloons to the front porch.

"No one will come," Darla had told me.

"Sure they will," Roz had said. "Free food."

Hopefully, no free drama to go with it.

I peeked over the railing to the floors below. Roz had been right. All of Wilfred seemed to be streaming into the library. I leaned back against the doorway to my living room.

Now what? Darla hadn't heard a peep from the judge. I could tell from her hesitant tone that she feared their suit would be dropped and the library's sale would go through. Before long, I'd have to leave—to go where? Home wasn't safe. I refused to put my family at risk by moving in with them. I couldn't afford to live more than a month without a job.

I wiggled my fingers and held up my palms to better feel the energy. The books' grumbling thickened enough to overpower the voices rising from the hall below, although I knew no one else could hear it. Say Toni was right, and I was a witch. What good was magic if it couldn't save the library?

I took a deep breath, pasted on a smile, and went downstairs. At least I could make sure the books were safe from stray cups of punch and half-eaten canapés.

"Josie," Ilona said the second I emerged from the stairwell, "glad you're here. You know how to run the projector? Or didn't they teach you that in library school?"

Ilona was decked out as hostess in a silver cocktail dress and rhinestone-studded wine bottles dangling from her ears that matched the charm bracelet dripping miniature champagne glasses.

Of course I could run a laptop projector. I shook my head. "Sorry I can't help."

I joined the crowd gaping at the model of the proposed retreat center. A miniature Wilfred was laid out on a card table with the Kirby River flowing through it in blue ink. Darla's tavern parking lot even had tiny cars parked at its door, although they were sedans rather than the real-life pickup trucks. Across the river, the Magnolia Rolling Estates' trailers settled in orderly rows dotted with oaks.

I raised my hand to touch the vaguely Native American lines of the retreat center. No library. Just a long, peak-roofed building with a picnic area overlooking the town. Lyndon's cottage was a parking lot. Big House hugged the property's edge looking more than ready to become guest lodging. The retreat center was nicely done, I had to admit. If it didn't mean the demolition of Wilfred's heart, I might have even liked it.

"Don't touch that." Ilona had come up behind me. "Please. We don't need your fingerprints on it. The investors haven't even seen it yet."

I backed up a few steps, and fingers grasped the backs of my elbows. I spun to find Sam. He dropped his hands instantly.

"Sorry," he said. "I was just coming over to see the model."

I looked away. "If the retreat center goes in, you sure benefit."

"What do you mean?"

The sincerity in his voice surprised me. He seemed to have relaxed over the past few days and looked more like the rest of Wilfred in worn jeans and a chambray shirt rolled up to his elbows. His expression still held the watchfulness I'd noticed before, and his mouth wore a faint smile, the smile he gave when unhappy. Trouble.

"Look how close your house is." I smoothed an errant curl as I spoke. "Turn it into a bed-and-breakfast, and you stand to make a bundle of money."

"I guess I could. If I stayed in Wilfred."

"You still have the house."

"He owns a lot of land in town, don't you, Sam?" Ilona slipped a hand under Sam's arm. Her lips shone frosted beige, a color whose name almost certainly contained the word "champagne." "The program starts in a minute. Don't miss it."

A crashing *thump* behind us drew our attention. A fat compendium of James M. Cain's crime novels had landed on the retreat model, flattening the miniature trees in the parking lot. Rodney's tail disappeared from the second-floor hall.

"Damn it!" Ilona yelled. "It's that cat."

Hiding my smile, I threaded my way toward the entrance of the house's old drawing room, where Roz stood, arms crossed over her chest.

"Darla's mad Ilona took over the meeting. She says the trustees will have to hold a proper meeting next week, and this time no showboating."

The library was now shoulder-to-shoulder with people. Some I recognized as library patrons—I waved at the man with the vegetable plot and wondered if the blonde with the toddler had started dog training lessons yet—but most everyone here tonight was a stranger.

Lalena, her hair wrapped in a blue silk scarf, made her way through the crowd. "I've been getting ridiculous amounts of business from people asking about the retreat center. Some want to hear that the center is a sure thing, while others are desperate to save the library."

"What do you tell them?" We stood close to hear each other.

"It will all work out. Eventually." She shrugged. "What else am I going to say?"

The squeal of a speaker interrupted our conversation.

Ilona stood near the Kirby Center model holding a microphone. Her earrings swung as she turned her head to take in the room. With her was a couple, a bearded man and a tall, elegant woman with almond-shaped eyes and a diamond nose stud. The buyers. Stock photos of laughing picnickers and women in yoga poses flicked on the screen behind her.

"May I have your attention?" Ilona tapped the microphone. "Welcome to the unveiling reception for Wilfred's retreat center."

The air itself seemed to tighten, although I wasn't sure anyone else felt it. I couldn't help glancing at Marilyn Wilfred's portrait. Was it my imagination, or did her lips just turn down?

Ilona fidgeted with the volume on the amplifier. "This is a joyous evening."

Darla muscled her way next to Ilona, and Ilona let the mike drop to her side. "What is all this?" Darla asked. "I thought we were having a trustees' meeting. Not a circus show."

"The town deserves to know what the retreat center is about. I didn't force anyone to come. They came because they wanted to."

"And because of the flyers you've been handing out. What's that about?" Darla said.

"Make it look good for the buyers," Roz whispered into my ear.

Ilona stepped away from Darla and lifted the microphone. "Dear fellow Wilfredians, I'd like you to meet Sita and Ruff Waters. The library's buyers and the founders of Wilfred's new Kirby River Retreat Center."

Clapping came from the crowd, some raucous and

some unsure. Other people simply clutched their canapés and watched.

"What about the suit against the trustees?" Mrs. Garlington said. I couldn't see her, but her wavering voice was impossible to miss. I hoped she wouldn't choose the next hour for organ practice.

Ilona shot me a stiletto glance. "I have it on good authority that the judge will be ruling on our petition tomorrow morning." She smiled. "I'm confident he will find in favor of the town's future."

I had no idea where Ilona's confidence came from, but I wouldn't put it past her to have bribed a few clerks in the judge's chambers.

Sita Waters stepped forward to take the microphone. Her dress—a half-Mexican, half-Indian affair with drippy embroidered sleeves—fluttered around her, releasing a hint of patchouli.

"It's so nice to meet you all." She spoke in firm, deep tones. "I'm Sita Waters. This is my husband, Ruff. His birth name is Raphael. Rafe. When we married, he took my last name, and, well"—she laughed and Ruff stroked his beard—"Ruff Waters it was."

"We've been wanting to establish a retreat center for decades," Ruff said. His wife grabbed one of his hands and clutched it in hers.

"We can't wait to share it with you. We'll have yoga retreats, vegan cooking weeks, meditation camps—all sorts of wonderful things. I hope you'll all visit."

I wondered how the Waters couple had ended up with Ilona as a real estate agent. I imagined Ilona wearing little Buddhas as earrings and feigning an interest in wildcrafted incense. Their business arrangement must have had more to do with Ilona's relentlessness than a soul-mate connection.

"We'll break ground as soon as the land is ours," Sita Waters said.

"In four weeks," Ilona finished. Her face was flushed. She produced a sheaf of papers and gold pen from seemingly nowhere and set them next to the retreat center replica.

"What's that?" Roz said in a low voice.

I stepped closer for a peek. "Some kind of legal document."

"No," I heard a children's book murmur in boyish tones. "No, no." Now a chorus of "no's" whispered through the library, deep voices, shrill voices, filling the air with shushing only I could hear. My breath quickened.

"Tonight, we have the honor of witnessing the signing of the intent to purchase." Ilona set the pen next to her documents. This was it, her moment of glory.

Sita and Ruff, their hands joined, signed where Ilona's finger indicated. She scrawled her own name further down the page and snatched the papers up.

"My signature makes this agreement binding. Would any of the library's other trustees care to add theirs?"

Duke handed his paper plate to the man next to him and pushed his way to the center table, parting the crowd like a fox-trotting bison. A crumb of cheese stuck to his mustache. He snatched the pen and traced a circle in the air before bending over the contract.

Darla backed toward Roz and me. "This is not a meeting," she told us. "It's a show. In very bad taste. None of it was approved ahead of time. Ilona orchestrated this whole thing so the buyers wouldn't back out."

A chilled rush of evening air hit my cheek as someone pushed open the front door. Murmuring washed through the crowd. Darla shouldered her way to the side of the man who'd just entered.

"Who is it?" I whispered to Roz.

"The judge." Her voice filled with wonder. "He's here."

CHAPTER TWENTY-FOUR

The crowd fell silent as Ilona and the judge stared at each other. A wide smile quickly replaced Ilona's frown. My heart fell.

"Why, Judge Valade, what an unexpected pleasure."

The judge was skinny and bald and wore a plaid wool shirt cut in a western style, giving him the look of an ascetic monk waylaid at the feed and farm store. The crowd silenced.

"Just thought I'd drop in and say hello." Although he was talking to Ilona, his gaze swept the rooms of books and landed on Marilyn Wilfred's portrait before returning to Ilona. "Haven't been up here in years. I got the amicus brief the new librarian sent and thought I'd drop in for your trustees' meeting. Quite a get-together you all hold."

By now, I recognized the look on Ilona's face. In this case, her insistent but timeworn smile reflected her intent to make the retreat center look like Wilfred's salvation and the library a crime-ridden dump.

"We were just concluding business," she said. "If you have anything you'd like to announce, we're all ears."

"Yeah," Duke added from the sidelines.

Roz and Darla edged nearer to me. Misery loves company, they say.

"Nope. Nothing yet. Need to do a little more investigation first."

Darla squeezed my hand. My breath came more easily.

Irritation flashed across Ilona's face. "Maybe I can answer some questions. Come have a look at the model of the retreat center."

"I may do that. I'd love to talk with folks, too," the judge said.

Ilona measured the judge's expression and that of the partiers. She made her decision. "Everyone was just leaving. It's not safe to be here after dark, anyway," she added and gathered up her documents.

"A shame," the judge said. "These must be the folks who want to buy the site. Maybe they'd let me walk them to their car."

Just like that, the party was over. Ilona and Duke cleared the library, and half an hour later I was left alone, washed in a slurry of despair and hope. The judge had arrived. He was being thorough about measuring the library's worth to Wilfred, and he might find in our favor. Maybe, at the very least, the suit would go to court and buy me time.

Then again, Ilona's train was gathering speed. The retreat center would bolster Wilfred's economy. The intent to purchase was signed.

I stacked half-ravished platters of hors d'oeuvres and

ferried them to the kitchen. Rodney popped through the pet door and sat at my feet. Unease fluttered in my gut. I placed a palm on my stomach to calm it. I returned to the atrium and took in the darkened floors above me.

The library just might be safe, I told myself, at least for a while. I might be safe. Why was I so tense?

An explosion ricocheted through the library, and the lights flashed. Then went dark.

A growl came from Rodney's throat, and a low buzz, like the angry noise from a faraway hornets' nest, rose from the bookshelves. Skin prickled on the back of my neck.

"Is anyone there?" I called.

Nothing.

I felt my way to the window in the old dining room and looked across the yard. Lyndon's cottage was dark, too, as were the windows at Big House. The birthmark on my shoulder burned, and I pressed a finger into it. The books' buzzing filled my head.

Through the veil of moonlight, I made out a man moving across the yard, quietly but surely, staying to the garden's edge. My throat seized. It was Sam. I knew it without a second glance. Were the doors locked? The windows?

Rodney's yowl pierced the buzz of the books. My whole body vibrated with energy, spreading from my birthmark and coursing white-hot through my bones. I held out a hand. It shook. I couldn't hear anything above the screaming of the books. Somehow fear had unleashed my magic. It was more than my body could hold.

Then I smelled it. Smoke! The library was on fire.

The shelves now rocked back and forth as books moaned and shook. I stumbled into the atrium to find the fire's source and saw flames ripping through the second floor. The library was built from old timber. In minutes, it would be a pile of glowing cinders.

Run, my brain told me. *Leave now while you can.* Louder than this voice of reason was the energy seizing my every cell. The air around me reddened to crimson with electricity. Above, flames devoured the railings.

Rodney leapt to my shoulders, his claws digging in against the chaos. Strangely, his howling had turned to a steady purr.

My power tightened to a burning cyclone, and I couldn't keep it in any longer. My arms shot up, knocking Rodney to the ground.

"No!" I screamed.

What happened next was beyond my ability to understand. As I watched, the smoke curled inward, like a movie running in reverse. It raced backward, sucking into itself, leaving undamaged wood behind.

I gasped. *I did this. I control fire.*

All at once, a paperback flew past me and thumped against the wall. Then, books, scores of them now, pierced the air at a machine gun's pace, slamming against the walls, shattering the windows. *Thunks* and crashes filled the air. The corner of a thick hardback ripped against my arm, drawing blood, but I was frozen. A storm of energy howled through the library, whipping the curtains, knocking paintings from the walls.

My power was out of control, and I couldn't stop it.

I flattened my palms over my ears and squeezed my eyes shut and screamed. Rodney nudged my leg, and at last, I opened my eyes. I collapsed into a chair among the torn and scattered books and sat, stunned, trying to understand what had just happened. The books were quiet at last. My whole body trembled with exhaustion and disbelief.

Someone pounded on the library's front door. "Josie! Are you in there?"

It was the sheriff. I made my way through the splayed books and unbolted the door.

"What the hell happened?" The beam from the sheriff's flashlight roved the chaos. "I was just headed into town and could have sworn I saw fire. Are you okay?"

I nodded and rubbed my shoulder where a book had hit me. It would leave a nasty bruise. Rodney crouched under the table and watched.

"I was cleaning up after the trustees' meeting, and the lights went out. After that—I don't know. The fire. Upstairs—" I looked up, and breath caught in my throat. The second floor landing was whole, unburned. Had I dreamed the whole thing? It was as if the fire had never happened.

"Upstairs," the sheriff said.

Dodging fallen books, we ran up the main staircase and circled the landing. Books lay helter-skelter across the rooms, and two bookshelves had toppled. A hint of smoke, almost like incense, hung in the air, but there was no sign of fire. I rested a hand on the polished wood banister I'd seen in flames only minutes ago. It was warm but undamaged.

The sheriff shook his head. "I could have sworn I saw fire. Let's check outside."

I followed him out the front door. The night was cold, and somewhere an owl hooted. The sheriff pointed to the power pole. "That's it. Look there. The transformer blew. But what happened inside?"

The sheriff talked to me, but I barely made out his words. The library had been on fire, and somehow I'd commanded that fire and made it stop. I hugged my arms. Not only did it stop, it was as if it had never happened. But . . . the flying books, the destruction—I'd made that happen, too. My power was greater than I knew—and massively more destructive.

"I don't see how a simple electrical accident could have caused this," the sheriff said as we returned to the library. "Was the crowd tonight that rowdy?"

"There were a lot of people," I said.

My eyes had adjusted to the dark now. Books lay scattered across the floor. I picked up a thriller with a cover of a policeman running away from a flaming skyscraper. A faraway siren grew closer, coming up the highway toward the bluff.

"The volunteer fire department," Sheriff Dolby said. "I called, but I guess there's no work for them here." He shook his head in wonder. "What a freaky accident."

"It wasn't an accident," I said. "It was Sam Wilfred."

CHAPTER TWENTY-FIVE

"Sam?" The sheriff leaned back, and his boots creaked. "No. Not Sam."

"You've said that before, but why not?" I said. "He's everywhere I go. Including tonight. I can't turn around without finding him watching me." Despite my exhaustion, my voice cranked to a higher pitch.

The sheriff sighed. "Let me go talk to the fire folks. Then I have something to tell you about Sam."

My body still shook as I picked up a few books and reshelved them. It would take hours to get the library back in shape. Books littered the central atrium and lay splayed beneath their shelves. And the windows—more than a few would have to be replaced. If they'd be replaced at all, given the uncertainty of the library's future. They'd need to be boarded up at the very least.

I stepped onto the porch. A man I didn't recognize

stood next to Wilfred's vintage fire engine, the sheriff with him, and pointed his flashlight toward the electric pole. The transformer was blackened. Melted Mylar stuck to it.

"It was the balloons. Blew out the power and started a fire."

At the unexpected voice, I clutched the railing behind me. "Sam."

"They must not have been tied very securely." He squinted toward the electric pole.

I was a few feet from the steps into the library. I inched toward them.

"Josie?"

I halted. "What?"

"What's wrong?" He stepped closer. From here I saw his smile. Remembering Roz's words, I knew something upset him. "You're not afraid of me, are you?"

I bolted for the stairs, and Sam grabbed the waistband of my pants. I felt the energy buzzing in me again. With it came a streak of fear that made me tremble.

All at once, Sam let me go, and I stumbled at the top of the steps. He rubbed the back of his head. "Whoa. Where did that come from?" He knelt and picked up a thick book.

The Rise and Fall of the Roman Empire. Impressive.

"How do you know the fire was an accident?" I said.

"You mean you think someone let the balloons go on purpose?" I couldn't read his expression in the dark. He lowered his voice. "It's just possible."

The volunteer firefighters returned to the fire engine and backed out of the drive. Sheriff Dolby joined us on the porch. Thanks to the moon, it was lighter here than it would be inside.

"Fried the transformer," the sheriff said. "Kids must have loosened the balloons. The electric company is sending someone right out to fix it. Won't be long."

I wasn't going back in the house, not with the windows blown apart and no power. To my relief, Lyndon's lanky form crossed the garden.

"I was down at Darla's after the party," he said. "Saw the lights blow. Swear I saw flames, too."

"The transformer," the sheriff said.

The library had been on fire, I remembered breathlessly.

"No kidding," Lyndon said. "What happened to the windows? Must have been some party after I left."

Somehow, I'd done that, too. "Broken," I said. Duh.

"Do you think you could board them up tonight?" Sam asked. "It's not safe the way it is. I'll help."

Lyndon was already training a flashlight around the first floor. "Looks worse than it is. Really only two windows and the French doors to take care of." Without waiting for a reply, he left for the tool shed.

"You can wait with me," Sam said. "Just until the power comes back. It will be safer that way."

"No." The word shot from me with force. "Sheriff, how about I stay with you? Or go down to Darla's? Can you take me?"

"She thinks you did it," Sheriff Dolby told Sam. "You'd better tell her."

"Tell me what?" I looked from man to man.

Sam pulled something from his back pocket. Instinctively, I stepped behind the sheriff.

"Here," Sam said. "It's all right. Look at this."

It was some kind of ID in a leather case. It was too

dark to read, but I felt the badge clearly enough. "Police?" I said.

"FBI."

Sheriff Dolby nodded. "It's okay. Sam's square. The Bureau coordinated with us. Sorry, Josie. I wanted to tell you earlier, but I couldn't." He shoved his hands in his jacket pockets and stared up at the power pole. "I could have sworn I saw fire." He shook his head. "Some kind of miracle."

"Are you all right waiting with me now?" Sam asked. "I'll fill you in."

"You'd better go," the sheriff said. "Until the power is on and the windows are boarded up. I'll stay and help Lyndon."

"Can I get a coat?" With the night, the temperature had dropped. The adrenaline dissipating in my bloodstream seemed to leach whatever heat had been left in my body.

"Too dark up there. All those books on the floor—too much chance of getting hurt," Sam said. He shrugged off his coat, a wool tweed lined in quilted fabric, and draped it over my shoulders. It was still warm from his body and smelled vaguely of something piney and green.

We crossed the garden and waved at Lyndon, who carried a large flashlight and a toolbox. The damp grass soaked into my shoes. At the garden's edge, overlooking the Kirby River, a gravel path led to Big House. We arrived at the back porch.

"Have a seat here. I'll grab a few blankets." He disappeared into the back door.

The porch was small—really only big enough for a

cook to pull up a chair and string beans. A table barely an arm's width and two wooden chairs were stationed to the right of the door. I took the far chair.

From here, I saw that Big House was on higher elevation than the library. Moonlight reflected off the library's upstairs windows. Below me, beyond the cottonwoods, flowed the Kirby, and the lights at Darla's and the trailer park lay like a pocketful of diamonds carelessly tossed on a velvet blanket. Beyond them, the valley disappeared into the coastal mountain range. Above the house—I drew in a sharp breath—the stars were crisp pinpricks of light. So many stars. Slowly, I relaxed.

"Amazing, isn't it?" Sam had returned. He handed me a heavy wool blanket and settled into the chair opposite mine. "I've lived in L.A. for years and had forgotten how beautiful the sky was. When I was a kid, we could even see the Milky Way." He stretched out his legs and folded his hands over his midsection. "I always thought Great-Grandad should have made this the front of the house. But no. It was like him to turn his back on the town."

"Los Angeles. That's where you live?"

"For ten years now. We moved there after the FBI academy."

We. He didn't wear a wedding ring. Not that it mattered, I reminded myself. "So, why are you here? You were sent to keep an eye on me, weren't you? That's why you've been lurking."

"Ouch, but yes. The Bureau has been watching you since you reported the conversation you overheard at the Library of Congress." He let out a long breath. "Your code name is Broomstick."

"What? You couldn't have chosen, say, 'Book Girl'?"

"Don't take it wrong. It's your hair. We always choose a two-syllable name. One of the agents said she got a witchy hit from all those red curls, and that was it."

"What's your role? Specifically? You're not here to take me in, I guess, or you would have already done it." The sound of a hammer and nails drifted across the yard.

"You're being what we call 'ghosted.' It's not easy to ghost someone in a small town, so the Bureau searched their records for a local agent. When they found out I was raised in Wilfred, they sent me the same afternoon."

"To protect me?"

"Yes. That and . . ."

"And what?"

"Let me start at the beginning. When you overheard the conversation between Senator Markham's aide and the lobbyist from Bondwell, we already had wind of possible graft. Your evidence is what moved the case from 'possible' to 'definite.' Then your colleague—"

"Anton," I said.

"Followed the lobbyist—"

"What?" I pulled the blanket more tightly around me. "He did what?"

"He tracked down Richard White and confronted him."

"I had no idea." Anton. "That's why he disappeared."

"Not disappeared. We know where he is, and he's safe. Don't worry."

Anton was safe. Deep in my chest, something softened and unwound. Maybe I was safe, too. At that moment, a star shot in a wide arc over the valley, vanishing in seconds.

"Did you see that?" I said.

"It's something, isn't it?" Sam's chair creaked as he

shifted. "Just think of everyone who saw that shooting star. Made wishes on it. Thought it was a sign. It's just a meteoroid probably no bigger than a loaf of bread."

"It's more than that," I said. "All those people who see a shooting star and wish on it give it meaning. It's more than space debris." I couldn't put my finger on it, but something in Sam's cavalier attitude about the star irked me. "Anyway, you didn't tell me what it was exactly that you're doing here, if it isn't to protect me." Then another thought occurred. "How did you find me, anyway? I haven't used my phone or my credit card."

"It wasn't difficult. You told your boss you were going on vacation in New York. As you said, you didn't use your credit card. How would you pay your hotel bill?"

He had a good point.

"And why would you withdraw so much cash from your bank account, if not to make a getaway?"

"But here? How did you trace me to Wilfred?"

"We found the job listing on your browser history at work."

He knew a lot more about me than I did about him. "I bet you found things in my apartment, too. I hope you at least watered the plants when you broke in."

A pause in the hammering told me Lyndon and the sheriff had moved to another window.

Sam's voice tightened. "Josie, we didn't search your apartment."

"Somebody did. The landlord told my sister someone had broken in and left the door unlocked."

"It wasn't us. I'm not surprised, though. Bondwell and White know where you are."

"How do you know?"

"Like I said, I'm here to keep an eye on you. Part of

that is to watch for anyone sent to keep you quiet—whether it's to bribe you, or—"

"I've got it. You don't have to say it." An angry humming filtered out from Big House. Books. Big House must have its own library.

"If we can nail Bondwell and Richard White, the case is closed. Slam dunk," Sam said.

"So, you're using me as bait?"

A moment passed, then two, without a response.

"I've been going about my business, and the whole time you're expecting someone to show up and pick me off, is that it?" I said.

"It's too late."

I closed my eyes and willed the books to rest. I didn't need another disaster like the one I'd caused at the library. "You mean they know where I am?"

"You know the body you found the day after you arrived?"

I nodded.

"January Stephens. She's been on our list for a while now, and she was coming for you."

"To do what?" The words came out as barely a whisper.

"To do whatever it took to shut you up."

All at once, lights flooded the library's ground floor and snapped on behind us in Big House's kitchen, along with the hum of a refrigerator and the sheriff's whoop.

"For me? Are you sure?" Even as I said the words, I knew he was right.

"Almost certainly. I can't tell you who hired her—if we knew that, we'd have all the evidence we need to close out the case—but she wasn't a small-time operative." Then, in a quieter voice, "I'm sorry."

"You're not here to protect me, are you?"

He didn't respond.

"Like I said. I'm simply bait." I rose from my chair on Big House's kitchen porch and dropped the blanket on the seat. I shed the coat Sam had lent me.

"I'll walk you back," he said. "With lights and secure windows, you'll be safe."

"Don't bother." I marched down the stairs, hugging my arms. I had some thinking to do.

"I'm here if you need me," he said.

CHAPTER TWENTY-SIX

The library's lights were on, but the place was a shambles. Lyndon and the sheriff had nailed boards across the broken windows. I dodged scattered books to close the curtains so I didn't face the damage.

I took the stairs to the second level to inspect once more where fire had scorched the walls and roared over the hall, and, once again, the undamaged railings and smooth plaster flabbergasted me.

I examined my hands, turned them in front of me. They were average enough looking. I filled my lungs with air and released it. Normal.

But I was not normal. I had some kind of unearthly power, and it had surfaced over the past week. An echo of the fear I'd felt earlier flashed through me. All that power, and all the destruction.

I hurried upstairs to the phone on my apartment's

kitchen wall. This time I didn't bother to hide my phone number. The secret was out. I settled into a wooden chair at my tiny kitchen table. It was almost 2 a.m. eastern time, but I didn't care.

"Hello?" my mother answered uncertainly.

"It's me, Josie." Of course she'd known that, or she wouldn't have picked up.

"What is this area code? Aren't you in New York?"

"No," I said curtly. "Oregon. Way out in the sticks."

"I don't understand. I—"

"Why didn't you tell me I'm a witch?"

My mother's choked breath in my ear sounded so close I could nearly feel it, yet she was thousands of miles away. "Oregon, huh?" she said. "That would do it."

"Do what?"

"Break your grandmother's spell."

Anger burned a hot track through my chest. She'd known my power. She'd known what I could do—what I could destroy—all along. I put my feet on the table's other chair and leaned back. This was going to be a long conversation.

Rodney had appeared from nowhere and leapt onto the table. He lay on his side and groomed a paw.

I forced myself to take a long breath through my nose, like Jean had taught me from her yoga training. "Maybe you'd better start at the beginning."

"Beginning of what?"

I knew this ploy. It was a way to buy time. "Oh, I don't know. Maybe when dinosaurs ruled the earth? Or, say, with the big bang?"

"There's no need to get smart."

I put my feet on the floor and sat up. "Well, how about this spell you mentioned?"

"That's too hard to explain without starting earlier."

"Something happened, didn't it?"

"Honey. I'm not sure where to begin."

I pressed a finger to my shoulder. "How about my birthmark? Why don't you start with that?"

"You were born—"

"I know!"

"Calm down, Josie. I'm serious." I heard her finger ticking against the phone, but her voice bordered on weepiness, not exasperation. "Are you calm now?"

"I'm fine. Go on." I softened my voice. Whatever had happened, Mom meant well. I knew that.

"You're right. You're a witch. So am I. So are your sisters, and your grandmother was, too, as were her mother and all the women back to Scotland."

I thought of Toni and Jean. Sure, we understood each other in a way many sisters didn't, but I couldn't imagine either of them busting windows by thought alone. All of those books flew across the atrium like the glee club from Poltergeist High had been let loose.

"The difference," Mom said, "is the star-shaped birthmark on your shoulder. You're marked. You have power none of the rest of us does. So did my mother—your grandma."

"You've always seemed ashamed of the birthmark."

"It wasn't shame. It was fear."

Fear, I could understand. A lot of raw power had rushed through me tonight. "I thought I was going crazy."

"It's like this. Each of us has a personality trait that defines our role in the world. You're a truth teller. You're compelled to help the underdog and right wrongs. You can't deny that."

"No. You're right. I wouldn't be way out here in the

middle of nowhere if I wasn't." Rodney rubbed his head on my hand, and I scratched his ears. He sure was affectionate tonight. "What about the rest of us? What are Toni and Jean's traits?"

"They're healers. Grandma was, too. She specialized in herbs. She could talk to plants, and they'd tell her what they could do for her."

A week ago, I would have laughed at this conversation. Talk to plants? How ridiculous was that? Tonight, I was rapt. "Books," I said. "Books talk to me."

"I thought that's the way it would be. It seemed inevitable. If Gerard didn't have so many books around—"

"You can't blame Dad for my love of books. I would have found them without him." Instinctively I reached for the closest book available, a Betty Crocker cookbook. A recipe for vegetable stew leapt to mind. Perfect for a fall night. "Why books?"

"I don't know a lot about being a witch. I—I deliberately left it behind. But from what I understand, in our family, witches gravitate to a source of energy to fuel their magic. You've always loved to read, so your energy comes from books."

"From the stories themselves?"

"From the authors and also from the people who have invested energy in reading the story. All that emotion evoked, you can call it up."

"What is your gift?"

"I'm a seer," Mom said. "Although I've done my best to ignore it. Some things you don't want to know. We live in a different world than even your grandmother did. My magic is minor compared to yours, anyway."

She saw something that had to do with me. I knew it. "What do you see in me? Tell me, Mom."

I felt rather than saw her shake her head. "Family legend has it that the last time a marked witch in the family was a truth teller, she was burned at the stake. In Scotland, a few hundred years ago. The town clergyman was abusing girls, and Grandma Ailith couldn't take it. She drove the clergyman out of town, but she paid for it with her life." Her voice faltered. "When you were in kindergarten and your birthmark began to appear, I saw horrible things."

The kitchen light, feeble as it was, glowed reassuringly, and the library's furnace chugged away, but I felt more alone than I'd ever been. "What kind of things?"

"You're an adult—just like you are now—and you're screaming. I felt—I felt . . ."

"Felt what?"

"Josie, you were going to die."

I was beginning to understand what had happened. Still purring, Rodney dropped to my lap. "What did you see, exactly?"

"Night. A creepy old house. Some kind of tower. You were struggling, and it was a long way down. There was a hand on your neck."

My fingers froze in Rodney's fur. Mom might have been describing the library's tower. I cleared my throat. "So, you had Grandma suppress my magical abilities."

"She didn't want to. She said you needed to learn to manage your power, that it was the best way to control it."

Grandma had been right. "What kind of spell was it?"

"A containment spell. You had to drink a tincture—I doubt you remember it. It was so long ago."

At her words, a chill ran through my body. I did remember. My dream. A full moon, Grandma's garden. They'd roused me from bed and walked me, still groggy, to the damp strawberry patch. Grandma pulled back my robe and let the moonlight fall on my birthmark. Then she wrapped a shawl around my shoulders and told me to drink from a small glass cup.

"Why?" I'd asked as a little girl. My hand had slid into my robe pocket, where I'd hidden a copy of *Grimm's Fairy Tales*. I wasn't supposed to be reading in bed, but under the covers with a flashlight I could finish a story or two, and Jean had never ratted me out.

"Just drink it," Mom had told me.

The breeze rushed at the shawl's fringe. *Grimm's Fairy Tales* shivered, and I yanked my fingers away.

I took the cup. The liquid smelled awful, rotten, worse than the cough syrup I sometimes had to choke down.

"I'm not sick," I said. "Why are you giving me medicine?"

In the end, I drank the cup's contents. Above me, the stars dimmed, and my book grew heavier in my pocket.

"Honey," Grandma said, "show me your book. I want you to read from 'Sleeping Beauty.'" The book fell open to the story. "Here." She placed a finger on a passage. "Read this. Aloud."

Mom pointed the flashlight over the page. I could almost hear my little girl voice now as I'd read:

In that very moment she fell back upon the bed that stood there, and lay in a deep sleep, and this sleep fell upon the whole castle. The King and Queen, who had returned and were in the great

hall, fell fast asleep, and with them the whole
court. The horses in their stalls, the dogs in the
yard, the pigeons on the roof, the flies on the wall,
the very fire that flickered on the hearth, became
still, and slept . . .

I didn't remember the rest. Mom must have carried me
back to bed.

Rodney purred under my fingers. "What's a containment spell?"

"It was the only way to tamp down your magic. In
essence, Grandma put a shell over you. It was big, but
stretched only as far as the Continental Divide. When you
flew over the Rockies, you broke it."

"Yes," I said quickly. Now I understood. "In the plane,
I felt like someone had yanked out my spleen. Since then,
things have been different."

My mother's sigh, quiet as it was, traveled the telephone wires to land squarely in my ear. "Tell me."

"I'm dreaming. Books seem to talk to me. Tonight . . ."

"What, honey?"

"Tonight the library almost burnt down, and it was like
my head was firing cyclones. Books flew everywhere,
breaking windows." I rubbed my arm. "Even hitting me. I
could have been killed. And the fire . . ." I swallowed.
"Somehow the fire sucked itself up and disappeared."

I pressed the fingers of my free hand against my face.
Cold as marble. I tried to breathe more deeply, but it was
like my chest was wrapped in iron.

"You have a lot of power, Josie. I don't know what to
tell you to do with it. If your grandmother were here,
she'd know."

"But she's not. Didn't you think the spell could be broken, and something like this might happen?" My anger began to simmer again. "What did you think I'd do?"

"Don't be mad at me. What choice did I have? I'd had a vision. Your magic would kill you, I saw it. I couldn't let you die."

I stood abruptly, and Rodney jumped to the floor. "It still might kill me. Did you ever think of that?"

"Listen to me. You have to lock down your power."

"I don't even know what my power is." A humming grew from inside me.

"Lock it down. Close your eyes and take your thoughts somewhere else. It's your energy that feeds your power. When you're calm, it can't use you. Right now. Close your eyes and steady your breath."

I clamped my eyes shut and forced my arms and chest to relax. *Inhale slowly*, I told myself. *Now breathe out.* The humming slowed and dropped to a breathy whisper.

"It's working," I said.

"Thank goodness," my mother said quickly. "Remember that. Can you do it?"

Eyes still closed, I leaned my head against the kitchen wall. "I think so."

"If you're serious about this, you'll need to repeat the containment spell. You'll have to do it yourself, though."

"How?"

"You won't have Mom's tincture to help, but you have enough power on your own now. Your power is in books. *Grimm's Fairy Tales* imprinted itself on you early. I'd try 'Sleeping Beauty' again. Go to a quiet place, summon your magic, and read that passage aloud with the intention of capturing your energy and the energy of the generations of readers." Her voice quieted as she composed herself. "You'll have to trust yourself to figure it out. I'm so sorry you don't have anyone to help. I'm nearly as useless as you."

I was having a hard time filling my lungs. "How will I know it's working?"

"You'll know." Her voice dropped. "I'm so sorry, honey."

I closed my eyes and clung to the phone, my only connection to Mom's comfort.

"There's one more thing that might help you," she said. "Mom's grimoire."

"What's that?"

"Her book of shadows. Maybe there's something in it that will give you direction."

A book. Her book. I remembered the leather book fat with notes and pressed flowers. "Send it to me."

"It's in a chest in the attic. I'll get your father to pull it down, and I'll have a look. I don't want to get your hopes up, though."

"Mom, it's all we have."

"I just don't want you playing around with your power. It's much safer to learn to keep the magic muted. You understand, don't you?"

I understood that tonight had terrified me to my very core. "I get it."

"Your magic is not a toy. It's viciously powerful." From the urgency in her voice, I knew Mom clutched the phone close to her cheek. "Don't let it kill you."

I made my way downstairs among the fallen books and settled in Thurston Wilfred's old office—the children's section. Here, no windows had been broken, and moonlight puddled on the desk and spilled to the rug. I didn't turn on a light—I didn't need to.

Despite the evening's drama, I felt good. Calm. I took the chair behind Thurston's desk and leaned back. Here's where he would have spent odd evenings meeting with mill workers while his family took dinner across the atrium. A fire would have crackled under the marble mantel. Maybe Marilyn, just a girl, played in the atrium, running between the kitchen, where the cook fired up the woodstove, and the gimcrack-laden parlor, where her mother stitched an embroidery panel.

I knew what I had to do. In another world, where I had a mentor, I could nurture my magic. Without direction, it was too dangerous. Tonight had proven it. I'd been fine in my old life. Sure, in Wilfred I'd lived richly, with every sense at full attention, but the cost was too great. I'd been fine before, I reminded myself. Just fine.

I looked down at the desk and found a copy of *Grimm's Fairy Tales* within arm's reach. No surprise. The books murmured as I touched it. Some books seemed to cry "Aha!" while others moaned softly. My heart rent as I leafed to "Sleeping Beauty." I was a witch—really, officially a witch—for so little time. What I could do, for good, even, I'd never know.

"No," a voice wavered in the background.

It didn't frighten me. It blended with the books' songs and made a part of the symphony playing in the background. Through the open archway, Marilyn Wilfred stared down at me. Rodney sat below her. He didn't move.

"Sorry," I whispered. I had to do it.

I reached for the book of fairy tales and found I didn't even need to read the words. They returned unbidden.

When the spell was done, the world shrank around me, stealing color, scent, and texture as it settled in my core. I sat at the desk, dull. *This is what it has always been like*, I thought. And, oh, how I missed my magic already.

I'd done the right thing. I had no other choice.

Then I set to getting the library in order.

CHAPTER TWENTY-SEVEN

I woke up groggy, with the sun coming through the windows brighter than it should have been. I'd slept in. Considering I'd spent half the night casting a spell on myself, then starting to clean up the library, it wasn't surprising.

Roz was already downstairs helping patrons when I made my beeline to the coffeepot. I hadn't dreamt. The room's colors grayed out. It was the old me, back again, and I didn't like it. I'd loved the sparkle of sun on the river and the sweet-balmy scent of cottonwoods. I clutched my coffee mug. Even its smell had been that much richer. Yet, the alternative—bursts of power with deadly force—was too high a price to pay.

"Good grief," Roz said. "What happened here? When I left last night, I figured the worst we'd have to deal with was onion dip on the parquet. Then I came in to this."

She waved around the kitchen, which looked pretty good, even given the sink full of dirty mugs. But I knew what she meant.

"You should have seen it before I went to bed," I said.

"I know. Lyndon told me. Figures Ilona's show would turn into the first phase of the library's demolition."

From her repeated glances over my shoulder, Roz was on the lookout for Lyndon. Irritation twisted in me. Was everyone in this town hiding something?

"Why don't you just ask him out?" I said.

Her head swiveled to me. "What are you talking about?"

"You know what I mean. Lyndon. You're obviously mooning over him, but you won't do anything about it."

Roz produced a fan from thin air and batted at her reddening neck. "Where did you get that idea?" She laughed a weak "*ha-ha-ha*."

I set down my coffee mug. "Roz, I know you're Eliza Chatterley Windsor, okay?" Last night's anger began to rise.

The fan batted more quickly. Roz dropped it to the table. She was ready to deny it. Then she surprised me by bursting into tears.

"How did you know?" she said.

I pulled her to a chair and put my arm around her. "It just—it just came to me. I'm sorry. I never should have said anything. Last night's events are getting to me, I guess. I'm tired of all the subterfuge. Plus, I want you to be happy."

"It's not in my stars."

"What?" I pulled up the chair next to her.

"I'm not fated to be happy. I'm not fated for love. Look at me."

I saw a curvy brunette with streaks of gray that gave her the air of an Italian starlet playing the role of a country girl. Her eyes were red, true, but they were wide and round and naturally dark-rimmed.

"I'm looking. You're adorable."

"Adorable! I'm in my fifties." She sniffed and patted her eyes with the hem of her shirt. "No longer fertile. No longer emitting pheromones. Who am I kidding? Why would an attractive man like"—she lowered her voice— "Lyndon even look at me?"

I sat back. "Well, you—"

"You have no idea what it's like to age as a woman. One day you're in the sun, and you see a little crepiness on the back of your hand. So you double up on lotion. Then a gray hair pops up. You pluck it. Your eyesight goes, but you get used to wearing reading glasses—except that with the glasses on, you notice that your neck doesn't look so good. And I don't even want to talk about the waistline." She pinched her belly. "You can't keep up. It's impossible."

"Why worry about it? Why not be you? After all, Lyndon's the same age."

Roz snorted. "As if. Spinsters age faster than dogs. I'm at least a hundred years older than Lyndon. Maybe more." Her tone had taken on a frenzied edge.

"What are you talking about?"

"It's like this. A woman ages normally—you know, one year per calendar year—until she's twenty-five. After that, she ages two for every one regular year until she's thirty-five. Then it's five to one. After forty-five, especially if she's not married, I figure a woman clocks in eight years for every one year. That makes me"—she screwed her eyes to the side while she did the calculations—"one hundred and seventy-three years old."

"What about men? How do they age?"

Roz had warmed to her topic. "They don't. They remain about thirty for life. Their bellies might grow and their hair might vanish—except for the ears, of course—but as far as they're concerned, they don't age a day. Bachelors are the worst. Bachelors and divorced men. If their bones feel a bit creaky, the next day they buy a sports car, and—bingo—they're thirty again."

"Impressive," I had to admit. "But bogus. You and Lyndon are the same age, and you've had similar experiences in life. You're perfect as companions."

Roz flushed, but she didn't reach for her fan. "Men aren't looking for companions. They want babes."

"Lyndon doesn't strike me as that type."

"You think so?" I'd never heard Roz sound so poignant. Her sharp tone came right back. "Anyway, I've given up."

"I don't believe you."

"Why not? What do you know about it?"

"You wouldn't have written that meet-cute scene with the dog walker—you know the one, where Forster Lyndon the billionaire helps Belinda find her toy poodle—if you didn't believe in romance."

She folded her arms. "Maybe I like to fantasize a bit. Why shouldn't I? I'm not hurting anyone, and the royalties help pay the bills."

"All I'm saying is that you have a live one walking around, and you refuse to see if it will go anywhere. If you want to sit and moon about it, that's your business. But I think you're braver than that. In fact . . ." I waited for the title of a helpful book to come to me. "I bet . . ." Nothing. My mind was blank. I took a shuddering breath. "Anyway, you should talk to him straight-out."

I'd lost it. I'd lost my magic with books. I still felt them, but they no longer spoke to me. This was the cost of suppressing my power.

Roz stared at her fan lying open on the table. "I'll think about it."

At the burst of rose perfume and clacking of heels, I knew Mrs. Garlington had turned up behind me. "Ms. Way, we're here to help."

I stood and smoothed my dress. "Help with what?"

"The Knitting Club has convened an emergency meeting to help clean up the library." Five women and a boy—no Duke—gathered behind Mrs. Garlington. One held a mop, and two had buckets. "As long as it's still standing, we're here."

By midafternoon, the knitters had left, and the library smelled of lemon polish. I had misjudged the bunch. Maybe they favored a retreat center, but until the wrecking ball swung, they stood behind the library one hundred percent. They left just as the day's patrons began to stream in in force.

"The book you suggested on putting babies to sleep was perfect," one young mother told me. "I don't know how you knew I needed it. I didn't even know." She adjusted the toddler on her hip. "I'm so rested. I feel like a new woman. Anything else you can recommend?"

The day before, I could have relaxed a split second, and a title would have been on my lips. Today, nothing. "Maybe there's something under 'children' in the card catalogue."

The mother didn't have to tell me how lame my help was. Her expression said it all.

I missed the books' company, too. Sure, I knew that a rich tapestry of stories and ideas populated the shelves around me, but I couldn't hear them. A hand on a book's spine drew comfort, but it didn't fill my mind with color and voice anymore.

What choice did I have? My power was enough to lay waste to several hundred pounds of books and a few windows and to land me with a bruise the size of Australia. Factor in my mother's vision, and, well, it wasn't worth the risk.

No matter what happened to the Wilfred library, in a month, if not sooner, I'd be back in D.C. and back to my old life. Back to sitting in the darkened stacks at lunch with an egg salad sandwich. My heart dropped. Either that, or watching my back every second, praying I didn't end up like January Stephens.

"Just loafing around? We pay you to work, you know." Ilona stood in the doorway, a hand on a black-clad hip. Her entire outfit was black: black pants, black crewneck sweater, and, her nod to country life, black cowboy boots.

"Catching my breath," I said. "There was quite a mess to clean up this morning, what with the hors d'oeuvre platters and all."

"I left that food for the people in town. No one can say I'm not generous."

"How can I help you?" Maybe not hearing books was good. A few snarky title suggestions just might have floated in.

"Is there somewhere we can talk in private?"

I was uneasy, but curious. "There's my office." As we passed the checkout desk, I asked Roz to keep an eye on things.

"I'll shut the door, if you don't mind," Ilona said.

Rodney squeezed in just before the door closed and leapt into my lap. Ilona perched on the desk. Up close, lines showed around her eyes, and her powder couldn't cover them. I guess I hadn't been the only one without much sleep last night.

"What did you tell the judge?" she said.

"What?"

"The judge. He was set to dismiss the lawsuit over the library. I had it on good authority." She leaned in, and the smell of rancid lilies of the valley wafted toward me. Even Rodney turned his nose away. "What did you tell him?"

"I wrote up the report on the library's benefits to Wilfred. You mean that?"

Her eyes narrowed from surprise to suspicion. "Plus something else, I bet. Money?"

I set Rodney on the desk, and he watched from behind the stapler. "You think we bribed the judge? Why? Is that something you'd do?"

My ire was rising, and a bare hum played low. *Be gone*, I willed. The hum ceased.

Ilona opened her mouth, then shut it. Her chest rose as

she sucked in a long breath through her nose. When she spoke, it was with force. "If I find out you've tainted this case at all, you'll be very, very sorry."

A low rumble came from Rodney's direction.

Ilona glanced at the cat and backed out of my office, leaving the door open.

"Remember," she said. "You were warned."

Every muscle in my body stiffened. This had to end. I had to find a way to bring the situation to a head.

Chapter Twenty-eight

As soon as the library closed for the day, I grabbed a cardigan and crossed the garden to Big House. The sun hovered on the horizon, but the moon hadn't yet risen, and the few leaves left on the oak trees rustled in the breeze from the river.

I paused beyond Lyndon's cottage. Should I take the front entrance or try the kitchen door, where Sam and I had sat last night? I headed to the house's front door. The brass knocker was shaped like a log. I rapped three times and stepped back, my heart beating a rumba.

It seemed like years before Sam arrived, pushing back the curtain over the front door's window.

"It's you," he said with a heartening frown. He wore a frilly apron smeared with something green. Chopped parsley, maybe.

"Surprised?" I pushed past him into the hall. "You shouldn't be. I thought you were keeping an eye on me. Oh wait. I forgot. I'm just bait."

He glanced at a grandfather clock in the hall. Despite the shrouded furniture I saw through doorways, the clock was polished and wound.

"I guess the library is closed now for the day. Just barely."

"Good thing an assassin didn't stop by to browse popular fiction."

As I spoke, I took in what I could see from just inside the door. Both the library and Big House were imposing structures, but the library, despite its size, had all the fussy coziness of a Victorian home. In contrast, Big House was heavy and chilly. We stood in a square hall with a staircase straight ahead and open arches off each side of the hall.

The rooms off both arches were dark, but the strains of an orchestra and soprano, and the smell of something spicy came from the house's depths.

"Come in." Sam led me through a salon and a dining room—now I saw the long table, big enough to seat twelve people.

As we approached the kitchen, the scent intensified. Cumin and cardamom, if I wasn't mistaken. Tomato. Along with the recognition, I felt a pang. In the week I lived with magic, these fragrances would have vibrated through me. Now they registered in my senses but didn't linger.

As in the library, Big House's kitchen was big enough for a couple of cooks and a maid. A pile of chopped cilantro and a lime sat on a chopping board next to a chef's knife. Something red burbled on the stove. Big

House's front rooms might have felt mothballed for decades, but here was a scene of real intimacy.

Sam tapped his phone, and the stereo's volume faded.

"You like opera," I said, feeling all at once that I'd intruded.

"Surprised?"

"I guess not. Cute apron," I added.

"It was hanging in the kitchen. You don't think the gingham makes me look fat?"

I laughed, and my unease melted away. "Indian food."

"Cooking helps me think. Indian food has lots of toasted spice and grinding and chopping, so it's especially useful for knotty cases."

"Like mine. How about Italian food?"

"A good ragù is useful when the facts are in, but answers haven't shaken out. By the end of a daylong braise, I usually have one or two ideas." He turned down the burner under the tomato sauce. "We used to have a cook, and as a kid I hung around and watched her. There are good trout in the millpond for frying up. Bert Dolby let me tag along with him sometimes when he went fishing."

"The sheriff, huh?" Wilfred was probably full of forest trails and swimming holes—a great place to be a kid.

"Do you mind if I cook while we talk? In fact, would you like to stay for dinner?"

At that moment, a thump announced Rodney's arrival through a cat door I hadn't noticed until now. He trotted over and wound through my legs. I knelt to pet him, but he retreated to the room's edge.

"Rodney! Does he come over a lot?" I asked.

"Never, actually. He must have known you were here." He sneezed and pulled a handkerchief from his pocket. "Allergies."

"Do you want me to send him away?"

Sam shook his head. "No. It's nice to have him around." Crockery clanked as he pulled two plates from an upper cupboard. "You might as well join me. Plus, I'm supposed to be keeping an eye on you, remember? This will make it easier."

"Okay," I said. "In fact, that's what I wanted to talk to you about. Keeping an eye on me."

"All right."

Rodney sat by the refrigerator and licked a paw. He felt so distant now. So far away.

"I can't take it anymore," I said.

Sam turned down the heat and set a lid on the big pot on the stove. "Have a seat." He motioned to the chair nearest me and took the one across the table. "Tell me about it."

I'd been working up to a fight, but his solicitude took the wind out of my sails. "What?"

"You can't take it anymore that I'm watching you. Tell me about it."

"Well . . ." My gaze wandered the faded curtains and the pendant light reflecting in the night-blackened window-panes. Yesterday at this time, it would have felt full of mood and depth. Tonight it was just a window. "I want to get this over with and go home."

"You don't feel safe in Wilfred? Is that it?" He flattened his palms on the table. For a second, I imagined what those fingers would feel like on my waist. I riveted my gaze to my lap.

"That's part of it. Mostly, I just want to get back to my old life."

"A town this small can be a real shock after a big city."

He pulled back his hands and leaned back in his chair. "Remember, I live in L.A. The traffic is a lot better here, though."

"And the nights are so quiet. Except for the bullfrogs."

"And the roosters in the morning. Can you hear them?"

"I think they're Duke's," I said. "Darla's threatening to ban roosters in the trailer park." I thought of the perfect poached eggs I'd had the morning before. "Thankfully, he can keep the hens."

Sam's gaze took a faraway look. "I miss being able to order Chinese food—good Chinese food—and I even kind of miss the crowds."

"Sometimes I love a crowd. You can simply vanish and watch people around you and imagine their stories. On a nice day, sometimes I used to walk to the sculpture gardens outside the National Gallery and watch people. It's almost as good as reading a book. Almost."

"So, you don't spend every lunch hour in the stacks."

"No."

"It would have been tempting."

Something splattered on the stovetop. "Your pan," I said. "The little one in front."

He leapt up and moved it off the heat. "Red lentils. They're ready now."

"You love books, too," I said.

Sam wiped around the burner with the spilled lentils. "Maybe not as much as you do, but I'd rather read or listen to music than watch TV."

"Why did you vote to sell the library?" This was something I'd wanted to know but certainly didn't think would come rolling out of my mouth.

His brows furrowed as he focused on scrubbing a spot on the stovetop. "Do you think what I did was right?" he asked finally, tossing the dish sponge into the sink. "I love the library. Always have. More happy childhood memories take place there than in this house."

The way he said "house" left it clear that his childhood hadn't been entirely happy. In Big House there wouldn't have been many places for a boy to roughhouse or even sit with pants dusty from the path on the river, except the porch off the back kitchen. No wonder he liked it there.

"Ilona and Duke made such good arguments," he continued. "Besides, it was my family that left so many people out of work. So suddenly, too. I know people still talk about it. I figured if I could help get the town going again . . ."

"You didn't think you'd ever be back in Wilfred, did you?"

He drew forks and spoons from a drawer and placed them on the table. "How about if I serve you from the stove?"

I nodded. I was hungrier than I'd thought.

"To answer your question, no. We still own land around here, but in case you hadn't noticed, the Wilfreds aren't very popular in Wilfred."

"I'm not sure that tearing down the library would make you much more popular."

He slid a plate of lentils and curry dusted with chopped cilantro in front of me. "Dig in before dinner gets cold."

"Thank you."

"We never did get to what you want to tell me."

I set down my fork. "Yes. Well . . ."

Complete dark had fallen now, and except for the rare car in the distance, the night was quiet. Rodney drowsed at the room's edge. The kitchen was a warm, yellow-lit oasis. Sam sneezed and dabbed his eyes with his napkin.

"I don't like all this waiting," I said. "Waiting for someone to show up to threaten me—or worse."

"It won't be long now. Given last night's attempt—"

"Wasn't that just an accident?"

"That's Sheriff Dolby's story, and we've agreed to run with it, but I don't think so. If it wasn't for the craziness when the lights cut—" Sam set down his fork. "Josie, what happened over there? For a moment, I swore I saw fire, but then, nothing."

I looked down at my plate. "Must have been the transformer. Anyway, I'm tired of the waiting, the lies, all of it. Too much has happened this week. I just want to go home."

The anger that had built in me fizzled to a near-sob. Rodney looked toward me, then leapt through the flap to the garden. Before—when I'd claimed my magic—he would have been in my lap.

Sam's voice was soft. "What would you have us do? You could go home, sure. I won't stop you. But the case against Richard White and Bondwell will be nearly impossible to prosecute. And you won't be safe. Just a few more days. I promise."

A fluttering settled over my chest. It had to be left over from before the spell had broken, I thought, when every sense and feeling was amplified.

"Okay," I said. "But I want it sped up. I can't go through my days as a sitting duck, not to mention the fact that soon I probably won't have a job here."

"What would you like to do?"

"The FBI sees me as bait. Well, fine. I want to draw out Bondwell. I have a plan."

CHAPTER TWENTY-NINE

The next morning I rose early, and as soon as the coffee-pot beeped, I laced a cup with cream and took it to the kitchen table.

Courage, I thought as I gulped a too-hot mouthful of coffee. *It's for the best.*

Washington, D.C., was three hours ahead. I wanted to catch my boss after she'd settled in for the morning, but before she was getting ready for lunch. I dialed her number and screwed my eyes shut.

One ring. Two rings. I was mentally preparing a voice-mail message when she answered.

"Folklife collections. Lori Moore speaking."

"Hi, Lori. It's Josie."

The pause on the other end lasted so long that I'd opened my mouth to check the connection when she responded.

"Josie! Where are you? I don't recognize the area code. I thought you were in New York."

"Oregon. Way rural Oregon."

"I don't understand."

"When Anton disappeared, I had to go into hiding. You get it, right?"

"An FBI agent was here asking about you." Even from the other end of the phone, I heard her fingers drumming on the receiver. This nervous habit had earned her the nickname Little Drummer Girl. The goal among her staff was to talk to her without starting the fingers going.

"I know." I couldn't tell Lori that I'd spent most of last evening with one, or I'd blow his cover.

"What are you doing out there? Are you safe?" The drumming picked up speed.

"I'm okay. I want to come home, though."

"It feels empty without you here. You and Anton."

I bit my lip then asked anyway. Sam had said he was okay, but I had to be sure. "Have you heard from him?"

The drumming stopped. "No. Nothing. Funny, though, the FBI never asked about him."

So, he was okay. Sam wasn't lying. "Anyway, I wanted you to know I'm fine and tell you my return might be delayed."

The drumming started again, slowly, then gaining force. She didn't reply.

"Lori? Is something wrong?"

"I'm so sorry." The anguish in her voice was real.

"What?" I asked.

"It happened just yesterday. They eliminated your positions. Yours and Anton's."

My grip on the handset tightened. So that's the way

they did it. I hadn't been fired; my job was "eliminated." A lump thickened in my throat. "Did they say why?"

"Budget cuts."

"Sure, but lots of things could be trimmed to meet the budget."

"I know." She sighed. "I can't explain it. The decision came from the top. It's effective as soon as your leave runs out."

"You're kidding."

"I'm sorry," she repeated. "You could get a lawyer and contest it under the Whistleblower Protection Act."

"I don't know," was all I could say. This had been my dream job. Now it was gone for good.

"I'll write you a great recommendation, of course. I have a friend who runs an elementary school in Arlington. I think they're looking for a librarian."

"I don't know what to say. I can't believe it."

"Is there anything I can do?"

Shock melted into sadness tinged with anger. I'd made the right decision by reporting the conversation, even if it had turned my life inside out. I couldn't have made another choice. My mother was right: I was a truth teller.

"Yes, in fact there is something. It's going to sound odd. Could you check the archives for stories on witchcraft, especially in the Maryland area?"

I gave her the Wilfred library's address, promised a lunch date when I returned, and hung up.

Then I called the *Washington Post*.

I took the stairs down to the library's kitchen, where Roz would almost certainly be brewing up the first of today's many pots of coffee.

My conversation with the reporter had gone well, but the success was bittersweet. My old job was gone for good. The kids cluttering Thurston Wilfred's office, Mrs. Garlington chugging through "Please Release Me" on the organ, the knitting club examining the town's events for sinister motives, even Roz's dour mood and hot flashes— I'd miss them.

Roz came in, humming something indistinct but upbeat. "What a glorious morning."

"Has Darla heard anything from the judge?"

"Not yet. I'm sure everything will work out okay, though."

I stared at her. Who was this person, and what had she done with Roz? "Are you all right?"

"Excellent. Better than excellent. I'm going to do it," Roz said triumphantly and pushed the coffeepot's power button. "I'm going to talk to Lyndon. I'm not going to dillydally around, either, with a suggestion of coffee or a walk. We've known each other too long for that. I'm going to tell him how I feel."

"That's great, but what made you change your mind?"

"It was the book you recommended for me a few days ago, *Trembling Rose*."

"It was a romance, then?"

"You don't remember?"

"There are so many novels," I replied. I'd recommended the book in passing when my magic was in high gear and my brain was a Niagara Falls of titles.

"Well, it wasn't a romance at all. It was a tragedy. If only Rosamund had confessed her love, Edgar would still be alive."

"I see," I said.

"What if Lyndon has loved me all along but didn't dare think I'd return his feelings?"

"He's definitely the quiet type."

"It's not easy. I admit, I'm terrified." Despite her emotion, Roz's skin stayed pale. No hormonal flushes. She must be truly committed. "But if it opens up something between Lyndon and me, it will be worth it. And if it doesn't, well, he has to be flattered, right?"

She smiled, her freckles and slight overbite making her even more adorable. "I can't see how he could resist you," I said truthfully. "When are you going to do it?"

"Right away. I can't wait. Do you mind if I take a bit of time off this morning?"

"Please do. I'll watch for patrons."

Lyndon would be starting his morning gardening by now. Usually he took care of the grounds in the morning and tended to whatever needed work in the library in the afternoons. Thus Roz's work sessions in the conservatory where she could keep an eye on him whether he was inside or out.

"Coffee ready?" Ruth Littlewood had brought her own mug. "I have a birding expedition to prepare. If anyone needs me, I'll be in natural history."

I caught a glimpse of Roz striding across the lawn and Lyndon straightening from his hunched position over the rosebushes. I silently wished her good luck.

Lalena Dolby was waiting for me at the sitting room-slash-circulation desk. If possible, she was beaming more brightly than Roz had. What was going on around here? Sailor tugged at his leash. A glance into the foyer revealed Rodney tormenting him from under the table.

"You'll never guess what happened," she said. "I need all your books on Paris."

"You won a prize?" I guessed. "An all-expenses-paid trip?"

"I found ten thousand dollars." She clapped her hands in excitement, and Sailor sat in response, clearly expecting a treat.

"You what?"

"This morning I was weeding, you know, putting the garden to bed for the winter, and I saw a loose cement block in the foundation. I was pulling it into place, when something glinted from under the trailer. If the sun hadn't been in that exact spot, I never would have noticed it."

"What was it?"

"A chest full of cash!" She lowered her voice. "I shouldn't yell, but I'm so excited. I'm blowing this town for good." Her smile lifted on one side. "You think Parisians like psychics?"

"How did the money get there?"

"It was Aunt Ginny's. I'm sure. She's probably been squirreling it away for years. She left everything to me, you know."

Sailor's whining rose in pitch. Rodney had wandered to the edge of the sitting room and sat down. His gaze bored into the dog.

"You're sure? I mean, that sounds risky, leaving cash under a trailer."

"Don't worry. I called Bert. He'll tell me it's legit. What do you think I should pack? Can I bring Sailor overseas? I've got a lot to figure out."

I bemoaned the loss of my magic. The books around me rustled in their shelves. *Ask us*, they said. *We'll tell her what she needs to know. You can help*.

To shut them out, I called to mind the drowsing court

from "Sleeping Beauty." I could do this. I could keep my power at bay.

"Come upstairs to the travel section. I bet there's something up there to get you started."

After leaving Lalena and Sailor on the window seat with a ten-year-old *Fodor's Guide* and a Paris map, I took the central staircase to the ground floor. Halfway down, I heard sobbing coming from the kitchen.

I stuck in my head, but saw no one. Another sob accompanied by a shuddering breath. Rodney pushed open the door to my office, where Roz was curled up on the armchair, her face in her hands.

Uh-oh.

"Go away," she said.

"It didn't go so well?" This was probably not the best time to tell her about Lalena's discovery.

Rodney leapt to the chair's arm and bumped his silky head against her ear. Without turning her head, she reached out an arm and felt along the desk. I pushed the box of tissues toward her, and she plucked one.

"He ran off like his pants were on fire. I don't think he'll ever leave his cottage again." She honked into the tissue.

"Are you sure?"

"Sure?" Her voice rose. "Am I sure? He tossed a sack of tulip bulbs in the air and hightailed it. You might want to put away his garden tools so they don't rust. It looks like rain."

I wanted to put an arm around her, but was afraid she'd throw it off, and, rightly, too. "I'm so sorry," I said. "I don't know what to say. I let you down."

She heaved a sigh. "I'm an adult. I make my own decisions. This has been coming for a long time, I guess." Her eyes were swollen and red and so, so sad.

"I'm horribly sorry," I repeated. "Do you want to take the rest of the day off? Maybe go home and read something comforting?" That's what I'd want, at least.

"Go home and pack is more like it. I'm too humiliated to stay. Right now, I need time alone. Shut the door behind you."

I meandered back to the circulation desk and absently refiled the cards patrons had left on top of the file. Wasn't there some way I could use just a bit of my magic to help people like Roz without blowing up the house? Frustration boiled in me. If only my mother hadn't made Grandma put that spell on me. She'd have been able to teach me how to work magic. I'd have the muscles to control it.

"Josie?"

I lifted my head from the index card I'd been twisting in my fingers. Sam, rumpled and smiling slightly, stood in the doorway. The smile meant trouble. Now what? I smoothed the card and gestured him in.

"Any news?" I asked.

"The reporter you called, the one from the *Washington Post*. He's been in touch with the Bureau. The story's set to run tomorrow."

"Oh." The word left my mouth in a wisp.

"I thought you'd better know. We could see results as soon as tomorrow night or the next morning."

I nodded numbly. I'd asked for it. Strange as it seemed, I wanted him to stick around a few minutes longer. Losing my job, crushing Roz's fantasies, and shutting down my magic was a lot to deal with on my own. "Have anything good to read? Maybe another Hardy Boys?"

"Funny you should mention it. I was just thinking about that."

I led him to juvenile fiction in Thurston Wilfred's office.

"They're all on the shelves, except number sixteen, for some reason," I said. "*A Figure in Hiding*." Now, wasn't that apt.

"Oh. I have that one. Since I was a kid, actually. I think it's in my old closet."

"Hey," I said, "did you hear about Lalena Dolby's money?"

"No. Tell me."

"You know her, right?" I didn't know who he knew and who he didn't.

"Sure, Bert's sister. Lalena. I remember her from elementary school. She was a few years behind me."

"She found ten thousand dollars in cash under her trailer. The trailer she inherited from her aunt."

"I would have thought Aunt Ginny would have kept her money in the bank. She did the books at the mill for years." He fingered the spine of one of the Hardy Boys mysteries and pushed it back onto the shelf. "She found it, huh?"

"By chance, when she was weeding a flower bed." I didn't want to get her in trouble. "She seemed sure it had belonged to her aunt. Plus, she said she was going to clear it with her brother."

"Hmm." He smiled, and his features sharpened.

This change in Sam from lazy to focused—and unhappy, the smile was a dead giveaway—was fascinating to watch. I wondered what he was like at meetings. Did he daydream, or was he as keenly aware as he seemed now? Cogs turned in his brain, that was clear. What they produced, I had no idea.

"Sam?" I said.

He snapped back to the moment. "I'll get back to you soon. In the meantime, don't open your door to strangers."

When he left, I wandered to the front desk as two teenaged boys and a bearded man walked past. Don't open my door to strangers? That's just about all anyone was these days.

CHAPTER THIRTY

This could be my last normal morning, I thought as I roused myself from bed. Today the *Post*'s article came out. Today I officially jumped from the frying pan into the fire.

The rising sun pinkened the window. I felt around for Rodney, but he wasn't on the bed. He'd stopped sleeping with me.

As I was stepping out of the shower, the phone rang. I wrapped myself in my chenille bathrobe and hurried barefoot to the kitchen to catch it.

"Josie!" Mom said before I even finished my "hello."

She would have read the story by now. I imagined her pouring coffee into her favorite mug with Letty's photo on it and preparing to fold back the page with the crossword puzzle. Then, eyes widening, seeing the article and shouting for Dad.

"What were you thinking?" she asked me. "I thought you went to Oregon to hide. But here you are, quoted by name."

"I did." This could be a long conversation. With my free hand, I filled the coffeepot with water and shook ground coffee into its filter. "I know what I'm doing, Mom."

"They'll come after you, honey. Look what happened to Anton."

"Believe me. I know. You have to trust me on this. I can't say much, but I'm . . ." I searched for the right way to get the idea across. "I'm not alone."

"What does that mean? You've shacked up with some guy?"

"No! That's all I can say. How's Dad?"

"You're changing the subject." Another of Mom's patented sighs whooshed through the phone lines. "At least there's one good thing. Your father and I searched the atlas last night, and we'll be danged if we can find Wilfred."

"It's not incorporated anymore. Anyone with a computer could find me, though." Coffee burbled comfortingly into the carafe. "I wonder, do you—?"

"Have I had any flashes about you, you mean?"

"Yes."

"The usual one. Nothing new. It's more of a feeling than something specific, but it worries me a lot."

I pulled the bathrobe closer. The flutter on my birthmark was as light as a mosquito's wings. "You're still having that vision?"

"Yes. It's back. It caught me last night again. Oh Josie. Why did you go and talk to that reporter?"

I hated to think what she'd do if she knew I'd actually

called him first. "It's inevitable. This whole situation. It needed to come to a head. I'm not being stupid about it, though. You have to trust me."

"When are you getting a regular phone? I'd feel better if I could keep in touch with you. You don't even have an answering machine."

"I'll be home soon, Mom. It can't be too much longer now." I cleared my throat. "Mind if I stay with you?"

"Of course not. You'll want to make sure your apartment is safe before you return."

"Actually—" I didn't want to say it.

"You lost your job, didn't you?" Having a witch for a mother had its advantages, I was learning. "Oh honey. We'll figure it out. You're—" Her voice dropped to a whisper. "You're still using the spell I taught you, right?"

"Yes." Yes, and the world is duller, including the sip of coffee I'm about to take. But it can't be helped. "Don't worry. It's all legit. No magic here."

Dressed and caffeinated, I walked down to Darla's for breakfast, as planned. The morning was cool and damp, and the air smelled of fir bark and the river.

I could understand how Sam would miss this part of the world after living in the concrete-paved mayhem of Los Angeles. I would miss it, too.

There were only a few cars in the parking lot, but the diner was warm and noisy, its windows steamed from conversation and platters of hash browns and eggs.

"Speak of the devil." Duke swiveled on his stool with the grace of Gene Kelly and faced me. "I saw the news on TV and picked up the article on my phone."

"Why didn't you tell us you were a fugitive?" Darla said.

I took a stool a few down from Duke. "Maybe for the same reasons you didn't tell me the library was set to be demolished."

"Ha-ha," Mrs. Littlewood said from her stool at the counter's far end. She was working her way through a dieter's special of cottage cheese, a hamburger patty, and a pineapple ring. Her bird-watching binoculars rested on the stool next to her. "Touché."

"Maybe I should order in extra provisions. We might be getting some press," Darla said.

"A great opportunity to feature the new retreat center," Duke said. When no one responded, he continued. "So, you were hanging out in the Library of Congress and you overheard this senator's aide cutting a deal with a lobbyist?"

"That's the gist of it." I waved away Darla's offer of coffee. I needed to keep the jitters to a minimum. "Poached eggs, please."

"We have some good salmon today. I'll give you a sliver on the side."

"If I were you, I'd be scared to death," Duke said. "Government's a bunch of crooks. Who knows who they'd send after you?"

"And what might happen when they did," I said, thinking of the woman's body I'd found.

"Girl has a point," a woman I recognized from the knitting club said. "When's the last time you went down to those bushes along the river?"

"Hush, Marcia," Darla said.

"There are good folks in government," Ruth Little-wood said. "Bad folks, too. Like just about everywhere, I suppose." She waved her fork toward the river. "This town is built on them. The Wilfreds didn't do us any favors."

"Sam's not so bad," I said. "I don't know about his family, but Sam signed off on the agreement because he thought he was doing something good for the town."

"Yeah, he's an all-right guy," Duke said.

Both Darla and Mrs. Littlewood looked at us as if we were a cat and a dog holding hands.

"He'll have to prove it," Mrs. Littlewood said. "Anyway, I want to hear more about this graft story. Insider stuff. Your colleague disappeared, is that it?"

"I really don't have much more to add, and I need to keep my mouth shut, anyway. It will all end up in court. In the meantime, as long as there's a library, I'm staying right here in Wilfred." The was the line Sam and I had prepared.

"That's it, then?" Duke said. "Nothing?"

Darla topped off coffees down the counter. "Leave her alone, Duke. It's not like we don't have enough news in Wilfred to talk about. There's the library, for instance. I have a good feeling the judge will see what a huge benefit it is to us."

"You haven't heard anything yet from him?" I asked.

"Not yet." Darla kept her gaze on Duke. "Soon, though."

"What good's a library when you don't have enough money to get a new roof? When people are leaving town faster than they're moving in?"

"Enough already," Mrs. Littlewood said. "I can quote both of you and have the argument myself. How about Lalena's money? Did you hear about that? Found ten thousand dollars under the trailer. Planning a trip to Paris."

That got people's attention. At this moment, the diner's grapevine was so heavy with fruit that I feared it would topple. It was about to get heavier.

The front door opened to Craig Burdock, rumpled and needing a shave. He took an empty stool and slipped off his shoes, rubbing his feet together.

The diner fell silent as patrons set down their forks, wiped their mouths, and watched.

"Craig. How are you?" I asked finally.

"Fine," he mumbled.

Darla slid a platter of biscuits and gravy in front of him. Surprised, Craig looked up, but didn't question his luck. He tucked in.

"Hey," Duke said. "That was my order."

"Craig needs it worse. The food at the county jail's awful."

"What's he doing on the loose, anyway? I can't believe he made bail. No bondsman would trust him for half a mil."

"He's right here, Duke," Ruth Littlewood said. "Don't talk about the boy like he can't hear you."

But Craig did appear to have shut us all out. He shoveled mammoth bites of sodden biscuit into his mouth and stared somewhere in the vicinity of the shake mixer.

"Craig," Darla said, "It's nice to see you—"

"Not," Duke said under his breath.

"—but I can't help but wonder what mercy brought you here."

"The sheriff made a mistake. They let me go." He said all this without turning once toward us.

"A mistake?" Ruth said. "I didn't think the Dolbys made mistakes. Unless he was sore at you over his sister and it clouded his judgment?"

"I still can't believe she found that money," Darla said. "Who'd have known Ginny could have saved up ten thousand dollars?"

Craig's fork hovered midair before dropping to his plate. "Lalena found ten thousand dollars?"

"Now, don't you get any ideas. She broke up with you for good reason," said Darla, hand on hip.

"Where'd she find it?" His words came thoughtfully.

"Why?" Darla said while Duke said, "Under her trailer."

Craig looked from Duke to Darla and back to Duke. "Just now? Like, this week?"

Darla shot Duke a warning glance. "What's it to you, Craig?"

He dropped his gaze to his plate and threaded a piece of biscuit through the amber gravy. "No reason," he said firmly and picked up the sausage patty, ripping off half with his teeth. Once he swallowed, he wiped his fingers and dropped a few bills on the counter while he slipped his feet into his boots.

"Leaving so soon?" Ruth said.

"Yeah." He looked at each of us in turn, a smile growing. "Tell the sheriff I said hi."

CHAPTER THIRTY-ONE

After breakfast, I trudged up the hill to the library. I'd accomplished my part of the plan. Everyone at the diner knew I would stay in Wilfred and carry on as usual. Any reporter—or fixer sent by Bondwell—who stopped by would know how to find me.

As I passed Big House, I waved. Sam waved back from a second-story window. He was on his phone. It felt good to know he had my back.

Yes, we had a plan, and, yes, so far everything was going fine. I was drawing out the enemy. Now it was the job of Sam and his colleagues to trap him.

One thing Sam had assured me was that it was unlikely I'd be approached at the library during working hours. To be safe, I'd always want to have someone within earshot. Right now, that person was supposed to be Roz. Frankly, after my failed advice about Lyndon, I wasn't sure Roz wouldn't happily push me in front of anyone waving a gun.

With that on my mind, I unlocked the library's front door. We were officially open for business. Patty from the This-N-That shop was waiting with an armload of westerns to return.

"About time you showed up," she said.

"I'm five minutes early," I told her. "Come on in. I set aside the latest Evan Lewis for you."

Lights were already on, which meant that Roz was here. I'd have to see her sooner or later, so I might as well get it over with.

She was shelving books in the history and natural science room and had her back toward me.

"Hi, Roz. How are things today?"

She responded with a grunt and refused to face me. I guess that meant Lyndon hadn't pledged his love since the day before.

"Lalena Dolby found ten thousand dollars under her trailer," I tried.

Another grunt.

"Craig Burdock is out of jail. I saw him down at Darla's."

This one didn't even get a response. Either Roz already knew, or she didn't care. The first plan Sam and I had come up with had me spending the night at Roz's. I'm glad we came up with a backup.

"Roz, I'm so sorry. I should have minded my own business. What do I know about love, anyway? Will you forgive me?"

"There you are." Lyndon's voice. He stood in the

doorway with a toolbox. I flinched as I heard first one, then several, books hit the floor.

"The furnace will be off for a few minutes while I change the filter. Oh. Hi, Roz."

Roz had come from behind the shelf and now stared at Lyndon with an expression sad enough to leave her usual Eeyore face in the dust.

"Need help with those books? Sounds like the shelf gave out." He talked as if nothing had happened between them.

Eyes wide, Roz shook her head.

I backed toward the door. Maybe if I just slipped out . . .

"No, Josie," Roz said. "Stay. I have something I have to tell you."

"Honestly, it won't take a second to help you with that shelf. It's the one with the tricky support, isn't it?" Lyndon said.

Patty appeared at the doorway. "The Wilfred boy is wandering around in the hall. I'm coming in here for some peace. Hello, Lyndon . . . hello, Roz."

Sam. I took this moment to exit. Maybe he had an update.

He was in the atrium and motioned toward my office. He pulled the door closed. I dropped to my chair. With both of us standing, he'd been less than an arm's length away. He leaned on the door frame.

"Something new?" I asked.

"Your interview has started things moving. For one, this morning Senator Markham fired Richard White."

My sympathy for him lasted only until I remembered Anton. "You said 'things,' plural. What else?"

"Bondwell is sending someone to Wilfred."

"Already?"

"They don't want you on TV repeating what you told the *Post*'s reporter. The sooner they can convince you to disappear—"

Or worse, I thought.

"—the better. An agent is tracing him from the airport. I want to be there when he's pulled aside."

"So, that's it? I'm safe, then?" I should have felt relieved, but I was vaguely disappointed. It felt too soon, too easy.

"No, you're not safe. Not until I tell you we've made an arrest. Until then, continue on as we planned, and don't take any chances."

"Oh."

He only had to lean forward a few inches to lay a hand on my arm. "You're still worried?"

"No." I forced a smile. "It's fine. Everything is working out exactly as it should."

Afternoon had come, and Roz and Lyndon were still MIA. I pictured Roz in her trailer with the curtains pulled closed and Lyndon shut up in his cottage.

I hadn't heard a peep from Sam, and although I wanted to stick to our plan of always having someone within earshot, thanks to Lyndon and Roz's encounter, it was only the occasional patron and me at the library. Rodney kept to the room's edges. I locked the kitchen and side doors and held my breath every time the front door opened. At lunch, I ate Roz's tuna sandwich while I sat at the front desk. Rodney was restless, and his cat door flapped every fifteen minutes or so as he stalked the garden then returned to pace the library's atrium.

Despite my nervousness, the day had been fairly quiet, except for a few Wilfredians who stopped by to ask me about the *Washington Post* article and opine about politics and corruption. One older gent who kept tipping back his baseball cap to scratch his bald scalp even found a way to link the Wilfred mill's closure to national politics. When he dove into criticism of Sam, I changed the subject and steered him toward a biography of Teddy Roosevelt.

Then Ilona showed up. Today she wore a fake fur–trimmed white suit with a matching tote, like something from a set of Doctor Zhivago–themed Barbies. Her earrings were tiny sleighs. It seemed early in the season for this particular getup, but I was no fashionista in the practical skirt and blouse I wore for the fifth time since I'd arrived.

"I don't get it," Ilona said. She stood in front me, a hand on a hip.

I remained seated. "Maybe I can help you. We have a good reference section. What don't you get?"

"You don't even care about the library. You just came here to get away from someone you snitched on." Her voice rose.

"I do care about the library. I care about it a lot." I missed hearing the companionable grumbling the books would have made on Ilona's arrival.

"You don't care about Wilfred, either." She stepped closer, and her tote hit the desk with a thud. "Why are you interfering? Why don't you leave us alone? For the first time in decades, good things are happening here, then you come and mess it up."

I stared at her in disbelief. "Why are you so worked up? All I did was give the judge evidence of how much the library matters to Wilfred." Could her commission from the sale really mean that much to her, or was it simply ego? Then it started to come together. "Wait. Has he ruled?"

She didn't reply, and her eyes narrowed.

"Ilona, if you know something, tell me."

"I have nothing to say to you."

Then why was she here? "Anyway," I continued, "since I've been here, patronage numbers have doubled, and people are checking out books on everything from Russian ballet to quantum theory. For instance, take Lalena. Now that she's going to Paris, I can help her with books and maps."

I knew how lame it all sounded, but all the same, I believed in the library's good. Ilona stepped back.

"Lalena's going to Paris?"

"I pointed out a few novels and a book on French history to her, and it fired up her interest. Then she found that money—"

"She found money."

"You haven't heard? Ten thousand dollars. Craig Burdock was—"

"Wait, did you say Craig Burdock?"

"Sure. He's out of jail." Was she going to repeat everything I said? "I guess the sheriff had been mistaken about him."

"I'd wondered . . ." Ilona said slowly.

"I guess they didn't have enough evidence to hold him."

She didn't wait to hear the rest. She hurried to the front door, and I watched through the window as she slipped into her white Mercedes. She knew something, and it had to do with Craig Burdock. What?

I ran to the kitchen and snatched the library's key ring from its hook. As the Mercedes disappeared down the drive, I locked the library's front door and ran to Lyndon's pickup. It was open.

Shoot. It had been a long time since I'd driven a stick shift. The truck stalled on my first attempt to shift into first gear, but it lurched ahead on my second try, and I bounced my way out of the driveway and after Ilona.

CHAPTER THIRTY-TWO

Ilona's Mercedes disappeared into the distance. What had I been thinking? The old truck groaned as I shifted into fourth. I'd never catch her.

I had a few things working for me, though. First, the truck looked like any number of trucks around Wilfred. I wouldn't stand out if Ilona should check her rearview mirror. Next, there was only one road through Wilfred until it hit the highway to Forest Grove. Finally, at this speed, she just might get caught in Sheriff Dolby's speed trap.

The speed trap was just on the other side of the copse of cottonwoods. The Mercedes beeped once but didn't slow. Figures she'd work an in with the sheriff. Thanks to the truck's laboring engine, I was barely at the speed limit. The sheriff waved as I passed.

Ahead, the Mercedes took a left at the highway. Craig Burdock could be staying with friends near Gaston. It wasn't out of the question. He might not be feeling welcome in Wilfred right now.

By the time I rounded the corner, the Mercedes had vanished. I rattled up the highway a few miles as farmland spread around me and the high arc of a field sprinkler shot streaks through the autumn sun. Black and white cattle grazed in another field.

No sign of Ilona. She was gone.

I pulled off the road into the parking lot of a small church and swung around to return the ten miles or so to Wilfred. I clicked on the radio to the station Lyndon had presumably been listening to and heard Frank Sinatra singing "Only the Lonely" to lush orchestration. Lyndon was full of surprises.

Would Sam be listening to the radio now, too? He'd have found a classical station, maybe. Or, better, he was listening to the confession of whomever Bondwell sent after me.

I slowed as I entered Gaston. I passed a bar and a block of cheaply built apartments called, strangely enough, the Armada. They probably weren't even nice when they were new forty years ago. Then I yanked the steering wheel to the right. Was that a white Mercedes I'd seen?

I backed up on the gravel shoulder and crossed the road to pull into the apartment building's parking lot. I slowed to a spot behind the dumpster. Here I'd be less obvious, even if I wasn't entirely hidden.

The two-story building had apartments upstairs and

down with exterior exits. Downstairs, the windows must have glared every time a car's headlights passed. Upstairs, the doors let out onto a concrete landing with metal rails shedding chipped paint. A sign warned that nonresidents would be towed. I wasn't sure who else would park here, unless it was for shady deals—probably right where I was stopped now.

In short, it looked exactly like the sort of place Craig Burdock would be holed up. What business did Ilona have with him?

I settled in to wait. A young woman with a thick pony-tail and a worn T-shirt that strained to fit dumped a plastic sack into the dumpster. She checked me out thoroughly but didn't say anything. When she left, I got out of the truck and stretched. Just then, a ground-level door opened, and Ilona stepped out, talking to someone.

"All right," she said. "You really don't think I should say anything?"

The reply was too quiet for me to make out.

"What else do we need?" Ilona said. "I saw we're out of paper towels."

She lived there? Ilona lived in this run-down, smelly apartment building? Couldn't be. But she sure talked as if she did. She couldn't be living with Craig, could she?

She turned, and I ducked behind the truck. Instead of the Mercedes, Ilona got into an older Ford sedan. I watched as she turned right on the highway.

Deep in thought, I opened the truck's door and noticed that the apartment Ilona had left was still open. A woman in a wheelchair watched me. The tubes of an oxygen tank snaked around it and into her nose. I saw no sign of Craig Burdock at all.

* * *

After staking out the Armada, I returned to the library to find the knitter's club angrily milling at the front door and Lyndon standing near the truck's usual parking spot looking perplexed. I apologized to the knitters and handed the keys to Lyndon.

"I had to borrow the truck for a bit," I said, not thinking of anything more original.

"Okay. You could have let me know. The clutch is a bit touchy."

"It was a last-minute thing. I didn't see you. In fact"—I met his eyes—"I haven't seen much of you all day."

"Been working on something," he mumbled and looked at his feet. No mention of Roz. Curiously, no mention of the *Washington Post* article, either.

When he didn't offer details, I said, "Well, I'll probably be turning in early tonight. You haven't seen Sam around, have you?"

"Nope. Not since this morning."

When the library closed that evening and I still hadn't heard from Sam, I continued with the plan. I punched up a few pillows and laid them out on the bed as if it were me, then set a timer on the bedside light. Then I stuffed a nightgown and toothbrush into a tote bag and crept out the kitchen door. I didn't see anyone as I darted down to the river path in the twilight.

I hesitated at the turnoff to the Magnolia Rolling Estates. My plan had been to go straight to Lalena's, but my mother's training was too strong. I couldn't show up without a hostess gift. I darted across the street to the PO Grocery and pushed open the door to an instrumental version of "Viva Las Vegas."

When I entered, the girl at the register was busy swiping screens on her phone and barely lifted her head. Fine with me. As far as anyone was supposed to know, I was in my apartment in the library.

The wine was in the back, next to the deli case. Above the shelves, WILFRED, OREGON and its zip code were still affixed to the wall in bronze letters. I grabbed a bottle of an Oregon pinot noir and was turning toward the cashier, when I heard Darla's voice in the next aisle.

"What does that say?" she asked. "I can't stand cilantro. And no extra picante this time."

"No cilantro," a male voice responded.

I pushed aside a few cans of pork 'n' beans and peered through the crack. Darla fingered her reading glasses and held a tub of salsa. Even though she regularly wore glasses on a cord around her neck, her vision appeared fine. She never wore the glasses. I'd seen her wipe up microscopic spills of gravy and grab the swatter to attack a fly across the dining room. She was faking a vision problem. Why?

I dashed toward the front of the tiny store and pulled a copy of the *Forest Grove News-Times* from its rack, then sauntered to Darla's aisle as if by accident. "Darla! Imagine seeing you here. I was just getting a few things before I head up the hill for the night."

"It's been a long day for you, honey." She turned to the man helping her. "Bye, Kevin. I'll see you around."

I flipped the paper open and caught an ad for a cheap oil change at Providence and Sons Garage. "Look here." I tapped the ad. "Think they're any good?"

She glanced at the paper, her expression mild. "I expect they're fine. You don't have a car. What do you care?"

Thanks to the logo featuring an illustration of a Model T, anyone could tell the ad was for a garage. "I just wondered if you knew the Prudence Garage."

She tucked the salsa into her basket. "You should ask Duke, but I haven't heard any complaints."

"About Prudence and Sons?" I pressed.

One eyebrow rose. She took the paper and brushed a finger over "Providence" then handed it back. "Sure."

I remembered the girlishly written note left for me my first night. Roz said Darla never texted. And she hadn't wanted to read the report on the library's benefits to Wilfred. Not to mention that, as far as I could tell, she'd never made use of her library card.

"Darla, you can't read, can you?"

She dropped off her readers to dangle against her chest. "I can read. Honest. I know how."

She was telling the truth. I sensed it. "Then what's wrong? You couldn't read the ad I just showed you. You couldn't read the salsa jar, either, could you?"

She turned away a moment, tapping her toe on the wavy linoleum. "Okay. I'm dyslexic. Severely so."

"I see."

"I can read, but I don't. Not much, and not without a lot of effort."

We faced each other, neither of us speaking. Her expression held a plea. I understood.

"I won't tell, I promise," I said. "But it's nothing to be ashamed of. Lots of people are dyslexic. You'd be surprised if you asked around."

"What would you know about it, anyway?" She looked up the aisle to make sure no one was listening. "For you, reading is like breathing, and from what I've seen, nearly as important. I'm not stupid."

"That's why you're such a big supporter of the library, isn't it? You don't want people to know about your disability."

"I'm going to reading therapy every week. That's where I was the night of the murder. Bert knows, but it's no one else's business."

"I get it."

She shifted her basket to her other arm. "Auntie Lyn knew I had trouble reading. She used to sit next to me after school and read to me, running her fingers under the words as she went along. It didn't help much, but I loved sitting with her, smelling her gardenia perfume, and hearing the stories. If it weren't for her, I would have gone home to an empty house. Dad was at the mill, and Mom had left a long time ago."

No wonder Darla loved the library. So many good memories were there for her. She probably felt she owed it to Marilyn Wilfred to save it. Plus, it gave her a front. Maybe that's why she'd accomplished so much, too. She had something to prove.

"You're not really going back to the library, are you?" Darla said.

I looked up in surprise. "How did you know?"

She nodded at my overnight bag. "Given what's happened with Roz, my guess is you're staying at Lalena's. You're taking her a bottle of wine. I've had years in the restaurant business, and I don't need to be a stellar reader to see you're making a huge mistake."

"How?"

She plucked the bottle from my hand and marched it back to the wine display. "Get a French one instead."

CHAPTER THIRTY-THREE

Lalena was waiting for me with a glass of something lemon-tinted, probably from the box in her refrigerator.

"*Bonsoir, chère amie*. Welcome to Chateau Dolby," she said.

"Sorry I'm late. I stopped to get this." I handed her the bottle of Vouvray that Darla had helped me select. "How's the vacation planning going?" I knelt to pet Sailor, who was jumping around my knees.

"Paris in the spring. Two weeks." Lalena drained her glass and set it on the coffee table in front of the pink couch. "Bert says he'll take care of Sailor for me."

I took the rose-hued armchair at a right angle to the couch. The living room furniture was crowded into an "L" shape to better watch television.

"Do you know anything about the Armada apartments?" I asked. Darla might be in the clear now, but Ilona's sudden drive to Gaston still weighed on me, especially now that January Stephens's murder was reopened.

"The Armada? Why that place hasn't collapsed on itself yet, I don't know. Why?"

"Ilona stopped by the library today. I think she wanted to blow off steam about my letter to the judge. When she heard Craig Burdock had been released, she sped to the Armada."

Lalena's eyes widened, then settled. "Oh. You thought maybe she was going to see him."

"I'd wondered. Something isn't right."

"Craig doesn't live at the Armada, if that's what you want to know. Ilona's mom does."

"You're kidding." So, that was the woman I'd glanced in the doorway. Ilona's mother. "How is it that Ilona drives a fancy car and her mom lives in a moldy hovel?"

"Right now, Ilona lives there, too, you know," Lalena said in a matter-of-fact tone. "Her mom needs regular care, and they don't have the money to hire full-time help."

"But the car. The clothes. Plus, she told us she was staying at a fancy bed-and-breakfast in wine country."

"Leased. Borrowed. Fibbed."

I let this sink in. "Essentially, Ilona is a fake."

"Oh, I wouldn't say that." Sailor jumped into Lalena's lap. "She's being more true to herself than she ever was. She's ambitious. She wants more than life at the Armada. The real her drives a white Mercedes."

Lalena might not be psychic, but she had spot-on intuition. "Was her family a victim of the mill closure, too?"

"Well, yes—and no. Her dad was a union organizer.

He was on the road a lot. One day, he simply didn't come home."

Ilona, poor and fatherless. As with so many Wilfredians, my view of her was changing. "How come no one ever told me all this?"

Lalena shrugged. "Why would they? You've only been in town a minute, and you'll only be here a minute more." She nudged the dog off her lap and rose. "Hungry? I made a salade niçoise, but with French fries instead of potatoes. And no tuna. Or olives."

"Thank you." The trailer was small enough that I didn't have to move from my chair to keep conversation going. "Why would the news that Craig was free set her high-tailing to her mom's house? I don't get it."

Lalena abandoned dinner prep and returned to the seat next to me. "Do you think they . . . ?"

"Would it bother you if they did?" I asked gently.

She played with the tassel on her belt. "Yes." She lifted her glass, saw it was empty, and returned it to the coffee table. "Craig has this—this charm."

"He's good-looking, for sure."

"It's not just that. He has a vulnerability people respond to. Women feel safe with him and want to nurture him. He can't help taking advantage of it."

I wanted to disagree—he could, indeed, help it, if he wanted to—but I bit my tongue.

"The vulnerability is real, Josie. It's what makes me so sure he didn't kill anyone."

"That and the fact that he was here that night, wasn't he?" At her surprise, I added, "I saw his moccasins."

She looked at her hands folded in her lap. "Yes, he was here. I know he was playing around, but when he stopped by—he said he happened to be in the neighborhood and saw my light on—I couldn't help it."

He couldn't help it, either, apparently. "Why didn't you tell your brother when Craig was arrested that he couldn't have done it?"

"I did." She scooted forward an inch. "I did tell him. He didn't believe me. He thought I was covering for him."

Some questions were answered, but others persisted. Darla, Craig, and Lyndon appeared to be in the clear. Ilona and Duke were still possibilities. Could Ilona have planted the murder weapon at Craig's?

While Lalena tinkered in the kitchen, I wandered to the front window and parted the pink curtains. Across the way, Duke pushed a lawn mower in the dark, illuminated only by his porch light. Lalena had told me she'd seen him leaving the trailer park on foot with a bag of something. I wasn't supposed to broadcast my location, but I'd been so successful at worming info from Darla that I decided to push my luck.

"How long until dinner?" I asked her.

"Ten minutes. I'm making the dressing now."

"I'll be back. I want to say hi to Duke."

Duke's push mower swished across the tiny lawn bordering his doublewide. The motion sensors on his porch light clicked on as he passed, then clicked off as he moved beyond their range. Duke turned at a tidy metal shed and mowed toward me with military precision.

"Hello," I said.

Obviously deep in thought, he lifted his head. He wore

a plaid jacket, and a hand-knit scarf circled his neck. "Josie. What are you doing here?"

"Having dinner with Lalena. You're mowing in the dark?"

"It's calming. My kind of meditation. This might be the last mow of the season."

Crickets chirped from the fields beyond the Magnolia Rolling Estates, and a cool breeze rose from the river. Some night soon, it would frost, and winter would move in. I wondered what the library would be like with snow outside and embers in the fireplace. I'd never know. The library wouldn't be here, or I wouldn't be here. Or both.

"I want to talk to you about the night of the murder," I said.

His expression shut down. "This again? I have nothing to say. And if I did, I wouldn't say it to you. My life is my business."

"No, Duke, I'm on your side."

"I don't know what you're talking about."

"That night, you were seen walking to the library." This was a stretch. It would work, or it wouldn't. "You were hiding something."

He shook his head. "You're making this up."

"I'm not." I lowered my voice. "You see, the night I arrived—the night of the murder—I was all keyed up from the flight, so I took a walk around the grounds."

He didn't respond, but he watched me intently. A sign I was on the right track.

"I found something of yours."

"What?" he said quickly.

Relieved, I continued. My gaze dropped to his waist. That would do. "A silver rivet from your belt. It caught the moonlight. It clearly hadn't been on the trail long—not a speck of dirt on it." I glanced across the drive to Lalena's trailer. Her form moved in the kitchen window, setting plates on the table. "I don't know what to do. I feel like I should tell the sheriff, but I don't want to get you in trouble."

"You have the rivet?"

"Of course," I lied.

"Show me."

"It's back at the library. Somewhere safe. But, Duke," I said, "you aren't a murderer. I know that. I'll toss the rivet. But I need to know why you were up there. You must have had a good reason."

He leaned on the mower's handle and gazed past me. "It doesn't matter anymore, I guess. Follow me."

He wheeled the mower to the shed and opened the door. I stood outside. Sure, Lalena knew where I was, but I wasn't taking any chances.

"In here," he said.

"No thanks."

"Good grief." Holding a grocery sack, Duke stepped onto the lawn. "Here."

I peered inside to see two canisters of spray paint. I sucked in a fast breath. "It was you. You've been spray-painting the library."

"Ilona gave me a hundred bucks each time I did it. I was going up there that night for another session. I knew Lyndon was out." He took the bag from my hands. "I'll deny it if anyone asks. The only reason I'm telling you now is that the library's sale is a done deal. Ilona has assured me."

He wouldn't meet my eyes. He wasn't telling me the

whole story. He was hiding something—something more serious than vandalism.

"That's not all, is it?" I said. "You saw something. Or someone."

Duke snatched the grocery sack and lowered his voice to a growl. "If you say anything, I'll deny it. We never had this conversation."

"Josie?" Lalena yelled from across the drive. Sailor barked in response. "Dinner's ready."

"I don't know what you're talking about." Duke stomped up his steps and slammed the door after him.

As I helped Lalena clear the dinner dishes, her cell phone rang from the kitchen counter. "It's Sam. For you."

"We have him," Sam told me. "The man Bondwell sent to silence you. And he's talking."

"Does that mean I'm safe?" I could hardly believe it. I'd been on the run for less than two weeks, but in that time I'd lived enough for several lifetimes.

"Definitely. You're in the clear. You can go home."

I couldn't tell if I heard a smile or a frown in his voice. "I'm having a good time at Lalena's, actually. I might just stay here tonight."

Lalena nodded and waved the corkscrew.

"I meant home, D.C. With the info we're getting now, Bondwell wouldn't dare try anything."

Home. Funny how Wilfred was feeling more like home all the time. "I want to see what the judge rules on our letter before I book my flight. It shouldn't be more than a few days." According to Ilona and Duke, it was a done deal.

An awkward silence arose. "Maybe you'll let me take you to dinner before you leave? There's a good place for sushi in the basement of the old Carnegie library in Hillsdale. It's not exactly big city, but it's good."

Warmth suffused me. "That would be nice."

"I'll see you soon, then. Give Rodney a pat on the head for me."

Still in a daze, I handed Lalena the phone.

"What's with you?" she asked. "It can't be the wine. That stuff has the alcohol content of Kool-Aid. Kind of tastes like it, too, actually," she added as an afterthought. "We'll open your bottle next. You're still staying, right?"

"Sam asked me to pat Rodney—Rodney! I forgot to give him dinner. Can you wait a few minutes while I run up the hill?"

CHAPTER THIRTY-FOUR

I borrowed a flashlight from Lalena and made my way over the bridge and up the hill. This time, I didn't worry about being seen. Sam had made it clear. I was safe.

From the bridge, all of Wilfred spread below me. The trailers on their curious cinder-block platforms, Darla's tavern and diner and its busy parking lot, the PO Grocery now shut for the night, the lone fire engine waiting in the back lot. Far off to the left was the black mass of the old millpond.

Across the highway, modest houses with roomy yards platted an area that would have made up a mere four square blocks back home. Many windows were warm with light. I envisioned Mrs. Garlington and her son dishing up a crusty-topped casserole and, a few blocks away, the Tohler clan setting its knitting aside for bowls of chili. Beyond them, farmhouses dotted the horizon. It's true that Wilfred wasn't the big city, but it had all the conflict and variety of any town fifty times its size.

I turned up the path to the library, toward the thickening woods of the coastal range. Big House was dark. No surprise there. I couldn't tell if light burned at all in Lyndon's cottage, thanks to his tightly drawn curtains. The truck was parked out front. And of course the library appeared tucked in for the night, just as I'd wanted it to.

"Rodney?" I called.

No sound of Rodney trotting through the leaves. Maybe he was out prowling the garden. Now that my magic was contained, I'd lost my connection with him. That knowledge drained some of the satisfaction from the FBI's arrest. I swept the flashlight over the lawn. A black cat wasn't easy to spot at night.

Seeing the library in the moonlight brought back the creepiness I'd felt the night I'd first arrived. I now knew the library to be a place of warmth, somewhere special, but it looked especially foreboding tonight. I could almost hear the books inside humming a warning.

"Rodney. Here, kitty, kitty," I said from the kitchen door. Besides the wind in the trees, all was quiet.

Then, a hiss.

"Rodney? Time for dinner. Come on."

Rodney edged from under the porch. His hiss stretched into a growl.

I froze. Rodney's eyes—now more citrine than amber—caught the light from my flashlight. "What?"

He didn't move.

I turned the key in the kitchen door's lock. As far as I could tell, the house was empty, but my neck prickled. The sound of the books had reached the muffled pitch of a flurry of violins. I knew had I not performed the containment spell, I'd hear nothing else. Yet the house was empty. Or was it?

I glanced at Rodney's dish. It was nearly full. That was all I needed. I backed out of the house and locked the door, double-speed, behind me. Within seconds I was back at the river trail, willing my body to relax. Whatever it was I'd felt, I wanted it to stay far away.

I stopped behind an old oak and leaned against its mossy trunk, catching my breath. What had gone on back there? I scoured the windows for a trace of light, a hint that someone was there, but the house stared back blankly.

"Looking for something?" came a voice I knew all too well.

I opened my mouth to scream, and a man grabbed me from behind, clapping a gloved hand over my mouth. I stamped at his feet and hit boot leather. It was Richard White, Senator Markham's aide. I went limp. Something hard—the barrel of a gun—jammed against my back.

"Let's go inside," Richard said. "We have some talking to do."

"Unlock the door."

The gun's barrel rose to press between my shoulder blades. A bullet would pierce my heart.

"Hurry up." Richard White nudged the gun for emphasis.

With surprising calm, I unlocked the kitchen door and turned on the lights. Richard flipped their switches off and pushed me forward.

"We'll go to the other side of the building," he said.

Because no one could see the light, he didn't have to add. I forced myself to breathe evenly.

We passed into the library's atrium, where Lyndon's arrangement of dahlias and golden maple boughs nodded.

"In there." Richard yanked my arm toward the house's old drawing room. He pushed me into a chair at the reading table and clicked on the side lamp.

I felt, rather than heard, the tension of the volumes of books around us. They tightened the air like metal bands. I had to force my lungs to draw breath. Had my magic been active, I knew I'd hear the books shrieking. I remembered my mother's vision. There had to be another way out of this.

"What do you want?" I said.

He swung a briefcase onto the table and opened it. A clip of bullets slid to the side. He withdrew a piece of paper and a pen. He wiped the pen with a cotton handkerchief and handed it to me.

"Hold this."

"Why?" My heartbeat rose.

"You shouldn't have talked to the reporter from the *Post*. Now you're going to have to recant your story."

Upstairs, the telephone rang. Its full-throated bell was only a quiet purr down here. Richard lifted his head but apparently decided it wasn't a threat. The ringing stopped.

"In fact," he said, "you're so sorry for all the lives you've ruined that you've decided to kill yourself."

Ice chips coursed through my veins. Rodney sat in the corner staring at me. Every muscle in my body was rigid with fear—fear of Richard and of what would happen if my magic cut loose.

For a second I imagined my body exploding with energy and books flying through the air as if caught in a vicious squall. Windows would shatter, furniture would rocket across the room.

Use it, a voice said. *Use your magic.* My eyes shot to Marilyn Wilfred's portrait, just visible outside the door. It was her. She was talking to me.

I screwed my eyes shut and said, "No."

"You don't seem to realize you don't have a choice."

My eyes flew open to Richard's voice. "Why? Why would I write what you say if you're going to kill me, anyway?"

He leaned in, a clump of gelled hair falling forward. "There are lots of ways to die. Some are more painful than others." He ran a finger down the gun's muzzle. "I'm not saying I like it. I went to some trouble to hire someone to stop you the first night you were here. She had a nice packet of money to offer you to change your story. Everything could have ended much more pleasantly."

"Ten thousand dollars," I said. Lalena's money. How had it ended up under her trailer?

Richard's eyes narrowed. "Too late now."

"The second man, the one from Bondwell. He was a decoy."

Before Richard could answer, the phone rang again. This time it was the library's extension in Thurston Wilfred's old office next door. Someone was trying to reach me.

Rodney's tail twitched. If I had my magic, I could ask him to knock the phone off the hook. Maybe someone would hear us. But I couldn't. I couldn't do it. It was too dangerous.

The ringing stopped.

"Pick up that pen," Richard said.

I picked it up and pulled the paper in front of me.

"Write what I tell you."

I refused to speak.

Use your magic, Marilyn told me. *Trust it.*

There had to be another way. Someone was trying to call me, to warn me. Someone—Sam? Lalena?—knew I was in danger. They'd come soon. They had to.

"We'll skip the salutation," Richard said. "Write this. 'I lied, and I can't live with it any longer.'"

The phone rang again. Richard spoke over its trill.

"'I never overheard any conversation between Senator Markham's aide and a lobbyist.'" He waved his gun. "Write faster."

I had been copying his words deliberately slowly. The longer I took, the more time someone had to find me. Besides, the pressure of the books' forced silence rushed in my ears like high tide and slowed my fingers.

"I'm shaking," I said. Writing these words went against everything I stood for. My mother had called me a "truth teller." Never had I felt this to be so exact.

"As you would if you were in an emotional state and planning to off yourself."

My mind raced. Marilyn stared me down. I felt like I was in the driver's seat of a stagecoach pulled by a dozen wild horses, leading me along a thin trail at a cliff's edge. The reins were slipping, and there was nothing I could do. If I let loose, we'd all die.

The phone rang again—the fourth time. Someone was frantic to get through. Richard abruptly stood, keeping his gun fixed on me. He backed into Thurston Wilfred's library.

"I'm taking the phone off the hook."

This is it, Marilyn said. *You can do it. Use your power to seal the doors. Trap him.*

Rodney heard the words, too. He mouthed a silent meow.

Even if I wanted to use my magic now, I didn't have time to release the spell. There had to be another way. I'd untangled Darla and Duke's lies tonight. Surely I could handle this. I leapt to my feet and grabbed the briefcase and stood hidden by a bookshelf just as Richard ran into the room. *You can do it, Josie*, I told myself. *Your own power is enough.*

I swung the briefcase. And missed him. It bounced off the wall and dropped with a thud.

Just then, siren screaming, a car spun gravel up the driveway.

Richard leveled the gun at me, his finger on the trigger. The slam of a car door seemed to change his mind, and he ran toward the kitchen.

The sheriff burst into the atrium. "Josie! Are you all right?"

"The back door. He went through the kitchen," I gasped.

The sheriff said something into his radio while running for the kitchen.

Richard White got away. He got away, and I could have stopped him. But I hadn't.

CHAPTER THIRTY-FIVE

A deputy sheriff sat with me for the next hour, and I walked her through the story, from encountering Richard on the river trail to his attempt to force a confession and fake my suicide. The entire time, words ran across my brain like a storm-warning banner on TV: *You could have stopped it. Richard White could be in custody right now. You had the power, and you refused to use it.*

The deputy didn't seem to think it was odd that Richard had escaped. She was gratified that I was okay and even surprised that I'd tried the briefcase maneuver.

The adrenaline that had torpedoed through my body had now evaporated, leaving me limp with exhaustion.

Her phone beeped. A text.

"It's from Sam Wilfred," the deputy said. "He says to pack a bag. You're spending the night with him."

* * *

At Big House, Sam opened a bedroom door. "This was my parents' room."

A four-poster bed was pushed against the wall in a large room decorated country-style, circa 1980s, complete with flowered wallpaper and ruffled everything. A vase of dusty silk roses reflected in the dresser's mirror. It had to be the house's grandest bedroom.

"You don't sleep here?" I asked.

"I stay in my old room. I'm comfortable there. Plus, it faces the library, so I could keep an eye on you."

Of course. He didn't have to know I'd kept an eye on him, too, hearing his faraway arias and taking comfort in his lit window.

He fetched a bundle of sheets from the hall closet, and together we made up the bed. I stole a few glances while he tucked in the bottom sheet.

"Come on," he said once the pillows were fluffed. "You've had a tough evening. I'll make you some chamomile tea."

I followed him down to the kitchen that was beginning to feel so comfortable to me now. Sam filled the kettle and sneezed. Rodney was curled up in his chair. He stretched his front legs, then leapt down and into my lap. I was grateful for his silky purring body. He'd been so remote since I gave up my magic. The magic that could have caught Richard White.

"I'm so sorry Richard got away."

"He had a car on a side road just west of here. We figure he waited until we'd headed toward Forest Grove before taking off."

"So he might still return?"

"Maybe. That's why you're here. My bedroom is right down the hall. Leave your door open." He had a tiny mole—just a raised bump, really—near his jaw that I hadn't noticed before. I was getting more attached to him than I wanted to. Darla was right. He really wasn't that much older than I. He'd simply lived more life.

"You'll fall asleep instantly, anyway. I'm not sure how I'm supposed to be safer than I would be at home."

He laughed. "I wake up instantly, too. Remember?"

I did. I remembered standing in the library's old drawing room in the kids' section in my nightgown and seeing Sam for the first time, an open Hardy Boys book in his lap. If I were a blusher, this is where my skin would fire pink.

"Don't worry," Sam said. "We'll catch up with him. We're monitoring every airport within five hundred miles. It's not Richard I'm worried about so much."

"What do you mean?"

"Remember, the sheriff still hasn't nailed the person who killed January Stephens, Bondwell's first envoy. He says he has a couple of strong leads, but something doesn't add up."

"He cleared Craig Burdock," I pointed out.

"True. But—"

His phone pinged, then pinged again a different tone.

"Two messages. Maybe they found Richard." He touched his phone and scrolled down, then down some more. Must have been a long message.

The kettle was boiling. I set Rodney on the floor and filled the teapot. "Anything good?"

He set his phone face down on the table. His expression alarmed me. It wasn't a smile or a frown, but something sadder, more hesitant.

"What?" I asked. "You don't want to tell me, do you?"

"It's from Ilona." His voice was soft. "She's seen the judge's decision. He's dismissing the case against the library trustees."

My heart sank. Somehow I'd been holding out hope against hope that the library would be saved, even if I wasn't around to appreciate it. I'd wanted a surprise happy ending, just as in the novels I loved so much.

"Is it for sure?" I asked.

"It goes public tomorrow." He sank to a chair. "I told her and Duke I'd withdrawn my support. I guess they didn't pass the message along."

"Then it's not too late," I said quickly.

"It is now." He drummed his fingers thoughtfully. "If I go public about it, it looks like I don't care about Wilfred's future. After all, the judge decided the library's sale is for the town's best."

I felt like an ashen hologram, and a breeze would dissolve me. How one day could hold so much emotion, I had no idea.

"The second text?" I said. Maybe there would be some good news this evening.

"Oh," Sam said. "That was my wife."

CHAPTER THIRTY-SIX

Of course Sam was married. Of course he wasn't interested in me. The strange thing is that until that moment, I'd never consciously considered the fact that he might hold any romantic fascination with me at all.

He pushed the phone to the side and handed me a mug of tea. "I'll call her tomorrow."

Why did I even care? I'd be leaving Wilfred soon. The library would be demolished—probably sooner than later now. I had a homicidal financial fraudster on my tail. And, if tonight's events were any indication, I'd struggle with being a witch the rest of my life.

"I guess we won't be going out to dinner tonight."

"Ha. No." He absently poured himself some tea, then set the teapot down abruptly. "I hope you didn't get the wrong idea about that. I'd told you I was married, didn't I?"

"I don't remember you mentioning a wife."

He looked at his mug, then a nonexistent spot on the table. Anywhere but at me. "It's complicated."

"I bet." I forced a smile.

"I hope you don't think I was misleading you. It never crossed my mind you'd have any sort of, you know . . ."

"No. No, not at all. Ha-ha-ha." I stood and lifted my mug. "It's been a long day. How about if I take this upstairs?"

I barely slept. From time to time throughout the night, I heard a door creak or the sound of feet on the stairs. Sam. Rain drummed on the eaves, and the sun took its time rising.

Had I done right by not using my magic? Maybe I could have stopped Richard White before he'd escaped. I turned in bed and tossed a pillow aside. It was also possible that thanks to my power I could accomplish the library's demolition without the help of a wrecking ball.

By morning, only the scent of strong coffee had lured me downstairs. I'd dallied with the idea of forgoing lipstick or even rassling my hair into a ponytail, but in the end pride won out. Big deal, since it looked like it could well be another day of house arrest, at least until Richard White was found.

Sam looked as if he'd been up for hours, but, unlike me, he wasn't the worse for it. I wondered if he'd called his wife yet.

"Good news." He handed me a mug of coffee. "Do you take milk?"

"If you have it."

"We might have located Richard White. He's not in custody yet, but reports have him nearing Seattle. He probably plans to fly out from there."

"So I can get back to work." Bittersweet. "It's going to take a while to pack up the library. A few weeks, at least."

"You still shouldn't be left alone. Until White is under arrest, and we're sure there aren't any more surprises—"

"Like last time."

Sam chose to ignore me. "—I'll stay here."

Despite its size, Big House oppressed me. I didn't want to be here, alone, with my complicated emotions. The library would hardly be better. "Can I go to Darla's for breakfast?"

"Yes, but stick to the main road and take this." He set a smartphone on the table. I greedily reached for it. I'd spent ten days with nothing but the library's rotary phones. "It's GPS-monitored. Text me every hour and every time you're at a new location until I tell you it's okay to stop. I'm the only number saved in the contacts."

I woke up the phone. No password. Sure enough, in contacts "Ghost" was the only entry.

"If you don't arrest Richard before tonight, then what?" I asked.

"Text before you go to bed, then again when you awake. If you sleep more than nine hours, you'll hear from me. Here's the charger. Keep the phone with you at all times. The timer starts now."

I slid the phone into my cardigan's pocket and gulped down half the mug of coffee before setting it on the table. "I need to feed Rodney—" I looked up. "No problem with that, I hope?"

"That's fine."

"I'll text you from Darla's."

I was out the back door before he could change his mind. It was too early for the library's furnace to have kicked in, and the house's damp air pierced to the bone. Rodney was nowhere to be found, but his dish was empty. I remedied that situation. I didn't make the trip upstairs, but pulled an umbrella from the lost and found box and hit the trail for Darla's.

Despite the early hour, the diner was full and its windows steamed with conversation from a dozen tables. Talk stopped when I pushed open the door. I stood still a moment, unsure of what to do.

"Right over here." Darla came from behind the counter. The lines under her eyes showed she hadn't slept any better than I had. "Biscuits and gravy on the house for you this morning." She sat me on a stool swiveled to face the dining room.

"Why is everyone here?" I said, suspecting the answer.

"We got final word from the judge." She forced a smile. I had the feeling she was working hard to channel Southern gentility. "Our suit to block the library's demolition has been thrown out."

"I'm so sorry."

Darla raised a hand. "He was very complimentary about your report, Josie, and he said he wished there was a way to replace the library sooner. But his decision was that the retreat center is the best option for Wilfred at this time."

Everyone watched me as if this were a reality television show. If only.

"Honey, you had a tough day yesterday. You know we have your back. Care to tell us about it?" Darla asked.

I surveyed the room. A friendly crowd. Roz sat near the front, although she glanced away when I tried to catch her eye. I winced when I thought of her failed declaration to Lyndon. Lalena had roused herself from bed. She hadn't changed into street clothes and wore a pink kimono with drippy sleeves. Mrs. Garlington and her son, the postman, sat in their corner booth. The Tohlers had arrived en masse, Dylan standing out in his natty suit. Craig Burdock was even here, alone against the wall.

No Duke or Ilona.

"Just a sec." I texted Sam. *I'm at Darla's. Okay here.* "The FBI gave me this to keep in touch."

"No kidding," Craig Burdock said.

"Well," I said. "You all know Sam works for the FBI, right?"

"Speak up," Mrs. Garlington said.

I cleared my throat and raised my voice. Darla pressed a tumbler of ice water into my hands. "Sam Wilfred works for the FBI. It turns out he's not here for old times' sake, after all, but for work. To keep an eye on me, in case someone arrived to shut me up. You all heard about the *Washington Post* article, right?"

"The what?" someone asked.

"Never mind," Darla said. "Most of us are up-to-date. Go on."

"The article was meant to signal where I was and to draw out anyone who might want to silence me."

"A trap," Ruth Littlewood said with appreciation.

"Exactly. And it worked. The FBI caught up with an operative hired by Bondwell. They had him in Portland, and I was pretty sure I was safe. I was spending the night with Lalena, just in case. Anyway, I dashed up to the library to make sure the cat was all right, and the senator's aide was waiting for me on the river trail."

Gasps arose across the room.

"What happened?" Mrs. Garlington's son asked. He was in his post office uniform, and his mail pouch sagged on the bench beside him.

"He marched me into the library and forced me to write a confession that I'd lied about him. Then his plan was to kill me and make it look like suicide. But Sheriff Dolby got there just in time."

The room cheered. I noticed the sheriff engulfed by the knitting club on the opposite side of the room from Craig Burdock.

"Speak! Speak!" Mrs. Garlington chanted, and soon everyone had joined in.

The sheriff reluctantly stood next to me. I was getting hungry and knew a platter of biscuits and gravy congealed behind me, but I wouldn't turn away.

"As Josie said, my sister, Lalena, was hosting her for the night. When Josie didn't come back right away, Lalena did what anyone should do when they suspect trouble is afoot—she called the sheriff."

"She called her brother," Roz said. "Big whoop."

"I tried phoning Josie first, but no one picked up," Lalena said, delicately pushing her kimono's sleeve aside to reach her coffee.

"It was lucky. I got there just in time."

In the warm diner with so many friendly people around and the aroma of french toast and bacon in the air, I could almost forget last night's terror. The look in the sheriff's eyes when his gaze met mine brought it all back.

"Richard White got away, but at least Josie was safe," he said.

"I stayed at Sam's to be sure."

"Ooh la la," Lalena said.

"Then I heard about the library."

Forks dropped to plates. The air grew windy with sighs.

"When . . ." Mrs. Garlington couldn't finish her sentence.

"When does it close for good?" Count on Roz to hustle out the bad news.

"The day after tomorrow. After that, we'll spend a few weeks packing up."

"We'll have a new library someday," Ruth Littlewood said.

"Someday? Ha. More like some year," a bald man added.

My throat thickened. I thought of all those shelves of books, their voices stifled, going into storage for goodness knew how long. Meanwhile, all the memories and knowledge that had imprinted within the library's walls would be destroyed. All the joy from story hours, the thrill of discovery, the pleasure of a well-told story—all that energy—would be locked away.

"But we're not going to let this keep us down," Darla continued. She wiped her hands on a bar towel and came around the counter. "Maybe we couldn't keep the library alive, but that doesn't mean we can't be grateful for what it's meant to our community over the years. We all have special memories attached to it."

"Definitely," one person said.

"Hell, yeah," another person added.

"So, tomorrow night after the library closes, we're going to hold the biggest party Wilfred has ever seen. I've already started making pies. I expect every one of you to be there."

Tears pricked the backs of my eyes. I turned toward the counter and poked my fork at a biscuit.

"Eat up," Darla said. "We have lots of work ahead of us."

Chapter Thirty-seven

Before I left the diner, Mrs. Garlington's son gave me the library's mail. I flipped through it as I made my way up the hill and over the Kirby River. Most of it was the usual—flyers, ads, an invoice.

We did receive something official-looking from the Western Oregon Library Association. I leaned against the bridge's rail and lifted the envelope's flap. It was an invitation to join. I refolded the letter and returned it to its envelope with a sigh. Maybe the trustees would want to look into it someday, if the library was ever rebuilt.

Among the letters was a padded envelope from my old boss at the Library of Congress. I felt a small, hard object—a flash drive—inside.

I passed Big House, knowing Sam was somewhere inside despite the lack of signs of life. The library wasn't due to open for another half hour. I tossed my purse and the mail in my office and wandered the library's rooms, so soon to become history. I flipped light switches as the old furnace groaned and kicked in for the day.

The mirror above the fireplace in the old drawing room reflected shelves of books waiting to release their stories. I breathed the rich scent of old paper and binding glue. I ran my hands over Thurston Wilfred's desk. Maybe Sam would take it now, if his wife approved, that is. Even the drawing room where I'd been held hostage welcomed me.

Maybe my senses had dimmed thanks to suppressing my magic, but I felt something I never had before: a rich love of place. I had to return to D.C., but Wilfred had changed me for good.

Roz was waiting for me in the library's kitchen. I paused, unsure whether she wanted to talk.

"Bad news, huh?" This time Roz looked me in the eyes.

I relaxed. "Horrible," I said, certain she'd like the direction this was going.

"That's life. You work your hind end off for a community, and they go and bulldoze your life's work before your eyes."

"Couldn't be worse," I agreed. "Positively heinous."

"Couldn't be worse unless you're trapped at gunpoint by an evil man," Roz said.

"Or you confess your love, and the object of your affection runs off like someone put a rocket in his shorts."

Roz snorted, then smiled.

I smiled, too, then laughed. Then I laughed so hard that my throat seized and I teared up. Roz got weepy, too, and hugged me, smelling of roses and baby powder. Rodney popped through the cat door and flattened himself against the opposite wall, which made me cry even harder.

Finally, I pulled away and blew my nose on a paper towel. "I'm sorry, Roz. I should have minded my own business. You were happy, and I wrecked it."

"No, you didn't. I needed someone to push me to take a risk. I spent years putting my emotions into novels instead of giving them air. Now maybe I'll be able to move on."

"Whatever happens," I said, "I want the best for you. You're wonderful. A man with any sense would adore you."

With that, the kitchen door opened, and Lyndon entered, carrying the hugest bouquet I'd ever seen.

This seemed like a good time to slip into my office and give Roz and Lyndon privacy. Between the moments I sidled to the door and pressed it closed, Roz gasped repeatedly, but didn't reach for her fan.

I checked the clock and texted Sam. *At library. All fine here*, I tapped.

Great, he texted back immediately. Not exactly an armload of exotic blossoms, but I'd take what I could get.

Then I ripped open the envelope my old boss had sent me. She'd included a note on Library of Congress stationery, driving a stake into my heart. How I missed that place, even if my job had been limited to cataloguing. Still, what fascinating documents to catalogue.

"*Hi, Josie*," the note read. "*We all miss you. I've always appreciated you as a steady, reliable worker, but now that you're gone, I realize how much we've lost. I'm so sorry how things turned out. Please keep in touch. Enclosed you'll find the materials you requested. Sincerely, Lori.*"

I fished a gray flash drive from the envelope. I glanced at the door. Was it safe to open it yet? I didn't want to take the chance of interrupting a love connection. I plugged the flash drive into my laptop and called up its contents.

My boss had named the folder simply "witch narratives" and had included some documents plus a few sound files.

I clicked on one labeled "Appalachia 1942."

"Folks used to warn that Aunt Pretty was a witch," a woman's voice said with a rich country twang.

I relaxed into my chair. How I loved these oral histories. I'd spent more time than I should have listening to them when I might have been slapping on subject and collection codes.

"Now, I don't know, but she did have folks coming to her back door late at night, and she did have that birthmark."

My own birthmark twinged. I pressed it with an index finger and turned up my laptop's volume.

"Tell me about her," the interviewer said. "Did you ever ask her about being a witch?"

"Ask her?" the voice replied. "Nobody asked her nothing. But once in a while, if you was working with her, say, she might tell you something."

"Such as?"

"She might start humming a bit. She might tell you something like the things you love, they're the things that trap your magic."

"Explain that to me."

I flinched a bit at the interviewer's staid tone, but it didn't seem to dampen the interviewee's responses. I hung on her every word.

"She told me, for instance, that I like babies. That's true enough. I do love babies. Anyone's babies, not just my own. Would I be a nursemaid otherwise? She told me the babies could talk to me, sure as I'm talking to you."

"You mean babies old enough to speak?"

"No, I mean nursing babies. She said if I paid attention, they would tell me things."

"Did they?"

"Once I was holding a little girl with hair as red as blood, and I was tempting her to eat. You know, sometimes those babies don't want to take the breast."

"Go on."

"Finally, she was eating real good when I heard clear as day the words, 'Take care of Jesse.' Jesse was our horse." She lowered her voice. "The voices are all around us, you know, talking all the time. We just can't hear them."

As the narrator prodded her, I reflected on my own situation. I understood. I'd always loved books, and they became the conduit for my magic. They talked to me. Or, at least, they did. Or used to.

I clicked to the next file. It was a song, low and melodious, punctuated with a woman asking someone to "put your money down." Zora Neale Hurston, Lori's printout said, recorded by a WPA worker during the Depression. Amazing.

I should have been getting the library ready for the day, but I couldn't help opening one more file. This one was scratchy and hard to make out.

"It's a gift to be a witch," a woman's voice said. Her accent placed her in the rural South. "You can't be selfish with this gift, or it will sour and poison you. No, I was wrong to call it a gift. It's a responsibility. If you're chosen, you must respond. It's the rooster's job to wake you when the sun rises, and the honeybee has to spread pollen, or the apple trees won't fruit. Same thing with us witches. We're a quiet part of the working of the world."

Maybe magic was a public trust, but my experience showed it could be a public hazard, too. I paused the oral history. I wanted to hear more, but not now. The library would open any minute, and I had a job to do.

The books counted on me.

That afternoon, the oral histories I'd listened to played in my mind as I sorted files. What could those documents teach me now, now that I'd tamped down my magic? I had to rely on my brain these days. I'd let Richard White slip through my fingers last night. Was there something I knew that could help bring him into custody?

When Richard wasn't after information to help the senator's staff research whatever bill he was drafting, I remembered he'd ask Anton to pull special files for him.

I leaned back in my chair and clasped my hands on my lap. What were the files? Anton made a special point of mentioning it, because it was so unusual. I'd never done any work directly for Richard or the senator, but I'd seen him perusing the stacks, something congressional staff rarely did.

I picked up the phone and dialed my old boss. She answered on the first ring.

"Josie, I really shouldn't be talking to you. I was taking a risk making all those copies to send." She lowered her voice. "How are you?"

I couldn't really say "fine." "Thank you for sending the package. I really appreciate it. I see you even mailed it at your own expense."

"I couldn't let it go through the mail room." She cleared her throat. "The patron relations team is stopping by for a meeting in a few minutes."

I got her hint to get down to business. "This is important, or I wouldn't have called."

"What is it?"

I imagined her, a finger tapping the desk, an eye on the little crystal clock she kept near her computer. I closed my eyes and went ahead with my request. "Can you get me Richard White's circulation records for the past year?"

Privacy was a big deal among librarians. If I'd been at work, with a few keystrokes I could have accessed his records myself, but I never could have shared them.

"You know I can't do that." Now she was whispering, even though no one could have heard her. "You're not even an employee anymore."

"But I am. I took two weeks of vacation, remember? It's not up until the day after tomorrow."

"After which your job—and you—vanish from the payroll."

"For now I'm still an employee." I scooted forward on my kitchen chair as if she was across the table. "Richard White was here."

"What?" Her fingers drummed rapid-fire.

"Here in Wilfred. The night before last he trapped me in a room in the library at gunpoint. He wanted me to write a confession that I'd never overheard anything, then he was going to kill me and make it out as a suicide."

"No kidding."

I gave the news a moment to sink in. "He's on the run now. I thought if he had an interest in a particular place, say, it might help the FBI find him."

"Why doesn't the FBI request the records directly?"

She was going to need to massage those fingertips when the phone call ended. "You know how long that would take. Every minute counts right now. They've tracked him toward Seattle." I bit my lip and waited.

"All right," she said finally. "I'll look up his records. But I'm not emailing you anything, and I won't give you titles. I'll just see if there's something suggestive. The rest the FBI will have to request themselves."

"Thank you," I said, letting out my breath at the same time.

Lori's keyboard was silent, but I knew she was typing, and I could picture the screens she scrolled through.

"Here it is," she said. "Lots of history. A political thriller. But this . . . oh."

"Yes?"

"Boating. He's checked out a few books on sailing and two how-to's on preparing for long trips. You might—" Lori's voice rose and turned cheerful. "Come on in, I was just finishing up this call. Bye, Mom. Hope your knee heals up soon."

She hung up. I didn't care—she'd given me the information I needed. At any point along the coast, Richard could easily skip to an island, or even Canada.

I reached for the phone Sam had given me. "Look for a boat," I said when Sam answered.

He sounded distracted. "Boat? Oh, for Richard White?"

"Who else?"

"Something isn't right with Craig Burdock's testimony. I keep thinking—"

"Listen, Richard White has done a lot of reading on sailing. He hasn't shown up at the Seattle airport, has he?"

"No." Now he was back to normal. "Nice lead. I'll pass it along right now."

I'd done it. I'd given the FBI information I felt confident would help them find Richard. And I'd done it all with my brain. No magic at all.

CHAPTER THIRTY-EIGHT

Darla was as good as her word. Over the next day, she'd filled the library's kitchen with pies. She'd also dropped off several bundles of flattened bankers boxes, which I'd been filling with library records stored away in the house's old laundry.

She'd kept up a uniformly cheerful attitude, telling patrons things like, "What a wonderful library this has been. Remember when Roberta had the idea of turning Wilfred into a Bavarian town and did all that research? I swear, she spent the better part of the early 1970s in the parlor."

Darla even made a point of patting my back a few times through the day, saying, "They'll find that dirty Richard White, don't you worry. I have a good feeling about it."

I caught her once, though, leaning against the doorway of one of the upstairs bedrooms, the one with the natural history collection. She was having a memory of her own, and it was clearly bittersweet.

She wasn't the only one mourning the library. I'd heard scores of stories from Wilfredians who trooped through the rooms for the last time and told me how they met their wives looking for a cookbook in the upstairs bathroom or used to sit under an oak tree outside and read Agatha Christie.

At the same time, Roz had found a book upstairs on the language of flowers, and she was busy dissecting Lyndon's bouquet.

"Carnations can mean 'fascination,'" she told me. "Or 'divine love.' Which one do you think he meant?"

The bouquet was beautiful yet otherworldly with its queer mix of blossoms. Roz had told me that Lyndon had pressed the bouquet into her arms and taken off. No wonder he had disappeared for a while. It would have taken time to gather lilies of the valley and blueberry branches in October, just to name a few of the bouquet's components. Roz was right—Lyndon had meant to tell her something with them. Meanwhile, he was nowhere to be found.

Neither was Sam. I'd continued to send my hourly texts along with the *good night* and *I'm up now* messages, and he responded with curt *OK*s.

Tonight was the library's grand closing party. Darla cheerfully called it a "celebration," but Mrs. Garlington's continuing dirges on the organ upstairs made the town's real emotion clear.

At 6 p.m. sharp, Ilona's heels clacked through the atrium, and Sita and Ruff Waters, the library's buyers, followed. Today Ilona wore a white jacket with blue vertical stripes over a short white skirt with horizontal stripes. The ensemble formed a sort of optical illusion, and I had to blink after looking at her. A few days ago, I would have scoffed at her outfit. Now I imagined her getting ready in her mother's dingy bathroom, and my feelings softened.

Sita and Ruff Waters looked as if they'd been lifted from a photo in a 1970s book about communes. Classy communes, I amended, noting Sita's chandelier earrings dangling what looked like real rubies.

"It's a sweet old building," she said. "You hardly ever see them in such good condition, except as museums."

"Maybe you'd like to keep some of the light fixtures for the retreat center?" Ilona said. "Or sell them? I can hook you up with a demolition team that specializes in salvage."

Ilona pushed past me to the windows and lifted the curtain to let in a quickly darkening twilight. "The view is unbeatable. If you take out a few of those oaks, you'll be able to see the river."

"What happened there?" Ruff Waters pointed toward a window boarded up after my magical disaster.

"Accident. Hoodlums, you know. The retreat center will be good for the town," Ilona said.

The three of them left the room without even acknowledging my presence. Roz, sorting books behind me, said, "Orange lilies, oleander, and nuts."

"What?"

"That's the bouquet I'd give Ilona. It means dislike, caution, and stupidity."

Upstairs, the organ started in on a mournful version of "Ain't We Got Fun?" The tearful vibrato rattled the windows. I would have asked Mrs. Garlington to turn down the volume, but what was the point?

"You should follow them," Roz said. "Make sure Ilona doesn't pinch the doorknobs."

I rolled my eyes at her. It was depressing enough without having to listen to them exclaim about how nice things would be in Wilfred when the library was demolished.

"Seriously," Roz said. "Maybe they have questions."

"About what?" I said, but rose anyway.

I found them upstairs in the business collection. Here, Mrs. Garlington's flourishes on the organ were almost deafening. It didn't seem to bother the student at the desk near the window. He was examining a chart of constellations and dragging his finger from star to star while he took notes. I pretended to straighten some old shorthand manuals.

"This will be the level of the rooftop lounge," Ilona said. "The view from here is even better." She angled her way past the desk to the window and in the process nearly knocked the student's book to the ground.

"Lovely." Sita Waters turned to the student. "What are you studying?"

"Astronomy. I'm applying for earth sciences camp," he said.

"Very nice."

"The application's not due for another month, but today's the last day the library will be open."

"You can study at the high school in Gaston," Ilona said.

"They don't have these books."

The student was likely right. Wilfred had a terrific science collection. The school could request books like them through interlibrary loan, but it was so much easier to browse through shelves and let it spark further investigation. I'd done the same thing as a girl. Stumbling over a book on Walt Whitman had led me to the history of the Civil War, which led me to books on nineteenth-century fashion.

"Josie," Sita said. "That's you, right?"

I nodded and almost dropped *Top Tips for Dictaphone* I was pretending to examine.

"Could you move Wilfred's book collection to the high school? At least some of it?"

"Their library's too small. The trustees have already looked into it. Plus, it would all have to be catalogued, and the school doesn't have the resources."

"A shame," Ruff said.

"A new library will be built soon enough. Anyway, it's too loud up here," Ilona said, eyes shooting daggers at Mrs. Garlington's back as it swayed on the organ's bench across the atrium. "Let's go down to the conservatory."

I took the service staircase and came out near the kitchen just as Ilona and the buyers reached the ground floor.

"What's going on here?" Ruff said, taking in a table of pies.

"Party," Ilona said. "Don't worry, we'll clear out before then."

"Why?" Darla emerged from the kitchen drying her hands on one of the library's old cotton dish towels. I supposed those would have to find a home, too. "Why not stay and celebrate? This old house has meant a lot to Wilfred. We want to say good-bye with style."

Upstairs, the organ had moved on to a bass-heavy dirge of "La Cucaracha."

"We'll let you celebrate in peace," Sita said. "We know the library has been important to the town. We hope the retreat center will be equally important. Once it's open, we'll throw another party for everyone. Another reason to celebrate."

The couple buying the library really did seem nice. They certainly meant well. I touched the banister's polished wood and ran my finger up the newel post, carved into a fist-sized acorn.

The group left to check out the conservatory, no doubt to lay out where the retreat center's parking lot would go. I hoped they wouldn't disturb the English as a second language class.

Darla joined me as I stared out the kitchen window. "Sad, isn't it?"

"Devastating. They seem like lovely people, but it's like tearing out Wilfred's heart."

She let her cheerful façade drop. "Yeah." She toyed with the dish towel, then tossed it onto a stack of plates she'd brought up from the diner. "Josie, I owe you an apology."

"For what?"

"I'm sorry for bringing you out here on false pretenses. You've been such a good sport and made such a great case for the library. In less than two weeks, you've really come to feel like one of us."

Strangely, I had. I'd come from the other side of the country—practically another world. Wilfred had welcomed me, protected me.

"I'll miss it here."

She patted my back. I hugged her, then went to my office. I needed a few moments alone.

On my desk, the phone Sam had given me flashed. I had a message.

"Good news," Sam's voice said. "We have Richard White in custody. Wilfred is cleared. You're safe."

I'd heard this promise before. This time I believed it.

CHAPTER THIRTY-NINE

By nightfall, the library was bursting with Wilfredians. Slices of pie disappeared rapidly, and rumors had it that bottles of whiskey were available for sampling, if you knew where to go. Everyone knew where to go.

Sam hadn't shown up. I didn't know if he was somewhere on the Richard White case, or if he simply wanted to be alone. He couldn't have returned to Los Angeles yet. Surely he would have said good-bye.

Roz was still entranced by her bouquet. She'd brought it home—must have had trouble edging it through her front door—and I even caught sight of Lyndon at some point. Darla led the kitchen brigade. Lalena was in the parlor at the center of a discussion about ghosts. Two patrons said Marilyn Wilfred haunted the library, but Lalena insisted she was at rest. The pro-retreat faction had tactfully stayed away. Maybe they were at Duke's trailer toasting each other. I didn't know.

No one seemed to notice when I fetched my coat and wandered outside. Rodney might have been somewhere near, but in my non-magical state, he hardly noticed me. I'd miss the little guy. It didn't make sense to fly him to D.C. with me now. I'd make sure Lyndon took care of him.

At Big House, a pale light glowed in the kitchen. I couldn't tell if it was the light Sam left on to greet him when he returned, or if he was home and simply didn't feel like a party.

"Will you miss us?" Sheriff Dolby, beer in hand, joined me in the stretch of garden between the library and Big House.

"I will. I haven't even been here two weeks, but my entire life has changed. Does that sound crazy?"

"Not crazy. Wilfred is special."

We both looked down past the river to the glow of porch lights in the trailer park and the speckled lit windows of the houses across the highway.

"This town has made me better," I said. "I came from D.C. thinking I knew everything I needed to know about life. I lived in a big city, after all, and the Library of Congress is about as hallowed a workplace as a librarian can get. But Wilfred has taught me so much about what people really need, and what a library can mean."

"I hate to see the library go." Bert Dolby drew a swig from his bottle. "But I'm happy you're more relaxed now that Richard White is in custody."

"There's just one loose thread, one thing that bothers me."

"What's that?"

"The FBI has Richard White locked up. The library's fate is sealed. Even Roz and Lyndon are working it out. But who killed Bondwell's fixer? In all the craziness of the last few days, it seems to have slipped everyone's mind."

"I guess it wouldn't slip yours, considering."

Considering that I'd found the body, he didn't have to say.

"We're close to making an arrest." He wiggled his bottle. It was empty.

"Who?"

"That's all I can tell you. You'll know soon."

When it became clear he wasn't going to reveal more, I looked toward Big House. "Have you seen Sam? He seemed kind of—I don't know—nervous, I guess, earlier. I thought for sure he'd stop by."

"Hmm," the sheriff said. It was hard to remember he was a sheriff in his jeans and western shirt. "I bet he's frying up the trout I dropped off this afternoon. He used to beg to go fishing with me when I was a teenager and he barely knew his ABCs."

"He does like to cook," I said, trying to picture Sam as a boy.

"You've gotten attached to him, haven't you?"

"He's married," I said flatly.

"It's not a bad idea to keep your distance. Maybe he isn't exactly what you'd thought."

I faced him. "What are you trying to tell me?"

"Nothing. Forget what I said."

"Seriously, Bert. You're trying to tell me something about Sam, and I want to know what it is."

He let out a bearlike sigh. "There's too much chance we'll be overheard."

He looked toward the trail along the river toward the woods. No way I was walking down there in the dark.

"Why don't we go up to my apartment? No one will bother us there. We can take the service entrance and by-pass the crowd."

"I guess that's all right," he said reluctantly.

We opened the Wilfred mansion's side door to a roar of conversation rippling with laughter. So much for libraries as bastions of silence. Still, it was good to hear happy people on what could have been a maudlin night.

As I'd figured, the service staircase was empty. I un-locked my apartment and invited Bert into the living room.

"Have a seat." I clicked on a few glass-shaded lamps and gestured toward the Victorian sofa.

"I'll stand, if you don't mind."

Probably a smart move, given his size and the sofa's daintiness. "So, what is it you want to tell me about Sam?"

Bert Dolby wandered to the window and lifted the lace curtain. Seeming satisfied with what he saw, he faced the room with the stance of a sheriff. "There's his heritage. He's a Wilfred."

"Of course. Great-great-grandson of the original Thurston Wilfred."

"He's not happy about the library's sale."

"True." This I was sure about, although I still wasn't clear on the sheriff's meaning.

"I just—" He turned to me. "Look, you'll be out of town soon. I just don't want you to be surprised about what comes up next. I owe you a warning."

"I don't understand." Hoots of laughter wafted up from the atrium. Someone else must have found the whiskey stash.

He shoved his hands in his pockets. They made the shape of balled-up fists. "I told you we were making an arrest soon."

"You mean . . . ?" Not Sam, I thought. Couldn't be. As I spoke, the library began to pull at me. Even with my magic shut off, I felt the books urging me to act. The thing was, I couldn't understand what it was they wanted me to do.

"Sam Wilfred," he said.

"No. Absolutely not."

The sheriff put up a palm. "Let me explain. You know he still owns the old mill property."

"No, I didn't know."

"Sam's going through a difficult divorce. He could use extra cash. He came to Wilfred to sell the old mill site."

"He's with the FBI. He's here because of me. They asked him to fly up when they found out he was from Wilfred."

"You were his excuse for being here. He petitioned for the assignment, not the other way around."

"How do you know?"

"The county sheriff's office has been working with the Bureau, remember? I was talking with one of the other agents, and she told me."

I let this sink in. "Why would Sam kill someone? That's what you're getting at, right?"

"He doesn't want the library to sell. He wants the old mill to be the retreat site."

I couldn't take this on my feet. I collapsed to the sofa. "The old mill?"

"Sure," the sheriff said. "He doesn't make a cent if the library sells. Say the library is tossed out of the running. The mill site is a contender. Sam is the sole beneficiary. Think about it. Big bucks."

"Then why did he vote for the library's sale?"

"It's his cover. Makes him look innocent. You were right about Craig being framed, by the way. Sam planted the murder weapon while Craig was at Lalena's. January Stephens had brought ten thousand dollars with her to bribe you. Sam hid that, too, intending to pick it up later."

"I don't believe it," I said. "Why would he kill someone? How does it help him?"

"It delays the library's sale, gives the area a bad reputation. Thanks to his connections, he knew the gal—the fixer—was coming to Wilfred. He could kill her and use it to his purposes."

"Ilona and Duke claimed the murder was a great reason the library should be sold," I pointed out.

"A miscalculation on Sam's part."

Lame. Super lame. How could the sheriff even think this was a good motive? I knew Sam. He didn't even seem to care about money. All he cared about was opera and cooking. And justice.

"I shouldn't have said anything," the sheriff said.

"What about the money? Why would he hide that under your sister's trailer, of all places? There must be a hundred safer spots."

"He couldn't keep it at his house, could he?" The sheriff turned toward the window and Big House. "Soon we'll know for sure—tomorrow at the latest. I can't tell you anymore." He crossed the room. "We should be getting back to the party."

"No," I said suddenly, remembering Darla's offhand

remark at the diner. "It couldn't have been Sam. He was in Forest Grove. Darla ran into him."

The sheriff shook his head. "Couldn't be. I would have seen him driving home. I was at the speed trap all evening."

"I really think you have this wrong. Let's go see Sam now, let him explain."

"Absolutely not." His voice, his stance, made it clear the discussion was closed.

I remembered back to my first night in Wilfred, Lyndon piloting the old pickup into town. No. Bert Dolby had not been at the speed trap. Lyndon had slowed down and made a note of it. The sheriff had lied to me. He was lying to me now.

I looked away. "Of course."

Pieces began to fall together. Duke, on his way to spray paint graffiti on the library, had stumbled upon something he refused to tell me. Could he have seen the sheriff?

Bert Dolby's gaze intensified, and his voice changed subtly. "You don't believe me, do you?"

"Believe you?"

"What do you think happened?" He took a step forward.

I caught my breath. Every instinct told me to return to the safety of the crowd. I stood. "I just don't see how Sam could be guilty, that's all. He's never shown a hint of it." I edged toward the door and fought to keep my expression calm. "Anyway, I guess you know best."

The sheriff turned toward the window overlooking Big House. I took another step toward the door.

"He's so high and mighty," he said. "At the first sign

of trouble, the Wilfreds skip town. There's a lot you don't know."

I froze. "Like what?"

The sheriff shook his head, and his tone took an edge of forged steel. "Forget I said anything. And now he's down there making dinner, thinking his life is just fine. I wouldn't be surprised if he's struggling with his guilt even now. By tomorrow, it will come to an end."

My pulse leapt. I needed to get to Sam. Now. "This is such depressing talk. Let's join the party."

"Josie. Stop." The command in his voice made me turn. "You want to run to Sam. I can tell. That's not going to happen."

"I just think it's time to join the fun. Come on."

I yanked open the door. An amplified guitar duo had joined the ruckus downstairs, and it was nearly impossible to hear. *Get downstairs—now*, the books urged.

I made it as far as the hall before Sheriff Dolby looped an arm around my neck, crushing my windpipe.

CHAPTER FORTY

The pressure of the sheriff's forearm made it hard to breathe and impossible to scream. He grabbed my hands in one palm and shoved me down the hall.

He wasn't going to throw me over the railing into the atrium, was he? I kicked, but he lifted me as if I weighed no more than a kindergartner and forged ahead. My flailing legs couldn't reach the walls, and my thwarted screams were too dull to draw attention against the party roaring below.

We passed the entrance to the service stairwell. There was only one place we could be going. The tower. My mother's vision. It was coming true. Fear ripped through my body. The sheriff planned to push me off the tower.

At the end of the hall, he pinned me against the wall, my throat still wedged against his arm. With his other hand, he felt above the doorway and drew down a skeleton key.

"Still there, after all these years." He pushed me in and bolted the door behind us.

I hit the floor and scrambled to a seated position to catch my breath. The tower clearly hadn't been used in years. Dust carpeted the floor, and mouse droppings scented the air. My birthmark seared my shoulder.

"You killed her," I said. "It was you."

The sheriff towered over me. Moonlight through the dirt-streaked windows half-lit his face. "You're right. It was me."

He didn't bother to hide it. He didn't mean for me to leave the tower alive.

"It was a mistake, wasn't it?" I said. "You thought she was someone else."

The sheriff ripped a filmy curtain from the window and tore it down the center. "A mistake. One you should be glad for." He snorted, as if laughing at a joke. "Funny how it all comes full circle."

Bert Dolby couldn't have known about the fixer ahead of time. No one knew, except the FBI. He'd told everyone he was at the speed trap. He wasn't. The sheriff had been at the library for a different reason.

Craig Burdock had been there, too—or he'd been intending to come, but Lalena had waylaid him. "You couldn't have confused the fixer with Craig," I said. I backed to the wall. Bert was between me and the exit, but I had to try.

He didn't reply. He twisted the curtain into a rope and tested it between his hands.

"What did Craig Burdock have on you?" I asked when I could finally speak. "He had something on you, something he thought you'd pay for. You thought the fixer was your blackmailer and killed her instead."

I made a dash for the door and flipped up the bolt. My hand had dropped to the doorknob when I was knocked to the ground. The sheriff pushed me toward the opposite wall and tied my ankles with the twisted curtain. I scratched and pounded, but my efforts might have been flies pestering him for all the difference they made. With the other half of the curtain, he tied my hands behind my back.

He raised an eyebrow at my screams. "I'm not going to bother gagging you. No one can hear you up here."

He was right. We could barely make out the sounds of the party below. I could yell myself hoarse with no effect.

"Why?" I asked. "Why did you do it?"

"Listen, I'm sorry, but it's got to be this way. The Dolbys have been Wilfred's backbone since there was a Wilfred. I won't have anyone blacken us."

"You're talking about your father, aren't you?"

"You're like everyone else and want to simplify it. Life isn't black and white, Josie. It isn't good guys and bad guys. My father didn't have a choice."

My brain whirred. There had to be a way out of here. But how? With my hands and feet tied, I couldn't attack the sheriff. The room held nothing but crates of rotting books, long forgotten.

"Does this have to do with the old mill?" I said.

"You think it's cut and dried. Not so. Unionizing the mill would have brought its end for sure. Mills were shutting down all around here. Add labor demands, and it would have been a matter of months, tops, Wilfred could have survived. All Dad did was help end it without violence. The Wilfreds aren't innocent, either."

Now it became clear. Someone died when the mill burned down and the Wilfreds skipped town. The sheriff was complicit. Somehow Craig Burdock had found out about it and had been blackmailing the sheriff.

"Murder is violence," I said.

"So is destroying the futures of generations of mill workers."

Sam and Bert were doubles, in a way. Yet Sam had taken a different route. Bert Dolby had cited honor as his reason to cover up his father's misdeeds. Sam didn't bother with that. He simply lived an honorable life.

"So, you're letting Sam take the rap," I said in a low voice.

"No. He won't be around to take the rap. Not after tonight's trout dinner."

The sheriff threw open the tower window, and my every muscle tensed. The sound of a few beer-loosened voices drifted up. He shut the window.

"We'll wait. I'll be back when the party's over. Too bad you'll have an accident."

The bolt thunked into place behind him.

I didn't think twice.

I closed my eyes and let my lips recite the words, ". . . and the King and Queen and the whole court waked up, and gazed on each other with great eyes of wonderment. And the horses in the yard got up and shook themselves, the hounds sprang up and wagged their tails, the pigeons on the roof drew their heads from under their wings . . ."

I couldn't remember the rest, but it didn't matter. Something inside me ripped open. The spell lifted. I choked in a breath as my every cell contracted and released.

In that moment, the world was enriched tenfold. The night sky deepened into a moist charcoal gray with ribbons of moonlight through the tower windows. The scent of old wood and mildewed pages suffused the room. My fear was sharper, too, and my throat filled with the taste of metal.

I was magic again. "Sam," I said involuntarily.

The sheriff was framing him for January Stephens's murder and planned to make sure he'd never be able to prove otherwise. I imagined Sam's shadow moving against the lit shade in Big House's kitchen like a puppet in a Kabuki show. He would be leaning over the stove, chopping parsley and tossing it with a spatula. He was making a dinner that would kill him. I could do nothing to save him. Or . . .

Rodney. I remembered how I'd slipped into his body accidentally. Could I do it now? Could Rodney feel that I'd reawakened my power? As if he'd read my mind, I heard Rodney's mew from beyond the tower door. I choked back a sob of relief.

I had to try. I closed my eyes and imagined Rodney's silky fur and stiff whiskers. I imagined what he would see and smell.

All at once, I was low, low to the floor like a cat. I raced down the service staircase, threaded my way through the crowd and through the kitchen's cat door with Darla calling after me. I raced across the wet lawn, my belly dampening and the smells of a thousand things I couldn't name filling my nose. A garter snake slithered through fallen leaves, drawing my attention, but I forced my thoughts toward Big House. I leapt through the cat door, its flap smoothing my ears.

The kitchen was warm and smelled of something good. Fish. Sam looked down at me and smiled and told me a shred of yesterday's roast chicken was in my bowl.

My vision blurred up close, but every movement in the distance was crisp. I absently noted a spoon under the refrigerator, probably forgotten long ago.

In the delicious wash of fishy fragrance, something smelled wrong. Very wrong. Rodney backed up, and I felt myself easing from his body. No, I urged him. We're going forward.

My muscles tensed, then released as I leapt onto the counter and landed as lightly as if a fly. The poison was in a cast-iron skillet, woven with the scent of trout, butter, and lemon. I recoiled from the toxin.

"That's hot, Rodster," Sam said. "Get down." He lifted me to the floor. As I watched from the linoleum, he scooped the trout to a plate and carried it to the table. And he sneezed.

That was it. I jumped to the table, then to Sam's shoulders. He reached for me, but I held tight and rubbed against his ears and neck, maximizing exposure between fur and skin.

It worked. He sneezed again, hard, and stretched an arm to the table for a tissue. I took this pause to shove my nose under the plate's edge and flip it to the floor. It felt only natural to raise a paw and knock the wineglass off the table next, mixing glass shards with Sam's dinner.

I sucked in air. I was back in my body on the tower floor and surprisingly calm. Below me, the party continued, its noise muffled by two floors of books and someone with a banjo and a microphone.

Magical energy pulsed through my system. The last time I'd used this energy, I'd nearly killed myself and destroyed the library. Now the library was full of people I could accidentally injure—or worse.

As the moon rose, light shifted, casting streaks on the dusty floor. Wooden crates of old books and magazines were pushed against the wall. Some moaned in low tones, as if they'd been sleeping and hadn't used their voices for decades. Old copies of women's magazines chattered like housewives. Outdated phone books recited numbers in a robotic tone.

I had little idea of what my magic could do. Could it unlock the tower door? I could roll into the hall and try to get someone to notice me. I closed my eyes and focused. "Bolt, unfasten yourself." The door was still.

At some point, cheers arose from the atrium, followed by "Happy Days Are Here Again" pounded out on the organ. Something joyous had happened. I couldn't imagine what it might be. Did anyone even miss me down there? Probably the sheriff had told them I had a headache and wanted to stick to my apartment.

My legs cramped, and my shoulders ached from being tied. My magic couldn't help that, either.

Eventually, voices filtered onto the library's grounds. The party was moving to Darla's. Then all was quiet.

This is when it would happen. When my mother's vision would become reality. I shivered, and not from the October night.

Footsteps sounded in the hall outside. The bolt creaked and the tower door opened, the hall light framing the sheriff's bulk. Before he had the chance to speak, I said, "Do you really want to do this? The Dolbys are about honor. This is not honorable."

He didn't speak, at least not with words. His eyes told about his shame, about how this would be the last time, this would finish it. Then he would go on being Bert Dolby, Wilfred's hero. He crossed the tower room in two steps and yanked me to my feet. He thrust open the window. Cold air rushed around us.

I opened my mouth to shout, but the sheriff covered it with his sweaty palm. "Silence," he hissed. "I locked up downstairs. No one is here. No one can hear you."

Within seconds, he'd untied my ankles and wrists. With one motion, he pushed me halfway over the sill of the old wood-frame windows, face-first. Far below stretched the porch's overhang, trimmed in jagged wooden gingerbread. If that didn't kill me, the gravel walkway below would.

The books screamed. My body heated with their energy. *Books*, I thought, *help me*. No—adrenaline fanned my energy into too broad of a cloud. God only knew what might happen. I had to tell them exactly what I wanted.

The sheriff heaved me further over the window. Only the crook of my hips held me in.

Books, I amended, *trap him*.

"What the—?" the sheriff said and loosened his grip.

Crates of books rocked side to side, creaking. One wooden strip peeled off a crate with a snap, then another. Dizzy, I pulled myself upright and watched in breathless wonder.

A book shot out of a crate and hit the sheriff in the Adam's apple. He backed toward the far wall as another book, then three, then a dozen whirled toward him with the velocity of boomerangs. The half-dozen crates splintered with the force of books seeking release.

My ears roared with energy. I'd done this. I didn't know if I should laugh or cry.

The sheriff shouted and turned his back. Books rapidly stacked on top of each other like leaden dominos, bricking him into a corner. He thrashed and pushed with his football player's body, but the steel energy of the books held him. My body churned hotter than lava.

"Josie," Sam yelled. "Are you up there? Say something."

Sam! "I'm here, in the tower," I yelled, keeping my vision and my magic focused on Bert Dolby.

Sam rushed through the open door. He halted a few feet from me. "Josie?" His voice was strange, quiet and unsure. "Are you okay?"

All at once, I went cold and let out a shuddering breath. A layer of books fell to the floor as the sheriff began to pound his way out.

"Sheriff Dolby," I said. "He killed Bondwell's operative, and he tried to kill me, too."

Another layer of books hit the floor. The sheriff's head and chest appeared as he punched a stack of magazines.

Each thrust of his fist came with a grunt powered by anger.

Sam smiled, belying his anger. With one hand, he calmly leveled a handgun at the sheriff. His other hand slipped handcuffs from his coat pocket.

"Bert Dolby, you're under arrest."

The books let out an exhausted breath. I sighed with them.

CHAPTER FORTY-ONE

I sat on my stiff Victorian sofa rubbing my wrists. Darla sat next to me, Sam relaxed in an elaborately carved armchair, and Roz perched on the coffee table. I'd never had guests in my tiny living room. This wasn't what I'd have planned for a housewarming.

Bert Dolby was in a squad car on his way to the county jail. I felt as if my innards had been ripped out, wrung dry, and replaced with cotton batting.

"Could I have more pie?" I asked Darla. One thing about having my magic back was that everything tasted so good again.

"Right here." She handed a slice of peach-blueberry to me.

"Are you ready to talk yet?" Sam said. "I brought Darla and Roz, as you asked."

I forked a bite of pie. "I think I'm about ready. Yes.

But I have a question first. When I was in the tower, I heard everyone cheer. You were celebrating something. What?"

"Oh," Darla said. "That's right. You weren't there. Sita and Ruff Waters backed out of the deal."

"They what?" I jerked forward so quickly that my pie plate would have slipped to the floor had Roz not been fast on the draw.

"They saw how much we loved the library," Roz said. "I guess your talk about Gaston High not being able to take our books, then the party—"

"They're decent people," Darla said. "You should have seen Ilona. Shut herself in the laundry room weeping."

"You mean the library won't be demolished?" I said with wonder. "Really?"

"And truly," Roz said.

This was going to take a while to soak in.

"We searched for you, wanted to let you know. We went upstairs to your apartment and everything, but you weren't here," Roz said. "You had to hear the news."

"That's when we went to Big House. Thought maybe you were hanging out with Sam." Darla cast me a meaningful look.

Fortunately, Sam didn't seem to have caught on to her insinuation. "We searched everywhere. The last car in the lot was Bert's. Then I figured it out."

"He told me he'd locked the place up. How did you get in? I took your key."

Sam gave a slight frown, a sign he was amused. "You think I'd give up the only key to the library?"

"Thank goodness," I said. "And thank goodness you didn't eat the trout the sheriff gave you." I might have looked at him a moment too long. "If it weren't for Rodney, you'd be on your kitchen floor about now."

"It was strange. I had no idea Bert tried to poison me. Then the cat goes and knocks my dinner on the floor, almost like he knew. At the same instant, the pieces came together in my mind. Bert had set up Craig to take the blame for the murder, and he knew I was close to figuring out why."

As if in response, Rodney jumped up to the couch next to me and purred.

"Good boy," I told him and ran my fingers through his silky fur. It was so good to have him back.

"You think the fish was poisonous?" Roz asked.

"Bert was too eager when he gave me the trout, and as greedy as I was, I took it. Anyway, it's on its way to the lab."

I set the pie plate on the coffee table. "The sheriff. What was his shame about, anyway? Someone was blackmailing him. I figured out that much."

"I can help with that." Craig Burdock stood in the doorway.

"What brought you here?" Roz said.

"Down at the diner, I heard that Bert was hauled off. I came up to get the story and add my two bits."

"I'm glad you're here, Craig," Sam said. "I planned on making a visit first thing in the morning."

He stood awkwardly in the doorway, barefoot and holding his moccasins in one hand. "He's really in jail, right?"

"Yes, and he'll stay there." Sam had turned investigator. His attention had telescoped to Craig in a calm but disciplined way.

"I, um . . ."

"Sit down." I gestured to the armchair near the fire-place.

He loped across the room and tossed the chair's needlepoint cushion aside before sitting. We all pivoted to face him.

"Here's what I know," he said. "When I was going out with Lalena, I helped her move into her aunt Ginny's trailer. That afternoon, I found her aunt's old diary. She wrote about the night the Wilfreds left town and the mill shut down. Remember? I was just a baby, but it was a big deal."

Roz snorted. "Yeah, a few of us remember."

"The aunt said that her brother—the other Sheriff Dolby—was called up to the mill site to deal with a union organizer." He nodded at Sam. "Your dad was there, too."

"Go on."

Craig took the plate of pie Darla offered and shoveled half of it into his mouth at once. After he swallowed, he said, "I guess they killed the union guy."

"What?" both Darla and Roz said at the same time.

"Yeah. There was a fight, and the guy got killed. Both Sam's and Bert's dads had a hand in it."

"By chance, he wasn't Ilona's father, was he?" I asked. "Ilona said he'd disappeared about that time. She mentioned he'd worked for the union."

"It's worth looking into," Sam said. "But you, Craig, you decided to cash in. Why didn't you hit me up, too?"

Craig looked at his feet. Had Sam been in town, he probably would have received a note. The sheriff was conveniently located.

"I'd arranged to meet Bert Dolby that night at the library," Craig said. "I knew Lyndon would be gone to get Josie, and it's out of the way enough that no one would see us."

"Bert didn't know it was you?"

He shook his head and curled his toes together. He really did have beautiful feet. "I think that was it. He made a mistake. He thought Josie's hit lady was me. Truth was, I stopped by Lalena's first, and, um . . ."

"I just don't understand why it was so important to the sheriff to cover it up," I said. "I mean, it all happened years ago. How could his father's reputation mean so much to him?"

Sam shifted his gaze to me. "I remember that day," he said softly. "My mom woke me up in the middle of the night. She had a suitcase. She put a coat over my pajamas and told me to take my favorite teddy bear. We got in the car and drove for hours. It was years until I knew we'd left because of the mill, but until now I never knew exactly why."

I resisted the urge to cross the room and put an arm around him. That was his wife's job. Wherever she was. Calculating her alimony, if the town's grapevine was right.

"Dude," Craig Burdock said.

"You'll have charges to face," Sam said. "But if you cooperate, my guess is the local police will keep them to a minimum."

"Sam," I said, absently eyeing Craig's empty pie plate. "Do you own the old mill site? The sheriff said you do."

He folded his hands over his lap. "I guess so. Yes. Why?"

"Do you have any desire to sell? Maybe Sita and Ruff Waters would be interested for their retreat center."

"It does have a good view," Darla pointed out.

"No flooding," Roz said. "And only a little farther over."

"Plus, the mill pond might be nice as a recreational area," Darla said.

If I were infatuated with Sam, my heart would have warmed watching his expression morph from clueless to keen. Good thing I wasn't.

"I guess I could do that. I mean, it's not like it's doing much for me now. There might be some environmental cleanup needed."

"Which would be good, anyway," Darla said. Unexpectedly, she laughed and slapped a knee. "Ilona would be thrilled to get the commission on that. Can we wait until tomorrow to tell her?"

Two days later, I walked out of the library's front door and inhaled autumn morning air. The sounds of hammer on wood and the grind of a saw came from the side of house where Lyndon was repairing the boarded-over windows. At last, the library would be made whole.

The woods seemed especially rich with the tang of fir trees and mulch. The river added its own mossy perfume. Country life was growing on me.

Darla had invited me to stay on as Wilfred's librarian. I told her I'd think about it, but in my heart I knew I'd stay. I was home. Rodney rubbed at my ankles.

Plus, now life in Wilfred was ramping up. Lalena had taken a loan from Mrs. Littlewood to visit Paris, and the PO Grocery offered a selection of French cheeses in her honor. The biggest news was that the Waters were putting an offer on the old mill site for their new retreat, which they were tentatively calling the Happy Trails Retreat Center. Ilona was over the moon. Suddenly, the library with its "glorious views" and "unparalleled placement" was second rate. Who'd want it when the "sweeping vistas" of the mill site were available? That was fine was me. It was first-rate as a library, although I'd have plenty to do to bring it into the current century.

Sam's last night at Big House had been filled with Verdi. *La traviata* floated across our common garden. Lyndon hadn't been around to complain about the noise. Darla said he'd spent the last two evenings at Roz's working on a thousand-piece puzzle of Dutch tulip fields.

Before Sam had left, he'd stopped by the library. "Think you'll stay?" He'd laid a hand lightly on my arm. I'd felt his touch all evening.

"Maybe. Probably."

He'd craned his neck toward the star-littered sky and back to Big House's dark windows. "I'll be back, too. I miss this place. I'm glad you brought me here, Josie."

Heat crept up my chest. "Say hi to your wife," I choked out.

He looked at me strangely—neither a smile nor a frown. "I'll be back. Alone," he said quietly.

Now he was gone. It was just Wilfred and me.

The sound of a car in low gear ground up the drive. Mrs. Garlington's son with the mail. "Package for you," he said.

It was from home. I lugged the box to the library's kitchen table. It wasn't as large as the bankers boxes I'd been filling with books, and, thankfully, now replacing on the library's shelves, but it was sizable. I cut away the packing tape and lifted a wooden chest from the cardboard. Green paint peeled from its exterior, and my grandmother's initials were carved into its lid.

Grandma's chest. I ran a hand over it, and my palm tingled. Mom had told me the chest was locked, and she couldn't open it. I fingered its hammered metal frame and touched the lock. It sprang open without a key.

Rodney jumped to the table next to the chest and peered in. Inside was the leather-bound book I remembered from Grandma's kitchen. I lifted it. It smelled of dried rose petals and hibiscus. Despite the kitchen's coolness, the book was warm in my hands.

Under the grimoire was a stack of letters sealed in envelopes. I lifted those to the table, too. Each letter was numbered and labeled "Josie." I found the first one and held it to my heart for a moment. "Grandma," I said. Hands shaking, I slipped a thumb beneath the envelope's flap.

"Dear Josie," the letter began in faded blue script, "if you're reading this, it means you've found your magic. I have so much to teach you."

Connect with  U s

Visit us online at
KensingtonBooks.com
to read more from your favorite authors, see books
by series, view reading group guides, and more.

 Join us on social media

for sneak peeks, chances to win books and prize packs,
and to share your thoughts with other readers.

facebook.com/kensingtonpublishing
twitter.com/kensingtonbooks

Tell us what you think!

To share your thoughts, submit a review,
or sign up for our eNewsletters, please visit:
KensingtonBooks.com/TellUs.

Grab These Cozy Mysteries from
Kensington Books